Table of Contents

The Ladies 1

When Will You Ever Learn? 17

Love Bites Are Frisky 28

A bitch, A Jerk and an Inmate 44

The gym and the park 61

Slut, Serial Killer or Lesbians? 76

Everyone Likes a Little Ass 88

She Made it Itch 103

Sundays Are For Eating with Family 116

When the Cookie Crumbles 130

Rice, Meatballs, Eggs and a Little Beer 142

All About the Balls 153

Inlaws 167

Lips, Sips, and Hips 179

Get Over Yourselves! 193

The Coast is Clear 206

Knock, Knock... 216

Sneaky Sneaky 227

Shh!.. 239

Monsters 252

I'm Starving 264

Best for Whom.. 275

Impulse.. 290

Get Away and Be Free 299

Restrooms 308

I'm Available... 317

Sweet Dreams... 328

Toxic 333

A New Day 341

Not for the Weak.. 345

Epilogue: New Adventures 348

The Ladies

Sam walked into the store, ready to buy the eighth bottle of her favorite perfume. It was the only perfume she ever purchased these days anymore. Sam loved the way it smelled. Besides, she had tried all the others, both expensive and cheap. The scents that did appeal to her never lasted.

Tonight, Sam was in a hurry. Traffic from the office had been a bitch. She knew her best friend Kyla would be waiting. It was their monthly get-together. She wanted to save time running errands before she saw Kyla. She chose to grab her perfume first. Unfortunately, that also meant running behind schedule.

Samantha Rose Dimartino herself was desirable. She had beautiful green eyes to match parts of the Caribbean Sea. Her hair was long with natural highlights and as thick as blood. Sam always met women who told her they wished for eyes or hair like hers. Sam was unique. She grew up in a rough neighborhood with her older sister and both of their parents. Growing up, they did not have much money, but she came from a big, close-knit family, and their holidays and parties were something! Sam knew how to handle herself in the streets and avoid bad situations. She became a wife and a mother who worked per-diem. In other words, Sam worked when she wanted to. She had a strong personality, dealing with difficult people, thanks to her upbringing. But she would drop everything in a heartbeat for those she cared about. For everyone else, Sam could care less. She had little patience for lazy, ignorant, and selfish people in Sam's world. Most of the population irritated Sam, and she considered them toxic. Unless you had something Sam wanted or needed, you could fuck off.

Most people envied Sam. She had a gorgeous husband with a body that a magazine editor should be advertising in a muscle magazine. His body was rock solid with bulging muscles everywhere. Sam got excited every time she looked at him. His personality, on the other hand, Sam wasn't crazy about at times. Sam did not care for or appreciated Sal's idea of humor. The good times have outweighed the bad, however. As for their lifestyle, they owned a five-bedroom colonial home in the suburbs. The house had an in-ground swimming pool, a lavish garden, and a four-door garage. Over the years, they even had the means to renovate several times. Their vacations, both with the kids and with not, were superb, sparing no expense. Sam always went after everything she wanted and ensured nothing or no one stood in the way. She was a strong and independent woman.

"Damn! I am late again"! Sam was late; about 20 minutes late. Her monthly get-together with Kyla was something they agreed to commit to and make a part of their already cramped schedules. They had had enough of the same dull days, making meals and doing household chores. They wanted more; a sense of "me" and not just "Mom" or "Hon." Kyla referred to it as "Titi Time"; no kids, no husband, and no distractions. They would get together for a few hours once a month on a Friday night. They would go for some mani/pedis, do some shopping in the Mall, and then it was off to a restaurant for cocktails to vent to one another about the bull shit in their lives. Sam and Kyla lived for this date. It was the only time they could honestly say everything on their minds without fear of being overheard by unintended parties, distracted, or judged. It was also the only time they could be true to themselves, share personal secrets, and behave however they wanted to without criticism from their loved ones. *Can she move any slower?* Sam thought as she stared at the girl behind the counter, who she needed to ring up. The little miss salesgirl was too busy talking to a co-worker about how her boyfriend put the moves on another chick at the club last night. While she waited, Sam decided to give her the once over. *Tits? Fake. Where did the makeup come from? I would bet money on it; it comes from the makeup aisle at the local convenience store. And girl, who did your highlights? the new hire fresh out of cosmetology school? The eyelashes? One could braid those shits. The lips? You definitely could cool the soup down with those. And let's not forget the wardrobe. Honey, who are you kidding, trying to put 20 pounds of shit into a ten-pound bag? No wonder why lover boy has wandering eyes. I would too!* When she was about to explode, Sam spoke up." Ahem! Ok, ladies, I hate to interrupt your deep convo, but I have an appointment. Can we speed this up, please?" Sam spat out as bitchy as she could sound as she rolled her eyes at both of the sales girls. "Sorry, Ma'am," Miss fake tits replied. Sam reached in her wallet for her debit card to hand the girl. *"Never spend what you don't have."*

That was Sam's motto. She didn't believe in credit cards. Why pay all that interest and make someone else rich? She learned her lesson long ago when she got her first credit card at age 17. Growing up, it didn't help that they lived close to a shopping mall. She went way over the limit, did not make the payments, and ended up destroying her credit. It took years to fix it. Her father was not happy, but Sam stood up for herself. She told her father he should never have gotten it for her then. Her father didn't know any better. He came here from Italy and wanted to make a good life for his family; make them happy. Only giving a teenage girl her credit card was a mistake. A collection notice came in the mail. His older daughter Kristen had interpreted the letter from English to Italian to her father. He responded by cutting Sam's credit card into pieces. She cried for a week.

Sam's husband, Sal, also criticized Sam often for her frequent spending—Salvatore Dimartino, her husband, for the last 14 years. He was gorgeous, but he could be so immature and stubborn at times. *Sam thought if only he could see what I see and feel what I feel. What an even better team we'd make!* Sometimes, Sam felt like marriage to Sal held her back from certain things and the person she wanted to be. She knew she did not have his approval on certain things. He just wasn't as generous or risky as she was with the things she did care about. Then again, maybe his reservations kept her from getting into trouble. Sam tossed the crumpled receipt into her Louis Vuitton bag and hurriedly fled the store. "God, Kyla is gonna let me have it tonight."

Kyla sat, patiently waiting at a table in the far end corner of the food court at the Mall, sipping on an iced coffee. *Damn you, Sam!* she thought. She had been sitting there for at least a half-hour, although it felt more like an hour. She was deep in "Teenage Hell." It was a Friday night, and the Mall was packed with many teens, just hanging out and being obnoxious and downright annoying. In addition to retail shops, the Mall also consisted of an arcade and movie theater. It was the local hangout for teenagers. Kyla watched these little teenage girls flaunt their toothpick bodies with heavily padded bras in front of barely out-of-puberty boys, trying their hardest to look sexy. They wore tons of makeup as well. And the language! Every other word was a curse. *Do you kiss your mothers with that mouth? Don't you kids have to watch Sesame Street or something?* Kyla wanted to ask them. She was getting more frustrated by the minute. It was 6:30, and Sam was supposed to meet her at six. *I might as well check in with the husband and see how he is coping with our children.* At 34, Kyla Joy Lovazzo was a stunning woman with an ass that was so hot; you could melt ice on it. She had black Spanish eyes and a radiant glow to her Puerto Rican skin. She was one sexy, beautiful Latina with a sweet soul. Kyla always gave everyone the benefit of the doubt. Something Sam would always scold her for. She had a nice upbringing with her parents and brothers in a nice house in Yonkers, New York. Her parents were strict Catholics and did not allow Kyla to do many things other kids got to do, like hanging out late, going to parties, and dating. But Kyla did not mind. She took pride in being a good student and devoted daughter. She always knew being a housewife, even with a college degree, was in her cards. She loved being a wife and a mother. Before the birth of her son, she was heavily involved in her career but chose to give it all up to raise Anthony and Francesca. Not that she cared, of course. Her role as a mom was her number one priority. However, Kyla often felt that a piece was missing from her life and spent much of her sleepless nights thinking, should of, would of, and could of. Her home life was pretty ordinary. While the hubby worked, she stayed home all day to care for the kids. They spent their weekends running errands. Home improvement stores were becoming the weekend routine for the Lovazzo family, and Kyla was becoming bored. She craved more out of her marriage, daily days, and life altogether. *Just once*, she thought, *I would like to hear Freddie say, "Babe, your mother is watching the kids. We are going to your favorite restaurant, then coming home to polish off some more wine and have great sex.* God! Did Freddie even know that there is more to sex than the missionary position? And think, Italians were supposed to be great lovers. Yeah right. Kyla sighed. Kyla' picked up her phone to dial her husband and did the Sign of the Cross as she dialed. *Pray for me, Lord.* "Hi, Hon. Is everything ok?" Kyla dreaded calling to check in with her husband. It was the monthly phone call where her husband would sound like he was at battle in the war and all his compadres were dead, and he was the last one standing, fighting for his life. It's not even like their children were babies. Anthony was eight, and Francesca was four. What was so hard to do to take care of them? All he had to do was give them dinner and put them to bed. He could even pull up a movie on Netflix, pop some popcorn, and call it a night. *Give me a break, Quejoso!* Kyla thought to herself as she listened to her husband bitch and moan. *I only want to be by myself for about four hours once a month while he stays with the kids, and you would think I asked him to jump off a bridge.* She took a deep breath before replying. "Yes, Dear. I won't be home too late. No, I won't be drinking and driving. No, Sam is not planning anything crazy. We are just getting together to share pics of the kids and have some girlie time." Never being aggressive, Kyla married a man who needed to be powerful by ordering Kyla around as much as he could without overstepping. It made him feel like a real man. He wasn't bad looking and could be condescending towards Kyla at times, but he made an honest, decent living and was a great father to their children. Given Kyla's history with men, Freddie wasn't so bad. However, he was in a bad mood tonight and wanted his wife to come home. Kyla on the other hand, wasn't having any of it. "You know it would not be right for me to cancel on Sam at the last minute. Besides, I am already at the Mall, and she hasn't yet gotten here. I won't make it a late night, Promise." Kyla told her husband she loved him and to give the kids kisses goodnight for her. With that, she disconnected the phone call and sighed once more. *Bitch, I need a drink, and I need it now. Get your ass here, Ahora!*

"Let's see; who shall I call to see if they are available for a little fun tonight?" Tina said out loud as she pulled her cell phone out of her knock-off designer purse. It was a Friday night, and Tina was feeling adventurous and energetic as usual. It had been two weeks since Tina last saw John, her latest conquest. "Mr., I have decided to do the right thing and go home to my wife." He was not returning her calls or texts. *How dare he!* Tina thought as she scrolled thru the hundreds of phone numbers for men she had fooled around with. She had them stashed in her phone in a "special" group. Ms. Santiago was not one you wanted to mess with! She and John had been having an affair for eight months, and all was going great! They secretly met at hotels, restaurants, and bars. John often lavished Tina with expensive gifts. The dinners were extravagant, followed by either passionate sex or a quick fuck. Their sex encounters were hot and steamy regardless. That is until John's wife learned about the affair and threatened to leave him and take the kids and the house.

"Tina, you just don't understand. She will take me for everything, leaving me with nothing." John tried to explain to Tina. "Well, you're stupid for getting caught in the first place!" Tina barked back. She wasn't hearing any of this bullshit, and with that, she tossed the rest of her red wine into John's crotch. Tina stormed out of the Presidential suite of the luxurious, upscale hotel in lower Manhattan. That was the last time she had seen or heard from him. Tina thought about that last encounter. *So what if I was the one that walked out? He should be on his hands and knees, begging for forgiveness and awaiting my calls. What sucked about the whole thing was that he was the entire package. And I envisioned us being together for a long time.* Tina frowned. John partnered with a prestigious law firm, bringing in lots of cash. He had the looks and the swag to bring Tina to her knees. She liked having their once-a-week rendezvous. Why would she want it to end? She got to stay in the best hotels around NYC, go to the best restaurants, and get those gifts!

Tina would miss those even more. Tina became pissed off. "Damn him! Eres un Hijo de puta, John Benecasa, and your ugly ass wife too!" Tina screamed into the bathroom mirror. "I guess I will have to start hunting again!" Tina then picked up her phone to call

Rick Valentin, her on-again, off-again fling. He had a bitch wife, too, always calling Rick's cell phone with some stupid shit. "I love you, Pookie, and when are you coming home?" Tina could vomit. "Voicemail, fuck!" Tina yelled as she threw the phone on the bed.

Tina slipped her long, curvy body into her bathtub, allowing the bubbles to float around her soft, sultry skin. She flicked the ones that landed on her nipples. At 34, Tina was a single, attractive woman. She had a regular daytime clerical job taking her nowhere but paying the bills. She resided in a one-bedroom condo in White Plains.

Although Tina would have preferred living in the city, she couldn't afford it. She had no choice but to reside in the suburbs. Tina chose this area for the location. She could walk to the train, shops and the bars! Tina had decided in her twenties that a husband and kids were not for her. She thought how any woman could be tied to one man and have to stare at him day and night was repulsive. Who wants to clean a house and pick up after a bunch of little pain in the asses that look like him? Plus, cook for him every night? Yuck. Tina did not want any part of that life. No, it was easier to have affairs with married men, having no attachments, no, having to hear that I love you and want to marry you. Tina was very decisive about who she slept with. They had to be rich, of course. And the men she did choose to fool around with; unless he was making six figures, no thanks. Their looks alone needed to make her drool with desire. Tina was a pro at finding these men too. She was a beauty with a killer body, having a knack for attracting men with her dress and body language. Tina looked hot wherever she went, providing men with just enough eye candy to make them want more. Luckily she could put on a whole ensemble that looked expensive and so sexy. She went to the best bars, attended the best parties, and networked herself as the best treat a man and his money could find and afford. It had always been this way for Tina Santiago. It just wasn't in her to be committed to one boyfriend and have him be her one and only. The idea of sneaking around and being the one the guys sought after excited her. What did she care? It wasn't her relationship to lose or the financial mess to get into over shared things like kids, a house, etc. Of course, this never went over well with her girlfriends. She had stolen many of her friends' boyfriends to fool around with them momentarily and then move on to the next one. In high school, she was hated by the females but adored by the boys. That suited Tina just fine. Only her sister's relationship was off-limits as far as Tina was concerned. That is one female that Tina wasn't messing with. Her sister was older, had the same man for years, and they shared a child. Tina adored her sister and niece more than anything. She finished bathing, stepped out of the tub, and wrapped herself in a long, black silk robe. Tina looked into her mirror again, brushed the hair out of her face, and smiled. "I guess it's time to get all dolled up and see who falls prey tonight," she said aloud as she chuckled.

Kristen ran down the ramp as fast as her five-inch stiletto boots would take her. She could feel that mini skirt she decided to wear rise to her ass cheeks. *God, please don't let any creepers be behind me!* The train would pull away from the track any second, leaving Kristen to wait an hour for the next train. *Damn! Why did I have to live back in the suburbs? It also didn't help that the girl took forever making my coffee. It's not rocket science! Plus, you did not want to be in the train station alone once it turned dark. Not to mention, being a female, wearing high heels and a short skirt. One could get mugged, raped, or even killed!* The train station was notorious for the number of drunks, homeless, and criminals that always hung out there, waiting to see if anyone would fall victim to their schemes. She could also be mistaken for a hooker. Kristen smirked at the thought of that. She practically pushed the woman standing in the middle of the ramp out of her way." Excuse me; I am so sorry!" Kristen shouted as she dived through the closing doors of the train car. *Ah! I made it!* Kristen said to herself as she found a seat next to the window. One of her stilettos couldn't say the same. The heel had cracked and was about to distance itself from the rest of the shoe. Kristen sighed. It was her favorite pair of stilettos, and she couldn't afford to buy another pair.

I can find a nice pair to accept one of those online services where you pay in installments. Kristen removed the heels and whipped out Silky Toes bendable, portable ballet shoes. She slipped them on her feet, shoved her heels in her bag, and put in her earphones. Now Kristen could relax. The local train ride on the Metro-North took a while, so she could sit back and listen to her music with a hot cup of strong coffee. After work, a few cocktails with her co-workers are always worth the hustling and long rides. She then closed her eyes and turned on her playlist while the train traveled from NYC to White Plains.

Kristen Ann Lapis had been through a lot in the last couple of years. She was 40 years old, seeking a divorce, and living back with her parents in their White Plains house with two kids in tow. She was a knockout with beautiful blonde hair, by a bottle. She had hazel green eyes and looks that women would pay a high price for. She had married her high school sweetheart and had two kids with him. Finances were always a struggle, but Kristen was so in love that she felt she had all she would ever need. However, that would all change. Kristen did not know that her husband was cheating and scheming behind her perfect world. These things would eventually catch up with them, rocking Kristen's world. Her husband went to prison for his crimes, and Kristen found out about all of his infidelities. She was not the only one who visited the state prison to visit Chris.

Christopher John Lapis had a few visitors. Kristen refused to be played for a fool and ceased the weekly visits and care packages she was bringing to Chris. He would no longer receive cigarettes, fresh socks, t-shirts, and more, not from Kristen anyway. Those packages were more money than Kristen could afford anyhow. With her husband in jail, no money came in. Kristen had no choice but to move her and the kids in with her parents and make the best future possible for herself and the kids. Her son was going to be looking at colleges soon. There was a little leftover from each paycheck to spend on herself. If she didn't have these nights out, she would lose it. She also tried giving what she could to her parents to help with groceries, electricity, and other things. God knows her kids used up a lot of electricity! Between their phone chargers, computers, and every other electronic device these kids had, it was no wonder why the monthly electric bill was insane. However, her parents would always refuse the money. All they wanted was to have their daughter and grandchildren taken care of, not to mention their home and privacy back. They loved Kristen and the kids, but there's a big difference between visiting someone and living with them. Sometimes they even had to intervene when fourteen-year-old Nikki argued with her mother. Those two could fight! But even with her parents' help, Kristen was still struggling emotionally and financially. Filing for a divorce would have to wait. The proceedings were costly, and so were the lawyer fees. There was no rush. The last thing she wanted was another husband, and Chris wasn't going anywhere. "Thank God I have the family I do." Kristen would often say out loud when she thought of them. Sam, Kristen's younger sister, was an excellent support for Kristen. They became much closer once since this all happened. Kristen thought about her younger sister as the train moved through 125th street. *It's funny how things are turning out. At my lowest point, I envied Sam, having her shit together, the perfect marriage, and a beautiful home. She seemed to have it all. Sam should have been looking up to me since I was older, yet I'm the one that envied her. But lately, she seems so unhappy. Sam looks as though she is jealous of my newfound freedom. She has mentioned feeling trapped sometimes. Yet, anyone looking in would think she has it all. When I tell her that she is crazy and that no woman should ever have to go through what I went through, Sam always just shrugs her shoulders and replies with "Whatever." Her once-a-month adventure with her best friend, Kyla, isn't enough for Sam. They say the grass is always greener on the other side, but not in this case.*

When Will You Ever Learn?

"I am so sorry! Please forgive me!" Sam begged as she sat down at the table Kyla had been occupying. *Boy, she looks pissed!* Sam thought as she stared into Kyla's eyes. Not to mention Kyla was busy tapping her stiletto-shaped fingernails on the table. "Sam, when are you ever on time?" *I've been stuck in*

teenage hell. Besides, Freddie is already asking me what time I will be home and where we are going." Samantha rolled her eyes. "Kyla, when are you going to set him straight? You are a wonderful wife and mother and devote all your time caring for them. Tell that husband of yours that you need a little time to yourself. You are not a child, and do not treat you like one. You need to tell him that it is neither a favorable nor attractive attribute in a man." Sam was tired of hearing the same old bullshit about the relationship between Kyla and Freddie. Kyla was a doormat that Freddie walked all over, and it pissed Sam off. Kyla was her best friend, and hated seeing her treated that way. She was never like this until she met that man. Sam despised Freddie; she thought Kyla was too good for him and deserved better. She'd cringed every time she crossed paths with him. *What Kyla sees in that man, I do not know!* Sam thought as she looked around the mall, staring at all the obnoxious teens. *God, I hope Natalia does not turn out like them!* Natalia, at age 12, was already turning into her mother. She had the same beautiful hair and an adorable growing body ahead of her twelve-year-old mind. "I know, Sam, but it is not that easy," Kyla was saying as she picked at a cuticle on her nail. "He tries his hardest to provide for us and is a good man. He lacks self-esteem and is needy. You know the situation with his mother. He needs me." Sam rolled her eyes again. "That's all fine and dandy, Kyla, but if this keeps up, it will destroy what YOU've got. Alright, enough of this depressing shit. Aren't we supposed to forget our marital problems and daily life during this time? Screw getting our nails done. Let's go right now and get some food and drinks!"

Sam and Kyla picked up their bags and proceeded to the nearest exit, leading them to the mall parking lot. "Ok, so where to Chick?" Sam asked as she opened the door to her Jeep. Kyla yelped. "Damn, Sam! Why did you take the top off? My hair will look like a bird's nest when I leave!" Kyla clamped both hands on her head to hold her hair down. "Stop Bitchin'. Grab the Yankee cap from the glove compartment and put it on your head. I say we hit one of the restaurants on Main Street. There are so many bars over there, and we can walk to one when we are done." Kyla reluctantly agreed. "Fine with me, but please, let's watch our time. I am not in the mood for Freddie's crap tonight!" Sam just rolled her eyes yet again.

Fagiola's was one of their favorite places to eat. They showed up without a reservation, but the manager knew they were regular customers and found them a table. It also helped that they were good-looking, which always makes any hangout more appealing. "It's good for business, and they tip well." the manager told the waitress when she complained about having another table to take care of. The food and drinks at Fagiola's were good, and the atmosphere was great. Many of the young hotties came here to eat just before heading to the bars for the night. Sam enjoyed looking at all the eye candy while she chowed down. Given the age difference, most of the guys were young enough to be a son of hers. She probably babysat one or two. Sam laughed in her head. Occasionally, some hotties would invite themselves over for a little conversation. Kyla would smile and pretend to be texting, but Sam enjoyed it. Nothing serious, of course. She believed in always being faithful to her husband, even if their relationship was flat. But boy, did Sam love to tease and flirt! She craved the attention she received from both men and women. From men, it was how they drooled over her, practically begging her to throw them a bone. For women, it was the look of envy as they looked her up and down, watching her every move. Sam could feel them picking her body apart, analyzing every part of her. She often blew kisses at them to see the reaction on their faces. Tonight was no different with the men or the women, except the flirting and taunting began after dinner. Once they had finished their meals, the women headed over to Vibes, one of the bars they attended frequently. They were there only five minutes when some twenty-something horny dude approached Sam and offered to buy her a drink. She kindly declined, explaining she was still working on her first one and had to drive in a little while. He smiled at her. "Oh, but what's your rush, Sexy? The night is young. We can have some drinks and then play. Your girlfriend can come to play too if she wants." Kyla rolled her eyes and pulled Sam by the arm. "Come with me. I have to pee." Sam willingly followed but was annoyed at the same time. *Fucking asshole! How dare he suggest they leave to go somewhere together"* Does anyone not respect the wedding ring anymore? It certainly wasn't the size of the gem that went down with the Titanic, but it was a big enough rock to be noticed. Sal had made sure of that.

"Do you believe that jerk?" Kyla asked as she pushed the door open to the ladies' room. Sam laughed."He's certainly an asshole, but I can't blame him. Look at me." Kyla rolled her eyes at Sam. "You know, you do that a lot, Kyla, Darling," Sam sarcastically stated. "Whatever and I could say the same about you, Samantha Rose," Kyla replied as she pulled out her lip gloss for some reapplying. Sam proceeded to do the same. While the two of them fixed their faces and gossiped, the door to the middle stall opened. Out walked Tina Santiago. "Excuse me," Tina said as she made her way to the center sink between Sam and Kyla. Both women glared at Tina. "Oh, my God! Tina?" Kyla said with her mouth wide open. Kyla and Tina were best friends many years ago. They both grew up on the same block in Yonkers when they were young. They remained close until high school. Tina went to the local public high school, while Kyla's parents made her attend parochial school. Sam was not a fan of Tina's. They had met several times when Kyla had both girls over at her house to hang out.

"Wow! Kyla? How long has it been?" Tina then turned and looked at Sam. "Samantha, you have not changed at all. I guess you and Kyla remained close." "Yes, we did remain friends... best friends," Sam spat back at Tina, acting like a teenager with an attitude. Tina ignored her approach. "Well, good for the two of you. I guess you both live close to White Plains, then?" "We live a little bit north of here, but we are familiar with this area, so we come here to hang out," Kyla replied. "Oh, that's great. It is a nice area—so many places to hang out. I live close by. I have an apartment not too far from here. The area is great, and it is so convenient having the train right here for me to travel to the city for work," Tina stated as she looked back at Sam, knowing Sam always had resented her. *Good, let the bitch see how hot I am. I was back then and still am. Although I must admit, Sam looks pretty good herself. But I will keep that to myself.* "And I see by both of your hands that you guys are both married?" *See, even a stupid bitch can recognize a wedding ring when she sees one.* Sam thought as she continued to glare at Tina. "Yes, we are, and we have kids too."

Tina smiled back at them even though she felt like slapping Sam. "Well, how nice for you guys. I never got married. My life is too hectic for a husband and kids." This time it was Sam who wanted to slap Tina. "So, who are you here with?" Kyla asked Tina. "Oh, I came by myself. I know the bartenders and the bouncers, so I have some drinks and chill with them." *I bet you do,* Sam thought. *She probably has gone home with every one of them and fucked their brains out. Fucking Buttana.* "I have a table near the bar if you girls care to join me," Tina offered. Kyla went to reply, but Sam cut her off. "Thanks, Tina. That's so nice of you, but we were getting our last pee in before we head home. Kyla's husband has to get up for work early tomorrow, so she needs to get home to the kids." "Oh, ok, next time then. Kyla, I'll give you my cell. "Definitely. I would love that!" Kyla exclaimed as she entered Tina's cell number into her phone. "I will call you, and we will set something up. "Cool.

I look forward to hearing from you." And with that, Tina hugged and kissed Kyla goodbye and kissed the air rather than Sam's cheek as she walked out of the bathroom.

"What the hell was that all about?" Kyla asked as she and Sam climbed into the Jeep. "One second, you're telling me that I should tell Freddie I need some space for myself, and the next, you're telling Tina that I have to get home to the kids because Freddie has to get up early. ¿Qué te pasa? Kyla was confused by Sam's actions. "Seriously, Kyla? You would want to hang out with her? Need I remind you about what a horrible person she was to you? Was there any boyfriend you had that the bitch did not try to fool around with? Why the hell would you want to hang with her?" Sam was annoyed. "That was a long time ago, Sam. People change. She seems like she has it together." Kyla was now annoyed with her best friend for scolding her like a little kid. Sam, however, was not about to back down. "Yeah, that's why she hangs out alone in a bar with twenty-somethings. Never been married either," Sam replied. Kyla became defensive. "Just because she is not married does not mean something is wrong with her, Sam." Now Kyla was angry. "Obviously, Kyla. But can't you see? Nothing has changed. She is probably still banging the first guy that comes along, married or not; Miss, my life's too hectic!" Sam looked straight ahead at the road before her as she drove up the parkway. Kyla almost felt sorry for Sam now as she stared at her face and could see the emotion all over it. "Gee, Sam, I think you hate her as much now as you did when we were teens." Kyla felt bad now. She didn't mean for Sam to get upset. "I could care less, Kyla. It's just that women like her are no good. They lie and backstab. They are homewreckers who don't care about anything but themselves. And for what? Worldly things, nice dinners? Who wants someone like that in their life? Especially when it concerns someone that I care very much about. She placed her right hand on top of Kyla's. You're not gonna call her, are you?" They had left the parkway by this time and stopped at a light. Sam turned and looked right into Kyla's eyes. "Look, I am sorry. I don't want to upset you. You are my best friend, and I'm just looking out for you." "I get that, Sam, and I truly appreciate your concern, but I just don't know. Tina and I had some good times together and go a long way back. Underneath it all, Tina is a good person. I want to get to know her as an adult." "Well, you do what you want, Kyla. You are a grown, intelligent woman who makes decisions for herself. But in my opinion, I'm just telling you, you are asking for trouble with that one." They drove the rest of the way home in silence, listening to Sam's playlist.

Kristen closed the door to the Uber and walked barefoot up the walkway to her parent's house. *Good, their car's not here. That means they're out to eat.* She did not feel like explaining why she had a broken heel. Her mother already hated the fact that she rode the subway, especially at night. And one look at Kristen's outfit, her mother would scold her as though she was fifteen. Once inside, she took off her coat and looked through the mail. It mainly consisted of junk mail and bills, but one envelope was addressed to her from the state prison. Kristen quickly opened the envelope and fell into the kitchen chair. Her ex-husband Chris had a parole hearing. Based on his good behavior, he was a candidate for conditional release. His release date had been set, and he would be released in three weeks.

She felt faint. Kristen started sweating and got an instant headache. She reached for a bottle of water in the refrigerator. *"This can't be happening. Not now. I am finally moving on with my life. His getting released will only complicate things. He'll want to see the kids, possibly demand joint custody, and bring his latest hoochie around them. Not to mention, I like Peter and was considering pursuing a relationship with him. I don't need interference from Chris. No, this can't be happening now!* Kristen started to cry and felt weak in her knees. She heard a car pull into the driveway and moved the curtain window to take a peek. Her parents had returned home. Kristen quickly wiped her tears and crumbled the letter with the envelope into her bag. *"I'm not ready to tell them. I'm still processing it myself!"*

As the key turned in the door, Kristen ran up the stairs into the bathroom to take off her sluty outfit and jump in the shower. If any redness was left on her face from crying, she could easily brush it off as it resulted from washing her face in the shower. *"I gotta talk to Sam. She will know what to do. She's probably busy with the kids and Sal now, though. I'll call her tomorrow."* Kristen finished her shower, wore her robe, and greeted her parents downstairs. She found them arguing over the cost of their dinner. Her father said it was too expensive. Her mother told her father he was cheap and that married couples should go out, even at their age. "Hello, parents. How are you doing on this lovely evening?" Her mother looked at Kristen and in her accent, she said,. "Your father, complaina about the costa of our meal. Please tell him that we are a no longer ina the Stone Age. Her father then spoke. "Kristen, Honey, pleasa tella you mother that she cana go outta to eat and nota order a few glasses of wine every time a!"

Kristen laughed. "You're both being ridiculous." Her mother smiled. "Enough about us. How was your night?

Love Bites Are Frisky

"Good morning. Are you up yet?" It was 10:00 in the morning on Saturday and Sam was texting her sister Kristen to see if she wanted to go to the mall with her and the kids. While she waited for the reply, she thought about the events that took place the night before. She felt bad about scolding Kyla. But they were friends and Sam did not want Kyla to get mixed up again with someone like Tina. "Damn! Why did they have to bang into that slut last night? If only that asshole did not hit on me, we wouldn't have gone to the bathroom and maybe we never would have seen her." The phone vibrated on the kitchen counter and Sam picked it up. Kristen said she would love to since she wanted to get out of the house for a while and also needed Sam's advice on something. Sam sighed. She immediately thought it had to be about the new guy in Kristen's life. *Maybe they are getting serious and she's nervous about it.* Sam snapped out of her thoughts just then. "Ma, can you take me to Sophia's house after the mall?" Natalia blurted out as she walked into the kitchen and reached for her Rice Krispies. Natalia was twelve going on twenty. She was a great kid and Sam adored her. It was hard to keep her innocent though. With all the latest happening on the internet, there was not much that Natalia wasn't being exposed to. Sal had a hard time with it too. *Damn you, social media!* Sam thought. *Although I gotta admit, some of it is entertaining.* "Not today, Tali," Sam replied. "Aunt Kristen is coming to the mall with us and she is bringing Nikki." The two girls were not only cousins but best friends even though Nikki was two years older. They shared everything. "Oh ok. Well, then can you buy me some new clothes and makeup?" My wardrobe could use a makeover and I am out of mascara."Tali, I don't know why your wardrobe needs a makeover. It just had a makeover last month and the month before that. Plus, I think you're too young to be wearing mascara. Not to mention, you have an allowance that we give to you each week. You're going to have to start saving it for the things you want. Spend it on the things you want that we don't already provide. We cannot keep buying several outfits this frequently "You need to start appreciating what you have and work for the things you want in life. That's how it works." Natalia sucked her teeth. "That will take me forever!" Sam shot her a look. Natalia smirked. "Fine. Whatever.. Can we just buy one outfit then?" Natalia then shoved a big spoonful of Rice Krispies in her mouth and proceeded to text her girlfriend. Sam threw a paper towel roll at her and shouted "Natalia Rose!" Sam poured some coffee for herself and sat at her kitchen table. *These kids today. They have no clue. At her age, we did not walk around with designer this and that. I had one wardrobe that needed to last a whole season if not more. I didn't dare ask my parents for more. And I didn't even have a phone. I shopped in stores I could afford and could care less about who I impressed. But now, if Natalia sees one of her friends with a $200 handbag, she has to have one too. Sal better get a second job!* As she was thinking about this, Sal himself walked into the kitchen to pour coffee into his to-go cup "Bye Babe, I will see you later," He then grabbed his car keys and headed out the door. Sal worked many hours and Saturdays were no exception. Sam was fine with it though since it left her with the day to do whatever she wanted. Not that she could with kids and all. "Bye," she mumbled, not surprised he did not kiss her before leaving. That was Sal. Romance was not a part of the Dimartino household. But when Sal was feeling frisky, look out! Sam would have to wear a scarf for a week with all the love bites Sal left on her neck, not to mention the rest of the bites and bruises on her body from having sex. Sometimes you could see the shape of his thumb in the form of a bruise on Sam's inner thighs. It happened every time he held on to her legs while he fucked her. "Well at least I can't complain about the sex," Sam thought, laughing to herself. Kyla could only dream about things like that from what she told me. But I'm willing to bet she gets kissed goodbye" Sam put her mug in the sink and kissed Natalia on top of her head, who didn't even know her father had left and headed for the shower.

The alarm clock began to sing loudly and Tina slammed on it to shut the alarm off. "Shit! Why does going to the gym have to be such an early project and on the weekend no less? Tina said out loud as she rose out of bed hung over from the night before. She knew why. If she did not go to the gym early, she would miss all of the hot married men who came in early for their workouts. Married men get up early and go to the gym so they can spend the rest of the day doing things that husbands do. "It makes me wanna vomit" Tina would often say when she thought about it. It was only the broke men with no lives who just went to the gym on the weekends that would show up in the afternoon. At least that was Tina's take on it. Tina would wear the tightest workout outfits she could find, sometimes even buying a smaller size. This way, her tits, and ass could stick out more. She loved sticking her physical assets out while using the workout machines and watching the muscle heads all around her, explode. It was a thrill to watch them try to bench press with their hard on's sticking out of the gym pants. She also got satisfaction from seeing all the women in the gym, staring at her as she worked each machine. *It's not my fault, I have a killer body while they can only dream of having one!* And these women were all the same. Many women were not blessed in the ass department. Their asses spread sideways while you could balance a mug on Tina's. *And those women that do have big tits? It's part of the fat that consumes their whole bodies. It must be something in the water. Look out boys! There's a new hot ass in town!* Tina grinned as she stared at herself in her full-length mirror.

Tina turned around and stared at the guy she took home last night. He was sound asleep in her bed. His arm hung over the side, exposing his hand. She could see the wedding ring on his finger. I wonder if the wife is wondering where he is, Tina thought. She threw a pillow at him. She hated when she had too much to drink and ended up passing out with someone in her bed all night long. Why did they hang around? We had great sex and a great time, but now it is over. What did they want? Didn't he have a wife to go home to? But when she was standing outside the front of the bar last night having a cigarette, she did take notice that this dude pulled up in a new Porsche. Tina could smell the money and determined that she had already had her last drink of the evening that she was paying for herself. It didn't take much effort to land this guy. All Tina did was flirt a little and bend over a few times to show this guy some cleavage and her derrière and wallah, bait, hook and sinker!

"Time to get up, um Mike is it? I have to go out. The guy from last night opened his eyes, smiled, reached for a condom and pulled Tina down on top of him. *Oh, what the hell,* Tina thought, *morning sex is the shit!* Tina removed her tank top and panties, allowing Mike to enter her, and proceeded to ride him like a champ. She threw her head back, moaning in sheer pleasure. They came together, thrashing back and forth, Tina digging her perfectly manicured nails into Mike's chest. When she was done, she climbed off of him and went into her nightstand, and lit a cigarette. "Thanks, Babe, you were awesome. I enjoyed myself. You can make some coffee for yourself if you want before you take off." "Are you kicking me out?" Mike looked perplexed. "Well, what were you expecting? We should get dressed, have breakfast together, and go for a walk in the park holding hands? Besides, I noticed your ring. Won't the little woman be wondering where you are? I am sure she's worried." Mike just glared at her. "I'm separated.

But, just in case we get back together, I wear my wedding ring when I go out to deter other women from approaching me." "I see. And how is that working for you, buddy? " Tina winked at him. "I was drunk and you're one fine-looking woman. I couldn't resist. Maybe getting to know you will make me forget about her." Tina started laughing. Was this dude for real? "That's nice and all, but I'm not interested. And I am not exactly sure if you're separated either. Maybe wifey is on a vacation somewhere. When the cats are away, the mice will play!" Tina winked and made the "ok" gesture with her fingers. I bet if you pulled that ring off your finger, there'd be a tan line since you probably never take it off. "Thanks tho." "Wow! You are something else." Mike replied with his jaw down to his knees.. *Women usually beg me to stick around, wanting to cuddle and all that crap. But not this chick. She literally wanted a one-night stand and she got one......from me!* Mike's ego was crushed. Tina frowned. "Aww, did I hurt your feelings, Boo? I'm sorry. You're a nice guy but I'm a girl who knows what she wants and I got all I wanted from you last night and just now. So thanks. ""I'd like to call you and see if we can meet up again," Mike said, confused. What the hell was going on here? The bitch was the one that was supposed to be saying those things and have her beg him! "No, that won't be necessary. Do you remember the way out?" Mike jumped off the bed, threw on his jeans, and walked out of the apartment. "Fucking slut! You are making a big mistake by turning me down!" yelling out as he walked out of Tina's place and onto the street and into his car. Tina sighed as she put out her cigarette. *Why must they get hooked all the time? It's cuz I'm a fine piece of ass, that's why!* She then proceeded to look for a provocative gym outfit, thinking about last night. *It was so good to see Kyla after all these years. She looked good. I'm happy that she found a life for herself, hubby and even spit out a few kids. At least she is representing us Latinas well. It was disappointing to see that she is still friends with Samantha however. What was it Sam had said, "best friends?" That Cabrona! I never liked Sam. How dare she think she is better than me? Sam thinks she is smarter than me and classier than me. Well, who the fuck is she? I hope her husband screws another woman, hotter than her, and she finds out about it. Oh, the fabulous Samantha Rose would be sooooo humiliated! She would get what she deserves.* Tina got dressed, grabbed her bag, and left for the gym. *"Tina stop wasting your thoughts on that bitch, Sam. There's work to be done. Hotties, here I come!*

"Kyla, are you awake? Ky?" She could feel his fingers slide up her leg. Then there was a tug at her panties. *Great.* Kyla thought. *It's eight am and he is in the mood for sex. The kids should be waking up any minute which means he will fuck me for two minutes, get off and then go pee. Then he'll want breakfast. Meanwhile, I will be stuck lying here, unsatisfied, trying to make myself decent as my older one barges in and asks me for breakfast.*

"Yeah, barely." she whispered. "I want you." *Is he drooling? I might as well get it over with.* "How do you want me?" she asked in her sexy voice hoping it would entice him to ask for something dirty and not the usual boring stuff. "Stay right where you are." *Great. Missionary position once again. I guess the earth won't be moving today or any day for that matter.* Freddie then began sliding her panties off of her. He took off his bottoms and climbed on top of her. He entered her and laid down on her chest. *Great, not only are we doing the same old position again but now I can't breathe either.* Kyla tried to focus on something else, anything while trying to sound like she was into it. "Oh, God! I am going to explode!" Freddie shouted as he rocked back and forth, panting like a dog that has not had water for days. *Yup! Was that even two minutes?* Kyla wanted to ask him. But instead, she chose to tell him to be quiet or the kids will hear him. Freddie got up and headed for the bathroom. Luckily, the kids were still sleeping. Freddie would be in the bathroom for at least twenty minutes, peeing, brushing his teeth, and doing whatever other shit men spend so much time in the bathroom doing. Kyla reached into her nightstand, unlocked the wooden box, and pulled out one of her closest and dearest friends. Her purple vibrator. *Well, if hubby can't do it for me, at least you will!* Kyla shut her eyes and pictured some hot stranger bending her over, fucking her from behind while other women watched with envy.

After having her morning delight, Kyla got up and put her robe on. She went downstairs and started making breakfast. The morning paper was waiting for her on the doorstep. The kids were still sleeping so she had a few minutes to herself to enjoy a cup of coffee. *I cannot believe I ran into Tina last night. She still looks good. She seems like she is happy with what she has going on. Maybe she is just not the settling down type. Sam shouldn't judge her for that. I am not even sure what Sam's problem with Tina is. Yes, Tina did a lot of fucked up things back when we were teenagers but we are all adults now and I am sure Tina has changed.* Kyla decided that she would give Tina a call and see if she was interested in getting together. I can still get together with Tina without having to involve Sam, Freddie, on the other hand, may need to be lied to. *If he knows anything about Tina's past, he won't let her come anywhere near me!* she thought.

"Thanks for showing a guy some love," Freddie whispered into her ear as he walked into the kitchen. "I have worked up an appetite. Whatta ya say you make your husband a nice breakfast?" *Worked up, my ass!* Thought Kyla. I, on the other hand, was not full. Now, that stranger that I was thinking about just a ½ hour before., would have left me satisfied and full. "Sure thing dear." She replied and proceeded to get out the pans. Freddie sat at their kitchen table and poured himself a glass of juice. "So I was thinking about running over to hardware store and getting some shelf paper. Want to come and pick it out?" Kyla whipped her body around, put her hands on her hips, and began to bark at him. "Oh how exciting Freddie! Should I get dressed up?" Kyla asked sarcastically. "What the hell is wrong with you?" Freddie asked, looking at Kyla in shock. "I am sorry Freddie. But just for once, I would like to forget about running errands and working on the house and instead doing something fun." "We did do something fun.......a little while ago, Freddie smirked. "Nice Freddie, but brushing my teeth would last longer than that." Kyla blurted it out before she had a chance to catch herself. She immediately regretted it and felt horrible. She did not mean to hurt Freddie's feelings. He was a lot of things but he was still her husband and that was cruel. "Are you saying you faked it, Kyla?" Freddie asked his wife as he felt a pang in his heart. Kyla paused and thought about what to say this time carefully. "What? No. I just would have liked it to last longer and maybe switch positions that's all. I was just worried about the kids waking up so I wasn't into it. I am to blame also. Besides, we were talking about our plans for the day, not our sex life." Freddie was upset. "Well, I want to talk about our sex life. Are you not happy?" "I don't satisfy you? Freddie looked like he was either going to cry or punch the wall. "Freddie, I am very happy and very satisfied. " Kyla lied. "Now can we please discuss what to do today?" "Well, apparently you don't want to do me! " Freddie yelled as he yanked the refrigerator door open, knocking all the eggs to the floor. "Daddy? Why doesn't Mommy want to do you?" Four-year-old, little Francesca asked, standing in the middle of the kitchen with egg yolk on her bunny slippers. "Freddie had not noticed or heard her come into the kitchen. "Great! Are you happy now Freddie?" Kyla asked as she bent down to clean up the eggs. Freddie bent down to kiss his daughter. "Mommy doesn't want to do my laundry today because she stayed out late last night and is too tired." With that, he turned to Kyla, beat red in the face. "I need some air. Kyla. We can discuss what to do this afternoon when I get back. I am going to the gym to blow off some steam!"

"Tell me again why we are shopping up here when there are two great malls by me." Kristen asked Sam as they pulled into the parking lot of the mall an hour past Sam's house. Natalia and Nikki sat in the back, clueless about their surroundings. Nikki had her headphones in, listening to her playlist and Natalia was texting her friend about what she should buy at the mall. "Because it is bigger and more open than those malls. Too many low lives go there anyway. There are so many cases of women being mugged or worse. It's not worth saving gas. Besides, this is the only mall that has lots of options for the girls. You know it is hard to find size double zero!" Sam said as she jumped out of the car. Truth was, Sam was becoming less of a city person and more of a suburban chick. She was tired of all the crowds and just people in general. "Girls! Andiamo! I want to get the bulk of the shopping done before it gets too crowded. The girls entered the mall through the department store entrance. Sam had to stop at the makeup department for mascara. Like her daughter, she was low on the stuff as well. "On our way out, I want to see if they have any new shoes. I need a new pair of sandals for a dress I just bought." Sam said as she tested the latest scents on display. Kristen frowned. I broke my heel last night while running for the train. So I'll look too. Not that I can afford to buy anything for myself. Nikki needs some stuff for school.' Sam looked at her sister sympathetically. "I will buy you shoes. A girl needs her shoes." Kristen shook her head. "Thanks, Sam, but I can't let you do that." Sam wrapped her arm around Kristen. "What are sisters for?" They turned and looked at their daughters. The girls were going to each of the perfume tester bottles and spaying them on the scent blotters to try them out. Sam paid for her mascara and the ladies headed out into the mall, shoe bound.

"No way Nikki! Those pants are too tight" Kristen yelled as Nikki strutted around the dressing room, checking out her ass in the mirror. "Ma, they look good and I want them!" "Sure Nik, if you buy the next size up. Camel toe is not an attractive look!" Nikki made a face and said, "Forget it. Please go outside so I can change." Her mother rolled her eyes and walked out of the dressing room. She joined Sam and Natalia, sitting on a bench, already having made their purchases. "I don't get that kid, " Kristen said to Sam, making sure she was out of earshot now so her daughter couldn't hear them talking. I try to teach her to dress appropriately and not give people the wrong idea. She obviously isn't aware of less being more." Sam looked at her sister." She's a teenager, K. They all dress like hoochie Mamas. Tali is the same way. "Um no I don't, but thanks Ma." Natalia put her hand on her mother's shoulder and gave her a shrug. Sam ignored her and continued talking to Kristen. "Gone are the days of one-store shopping. Our mother used to love shopping at Gimbels and Wannamaker's in Cross County." Kristen laughed at the memory and then frowned. "I hear ya and it is not easy raising her without the support of her father. God, I hate him!" Kristen clamped her mouth shut then as Nikki came out of the dressing room. The woman left the store.

"Ok, so where to now ladies?" Sam asked. "I am starving," Natalia replied. "Can we go to the food court?" "Yea, I could eat something too, I am starting intermittent fasting and it's rough!" Kristen said. "Ok, let's go," Sam headed for the escalator. They chose a table in the corner. Nikki and Natalia opted for McDonald's, while Kristen and Sam chose a deli that made delicious turkey sandwiches. "If only we had the same metabolism as our daughters, Sam thought as she inhaled the delicious aroma of Natalia's french fries. It was getting harder and harder to look ten years younger than her actual age. Natalia and Nikki finished their meals before their mothers even had a chance to make a dent in their sandwiches. "Can we walk by ourselves and meet up with you guys in an hour?" Nikki asked. Their mothers agreed and the girls were gone. "I guess it's not cool to be seen with us old women," Sam laughed. "Speak for yourself!" Kristen replied.

Sam and Kristen finished their lunch and headed for Lululemon for some yoga pants. It was Sam's favorite store, that and Victoria's Secret. "Hey, I didn't want to say anything with Nikki around but if I don't tell someone, I might explode!" Kristen said to Sam. "You're pregnant? Sam spun around and looked at her sister. "No, you jerk!" Kristen replied. "And by who or what? Immaculate Concepcion? It's worse. I received a letter in the mail the other day. It's from the prison. Chris is being released. "Oh my God! When?" Sam got goosebumps. "In about three weeks." "And you haven't told Nikki yet?" "I was going to tell her tonight. For once, I don't have plans and neither does she so I thought I would take her to dinner and tell her." "Oh wow! I hope she can handle that." Sam sympathized with her sister. She knew how hard Nikki took it when her father was sent to prison and everything that happened after. Kristen put her head down. "She is upset with him but I think she will get over it. As much as she is mad at him, she has missed him. As much as I prefer him staying put, he is still the father of my children. I could never wish him harm. Besides, It will be nice to have someone else in my corner to help with the discipline and the finances." Sam sucked her teeth. "Yeah, well, let's see if he contributes first," she said sarcastically. Chris was another man that Sam did not care for. Why were the closest ladies in her life involved with such losers? "Can I help you?" The sales girl asked them as they walked into Lululemon "No thanks, just browsing" Sam answered as she walked by her, headed for the back of the store. "The last thing Sam wanted was a cute twenty-something with an adorable figure, helping her. So I can look old and fat? Sam shuddered at the thought.

A bitch,
A Jerk and an Inmate

As she threw the paper towels covered in egg yolk into the trash, Kyla could not help but cry. "When did her life become so ordinary? She thought. "I did not live the life of a movie star but I had my moments. I attracted guys from all different species. How did it end up like this?" Kyla truly loved Freddie, but now in her thirties, she was becoming more and more depressed as well as bored. "I did not mean to hurt his ego but I certainly would want to know if my partner was losing interest. That way I could work on it and improve it before they sought satisfaction elsewhere." Not that Freddie was the type. His self-esteem was too low to try anything like that. "Is a life filled with sexual desires and excitement as well as romance supposed to end just because you get married and have some kids?" I need Sam's advice. She always has an answer. Sometimes it has gotten her into trouble though." Kyla smiled, thinking of a few times Sam had worked herself into a mess with Sal and how she managed to work herself out. "I think I will call that crazy mujer and see what she is up to." Kyla reached for her cell phone and selected the first contact on her phone, "Best Bitch."

"Hola Chica! Que Pasa?" Kyla laughed at Sam's atrocious way of speaking Spanish. The funny thing was however, Sam thought she was good at it. "Stick to English," Kyla would always tell her. "Leave the Spanish to me." Sam had picked up on the first ring but Kyla could barely hear her. There was so much noise in the background. "Where are you? It is so noisy." "The mall with my sister and the girls. We promised we'd take them shopping." "Aww, that's nice you guys all have mother/daughter/sister time. I am jealous." Kyla had two older brothers, who both drove her nuts. "Trust me, the way Natalia and Nikki act sometimes, you should be grateful that Francesca is not this age yet. Everything me or my sister does or says is wrong. It is like having another husband." "Oh, God! What you're describing could be summed up in two words, "Teenage Hell!" Both women started laughing. "Ok, I will let you get back to them. I just wanted to know If I can come by with Francesca and Anthony later. Freddie has to step out and I could use some girlie time with you." "Yea, sure. I am not sure what Sal's plan is for later but I am sure it will involve doing some project with the house and we won't see much of him. Besides, the girls would love to see your kids. You know how they love to dress up Francesca and play with Anthony" "Ok, I will call you in a few hours. Talk to you later." Kyla hung up, feeling a little bit better, knowing once she saw Sam and they had a pep talk, all would be ok. "Francesca, let's get you dressed. Mommy needs to get out of this house for a while!"

Francesca was sitting on her bed, pouting. "What's wrong Mija?" Kyla asked as she sat down beside her daughter on the princess-themed bedding. "I hate when you and Daddy fight. It makes me sad." "Oh, baby. We are not fighting. Sometimes adults don't agree on certain things, that's all. You have nothing to worry about. Mommy and Daddy love each other very much and we both love you and your brother more than anything else in this world. Ok?"

Francesca hopped off her bed and picked up her favorite doll."Ok, Mommy. I love you and Daddy too!"

"Ok, play for a little while and then we will go to the park for a bit. And guess what? Later on, I am going to take you to Aunt Sam's to play with Natalia. Her cousin Nikki is there too! Would you like that?" "Yes!" Francesca yelled as she ran around her room. "Ok, I am going to go get ready now." "Mommy? Francesca turned to look at her mother. "Daddy said you did not want to do his laundry because you stayed out with friends. That's not nice. You should stay home and play with Daddy. Kyla, in a bit of shock, replied, "We just had a misunderstanding, Honey. Now go play and then we will go out." She walked out of Francesca's room and headed for her room, thinking, *I am going to kill Freddie!*

"Woo hoo! The gym is packed with hot, sexy, sweaty bodies already!" Tina thought excitedly as she put her gym bag in a locker. As this hot muscle head walked by her, Tina pretended to drop her water bottle onto the floor. She bent over in front of muscle head, sticking her ass in the air as high as she could. She timed it perfectly so that his crotch went right into her ass. "Oh excuse me! " She replied as she stood back up. " I didn't see you behind me." "Well, I saw you!" Muscle head said as he stared at her overly exposed cleavage. Tina smiled and batted her eyes. "I guess I will see you around. Maybe you can give me a spot or two." Tina said, in her most flirtatious way. "Sure!" Muscle head said. He then walked away and headed toward the weight bench. *Bait, hook, and sinker! This is too easy.* Tina said to herself as she walked over to the treadmills.

Tina chose a machine between two fat women who were sweating so much you would have thought they just finished running the NYC Marathon. Tina always chose the most unattractive women she could find to be near in the gym. The uglier they were, the hotter she looked next to them. She was like that when she was younger too. She chose to be friends with girls that scored low in the looks category. Except for Kyla, all her friends were dogs. Tina was always the one who got the phone numbers and asked out on dates. It sucked when Kyla started bringing Sam with her to hang out with them. Tina may have been hotter, but that bitch Sam was prettier.

On the other side of the gym, Freddie was walking in with one of his high school buddies, Tim. Freddie and Tim did a lot of things together. They worked out together, watched both the Yankee and the Giants games together, and occasionally would get together for dinner with the wives. Tim's wife, Lisa was a down-to-earth, the girl next door type. Kyla got along great with her. *Thank God for that,* Freddie thought. *If Kyla was like Sam, who hated most women, it would have been a problem. Sam is a bad influence on my wife.* Freddie thought. She is so independent and thinks that Kyla needs more time to herself. *Well, who the fuck does that cunt think she is?"* *She is a wife and a mother and needs to stay home and take care of her family. She shouldn't worry so much about getting her hair and nails done. Who is she trying to impress? Certainly not Sal! Sal......what a wuss! If he had any control over his wife, he wouldn't let her run around so much, going God knows where and doing God knows what! And those piercings! A grown adult as well as a wife and mother should not be walking around with her nose and stomach pierced. And now, Kyla wants to do it too! Over my dead body!* His attention was brought back to Tim who was asking him a question. "Do you want to do arms or legs today, Freddie?" Tim asked as he took out his headphones from his gym bag. "Let's do arms. I did cardio yesterday and my legs are sore. Besides, I want to do as much as I can with my upper body. I have a feeling Kyla is looking for a little more excitement." "And you think having a bigger chest and some big guns will achieve that?" Tim asked Freddie with a puzzled look on his face" I don't know but she seems bored with me lately, in all areas. She thinks we don't get out enough and then she made some comments about our sex life." "Are you not doing what you're supposed to?" Tim asked, trying to hold back his laughter. He did feel bad for Freddie though. Freddie always lacked self-esteem. Tim was shocked that he landed a looker like Kyla. " Don't be a dick. Anyway, I thought I was, but maybe I'm not in her opinion and her needs."

Freddie replied. "It is probably that bitch Sam putting shit into Kyla's head." "Why? You slept with Sam and she's telling Kyla how bad of a lay you are?" Tim was laughing now. Freddie grew angry. "Fuck you douchebag! No way! Sam is hot but I can't stand her! Kyla is probably confiding in Sam about us and Sam is probably giving her bad advice. For all I know, Sam could be telling Kyla to tell me they are getting together to do some shopping, while persuading Kyla to find someone to have an affair with, instead. I wouldn't put it past Sam." "Freddie, I don't know Kyla as well as you do, but from what I see, Kyla loves you very much and she is not that type of girl. I know Sam too. She is headstrong but has her morals intact. Kyla is probably just going through a rough patch. You two have been together a long time. Having kids also will put a strain on a marriage. It's probably tough to stay home with kids all day and cater to them. That is why I don't have any. Lisa is focused on her career and so am I. We have no desire to have children. But I will tell you that I do keep it interesting so that Lisa's eyes do not look beyond me." "Ok, so what is so interesting is that Lisa would never want to fuck another man besides Big Timmy?" Now it was Freddie's time to laugh. This time, Tim made a face, "Who's being a dick now? To answer your question, we don't do anything crazy, nothing special. We get dressed up, go out to eat, and then have some drinks. She gets into a wild mood after a few drinks. We go home, watch porn, and play.

We try new things and shit. Lisa is actually into trying new positions and playing with toys. If you can believe that! Anyway, I've said too much. If Lisa ever knew I was talking about this, she'd ban me from her vagina. Both guys laughed at this point. Freddie put on his headphones and grabbed his water bottle. "Enough about this shit! Let's go work out!

The gym was crowded at this time. All the weights and benches were being used so Freddie and Tim decided to kill the wait time and headed to the cardio section of the gym which consisted of bikes, treadmills, and ellipticals. It was crowded there too and the only thing available was two ellipticals in the second row of machines behind some ugly, sweaty women and one petite attractive one. "Shit Freddie, we gotta stare at these backsides? "At least there is one fine-looking ass in the middle of it!" Freddie and Tim proceeded to get on the ellipticals located directly behind Tina Santiago. Tina looked over her shoulder and smiled at them. "Damn, I think she heard us." "Trust me, that girl does not need to hear it from us. She probably tells it to herself!"

For the next two hours, both men did their workouts, pushing as hard as they could. When they were done, they headed for the locker room to wash up. "So what's your plan for the rest of the day? Tim asked Freddie. "Oh please. That is how my fight started with Kyla this morning." Freddie mumbled. "Well, good luck with that. I'll catch ya later." Tim walked out of the locker room. Freddie finished changing and headed out of the locker room. He pulled his cell phone out of his gym bag to check for messages. He was looking at his phone and not paying attention when he banged right into someone. "Oh, I am so sorry. Please excuse me!" Freddie said, embarrassed. "That's ok, I don't break easily." Freddie was staring into the eyes of Tina Santiago.

Sam dropped Kristen off at home after the mall and headed back to her own house with her daughter and her niece. Nikki was spending the night with them. She would do anything to get away from her mother and grandparents for a night. They harped on her too much. She would have been forced to go to dinner with all of them. Her grandfather would embarrass her by asking her if she is seeing any boys. Her grandmother would scold her for the way she dressed, spoke, and maybe even the way she was breathing! And her mother, well she was just plain annoying to Nikki. Yes, a night at Aunt Sam's would work. Aunt Sam and Uncle Sal were not like other parents Nikki had observed at friends' houses. They were laid back and let Natalia pretty much do whatever she wanted as long as she did as she was told. Kyla was coming over too. Kyla was a lot of fun. She was bringing her kids. Both Nikki and Natalia loved to play with them.

Once they got back to the house, the girls headed for Natalia's room. Sam knew she wouldn't see or hear from them for a while. *How those two can stay on a computer for hours and not get paid for it, I will never understand!* Sam thought as she put away all the stuff she bought at the mall. *Sal should be home in a little bit. At least that will give me some time to relax before he gets here and starts ranting and raving about what we didn't put away or what has broken in the house this time.* Every time Sal bitched, Sam would say," Hello? We have kids. Things will get messed up." Did Sal think they should sit on the couch and not move from the time they got up until they went to bed? *I would love to switch with him for a day. I would work all day while he stayed with the kids. Let's see how he will handle it! I bet he wouldn't survive!* Sam did love Sal though. He was a great father to the kids and took care of them well. Sam did not hurt for anything. She just wished his attitude toward life was a little better. He was a bit too high-strung for her. *He has to learn to relax before he has a heart attack!* Sam jumped onto her social media networks to check what everyone else was up to. She liked to go on before Sal got home. He had a problem with the whole internet thing. He did not like their private family life to be exposed. It also didn't help that several of Sam's friends were ex-boyfriends. "It does not mean anything Sal," Sam often heard herself saying. "We shared a past and we are friends on here, that is all." "Well, I don't understand why you need to be friends with them. Why would they need or want to talk to you unless they were interested in getting together with you?" That was always Sal's reply. He just didn't get it. He did not have any accounts online and he did not want any either. As far as he was concerned, it caused nothing but trouble. He was right to some extent. They both knew that just from having Natalia and Nikki around. Kids could be so cruel. More often than not, when kids were in a fight, one of them would write mean things about the other one on social media. From what they would see on the news, some kids committed suicide over it. Sam reminded herself to go on Natalia's page just to look around and make sure all was innocent.

By the time Sam had finished reading through all the comments left on both her page, Natalia's page, and Nikki's, Sal was home. Sam shut down the computer and went downstairs to greet him. "Hi, Baby. How was your day?" "Busted my ass again as usual. Two guys didn't show up and one of the machines broke. I am never gonna finish this job and the owner is bitching. "I'm sorry honey," Sam said as leaned toward Sal to kiss him. "Not now, Sam. I am filthy from work. Sal then walked upstairs to put his stuff down. "And how was your day Baby? What's new?" Sam said sarcastically as she watched Sal walk away. "Thanks for asking, Jerk!" she whispered.

"Yo Ma, when is Kyla getting here?" Natalia and Nikki both bounced into the kitchen, headed for the refrigerator. Sam gave

Natalia a look for "yoing "her. "I made cupcakes this morning. They are on top of the microwave. Kyla will be here in about one hour. Tali, I hope your room is neat. If not, go clean it." "After I eat a cupcake." Natalia poured two glasses of milk for her and Nikki. "Did you see what Tara wrote about Jen?" Natalia asked Nikki while shoving almost the whole cupcake in her mouth. "Yup! What a nasty bi-atch!" "Watch your language!" Sam spat at Nikki. "Sorry, Aunt Sam." "You guys have to be careful what you put on the internet. It is considered bullying. It has hurt a lot of people and gotten people into trouble." "Then why do you have it, Mom?" Natalia asked her mother sarcastically. "Because I am an adult, Tali. And I only deal with adults on it. I don't post every day, gossiping about someone. Natalia rolled her eyes. "Whatever, I am going to clean my room. Coming Nik?" "I wanna finish my cupcake first." Natalia left the kitchen, leaving Sam and Nikki to clean up. "Oh, that child!" Sam threw out Natalia's plate and wiped up the crumbs.

"So did you hear, Aunt Sam?" Nikki was asking her Aunt. "Did I hear what? Tali is a slob?" Sam laughed. "No seriously. My dad is being released from prison." Sam stopped laughing and looked at Nikki. "How do you know that?" "When someone is in prison, you can go to the county website and request to be emailed when there is a status update on an inmate. I had Daddy's DIN number so I signed up for it. I received an email letting me know he is about to be released. I am not sure if Mom knows." Sam looked at her niece. "Mom does know Nikki and she was planning on telling you tonight until you requested a sleepover. She did not want to disappoint you, so she was going to wait until tomorrow to tell you." "Well, now she won't have to." "How do you feel about Dad getting out?" Sam put her hand on Nikki's shoulder and looked at her. "I don't know. I am so mad at him for disrupting our lives. We had to give up so much because of him. I don't think he even realizes it. But then I think about all he had done for me before this happened. He was at all my games, my plays, everything. Should I fault him for trying to provide for us? Mom and dad struggled for so long. He just wanted a chance to give us anything we wanted." Nikki's eyes started to well up with tears. Sam put her arms around Nikki and hugged her. "I don't know what the answer is, Honey. It is up to you to decide how you feel and if you can forgive him. That is not for me, your mother, or anyone else to decide for you. "I guess I will have to think about it. Mom finally started having a life again and showing signs of happiness. I don't want this to ruin it. We are starting to get along again." "I know, baby. You two will get through this together." "Thanks, Aunt Sam. I am going to go help Natalia clean her room before the rugrats get here!" Nikki kissed her aunt and walked out of the kitchen.

Now what am I gonna do tonight? Kristen wondered as she put all her packages away. She planned to stay home and tell Nikki her father was being released from prison. Nikki pleaded with her to stay at Sam's overnight so Kristen gave in. She liked making Nikki happy. *That kid has been through so much and now that her father is getting out, who knows how she will react. "* Kristen had tried everything when Chris went to prison. She had Nikki see a therapist. She even took a leave of absence from work to spend more time with her daughter.

"Kristen is thata you?" her mother called as she opened the door and walked into the house. "No Ma, it's a burglar!" Kristen joked as she kissed her mother. "Don't geta smart!" her mother scolded. "Remember, your father and I always be cautious. We always make sure all is ok, when we hear a noise!" "Yeah, yeah," Kristen replied as she grabbed the packages her mother was carrying and put them down on the kitchen table. "Where is Nikki?" "She wanted to stay with Sam tonight." "Oh ok. Will you a be going out again tonight or should I includa you in our dinner plans for thisa evening?" "I am not sure yet. I have to give Peter a call and see if he is free now. Nikki staying at Sam's was unexpected." "God forbid youa stay home!" Her mother scolded.

Kristen sighed. "Ma, please. Seriously? What is there for me to do here? I am sure you and Dad like your privacy. Nik is not here. Going out and having fun keeps me sane and helps me to forget everything I have been through. Speaking of which, there is something you should know." "Oh?" Her mother turned and looked at Kristen with a worried expression." "Chris is being released from prison." Kristen turned away from her mother and pretended like she was cleaning the counter. She couldn't bear to look at her mother's expression and feared what was about to come out of her mother's mouth. "What? When? How dida this happen? You mean to tell a me that that no good, poor excuse a for a husband and a father is getting out? I never did a believe in our justice system!" "Ma, don't go there. Yes, what he did was wrong but he was always good to the kids. And please, don't ever talk like that in front of them about their father." Kristen's mother looked at her like she was crazy. "Kristen, I don't have a to. Surely, they cana see what an asshole he is, stronza di merda! " Kristen started to open her mouth to protest but her mother stopped her. "Kristen, how cana you defenda that man? Not only did he cheata on you, but he was involved in a criminal activity, sending him to prison. You and a your children were forced to leave your home. You options were to either go on welfare or move ina with your father and me. If anything, I woulda think that you woulda be hoping someone would kill him while a he was inside!" Her mother was beat red in the face now. Kristen was also. "Mother! How could you say something like that? I have known Chris since we were teenagers and things were good for many, many years. So what if we did not have much money? We were happy. Things fell apart financially and he got desperate. Because of the financial problems, we fought a lot and he found comfort in another woman. He is human, Ma. I don't forgive him but I can understand why he did what he did. Kristen was crying now. *Why did it have to be like this she thought? Am I ever going to find happiness again?* "Kristen, I raised you a better than this. Che diavolo c'è di sbagliato con te? What Chris dida is unacceptable and wrong. You needa to see that. There is a no excuse for his behavior and I willa not allow you to defenda that piece of shit in mya house!" With that, her mother stormed out of the kitchen and into her bedroom, slamming the door behind her and cursing in Italian. Kristen sat at the kitchen table and put her head in her hands. "Someone, please rescue me from this hell I am in." she whimpered.

While all this was going on, Kristen hadn't noticed her cell phone went off. She reached into her bag for some tissues to wipe her tears and noticed she had missed a call from Peter. "Ah, Peter. Sweet, adorable, and sexy Peter." Kristen felt better all of a sudden, thinking about her latest fling. She had met Peter on a singles website. He was divorced with one child. He and Kristen had gone out a few times and had hit it off. Kristen found herself thinking of Peter frequently and this shocked her.

In the last few years since her former husband went away, Kristen had dated quite a few men she met both on websites and through the workplace. She always had a good time, but up until now, there was no one Kristen took seriously. She had even booked a hotel room to have casual sex with a few, just out of pure woman's needs and for fun but nothing more than that. Peter was different. He treated her like a lady and they had similar interests. Nikki had met him a few times and liked him as well. Things with Peter were developing into something more and rather quickly at that. Kristen did not know whether to feel excited or nervous about it.

The gym and the park

"I think I should attend the gym more often," Tina said out loud to herself as she left the gym and headed toward her car. She had just banged into someone she did not know but had caught her attention with more than just his physical appearance. Being this normally did not happen, Tina was intrigued by it. She had no idea if he had money, what he did, who he was, or where he was from. Shit, she did not even know if he was married! "Like that matters anyway!" Tina laughed as she turned the key into the ignition. She did catch a glimpse of him earlier when he was behind her in the cardio area. His friend gawked at her while this guy paid her no mind. Freddie, he said his name was, banged right into her as she was leaving the gym. Their eyes had met. She had never seen eyes bluer than his. He had a nice tone to his body and when he smiled at her, she felt herself melt a little. *What is happening?* She thought as she drove back to her apartment. She had never seen this guy before but wanted to see him again. Tina found herself thinking about this guy and it gave her butterflies. She did not like it. "Never involve feelings. That's how you get hurt," was Tina's motto. Yet, she couldn't help it. *Yes, I will definitely have to make more attempts to get to that gym and see if that guy is a member! Oh, wait! I could ask Brielle!* Brielle was the receptionist at the front desk. Tina was friendly with her and if anyone knew who was who in the gym, it was Brielle. "Yes, I think I will give Brielle a call and find out exactly who Mr. Blue Eyes is!"

Tina pulled into her parking space at the tenement where she resided. She stopped at the mailboxes to get her mail. Nothing. "Stupid piece of shit mailman!" Tina's mail never arrived until late afternoon on a Saturday. *What does he do all day? Jerk off in his mail truck?* Tina chose to walk up the steps instead of using the elevator. *Might as well keep it tight!* Tina swore her ass was her best asset and would make sure it stayed that way. She walked into her apartment and set her gym bag on the kitchen counter. She pulled out her cell phone which was displaying a voicemail message. *I guess I never heard it ring,* she thought as she entered her password on the phone to listen to the message. It was from John, "Mr. I have a wife and cannot leave her." Tina smiled at first. *I knew it was only a matter of time!* But once she started listening to the voicemail, she became disinterested. John began to tell Tina how he missed her and wanted to see her. He figured out how he could sneak away for a bit without his wife knowing. He wants to take Tina out for dinner...to talk. "Yeah, and to fuck my brains out and then go home to his wife! Pendejo!" Tina threw her phone on the couch. *Screw him! You don't get to decide to walk away from me, realize you made a mistake, and think you can just waltz right back into my life! What did he take her for, some cheap whore that he can just call whenever he feels like it? Does he not know how I operate? He must not know me at all! It would serve him right for me to contact his wife and play this message for her!* Tina picked up the phone to see if she could find any way to get in touch with his wife but then decided against it. *I did have some great times with him and it is better to never burn bridges.* John was pretty powerful and popular. It was better to have him on her side than to be enemies with him. *Besides, I can always use what I have between my legs as a bone for that dog! I'll make him sweat it out and beg a little before I return his calls. Maybe he will even try to bribe me a little with some nice gifts.* "Yes, I think I will hold out for a bit. Tina deleted John's message and then noticed she had a text message. It was from Kyla, telling her how great it was seeing her after all these years and how she would love to get together. *Wow! I guess she has forgiven me for all those rotten things I did to her when we were teenagers. I guess I could have avoided seeing anyone that Kyla was involved with. I was young and stupid though. Besides, none of those guys mean anything now anyway.* Tina smiled. "I would love to see Kyla again. We used to be best friends." Tina had missed having someone in her life that was easy to talk to and to whom she could reveal all her dirty secrets too without judgment. "Now if I can just keep that bitch, Sam, out of the picture, it would be perfect!" After all, Sam was a hater and Tina did not want to have to deal with that or have Sam's opinion of her influence Kyla in any way. Truth was, most women were intimidated by Tina and weren't a threat, but Sam was different. Tina knew she had met her match with her all those years ago when she met Sam and certainly did not want to go there again. Sam was the only one that had the balls or tits for that matter, to tell Tina off and threaten her if she came anywhere near the guys she was seeing. Tina was somewhat afraid of her then. *Now as an adult, Samantha*

Rose may be even more vicious! She would be a challenge and I am not so sure I'd win. But for now, I think I will shower and then give Kyla a call so we can set something up. "But before anything, I am going to call Brielle and get the scoop on that guy I met earlier", she told Diamond, her cat, named after Tina's best friend. *I think she is working now.* Tina dialed the phone number of the gym. " I need to know who that guy is!"

The park was filled with many strollers and stay-at-home mothers sharing their latest recipes and remedies for when the kids get sick. Kyla was usually kept to herself, away from these types of moms. She loved being a mom but she wasn't exactly like the other moms that congregated in the park. Today, she really wasn't in the mood to be social. She was desperate for some alone time. She did not want to hear about who did what in school last week and whose marriage is falling apart. To ensure she got her much-needed quiet time, she chose a bench in the park away from everyone but where she can still watch her kids on the jungle gym. Kyla put her headphones in her ears and opened up a book. Francesca and Anthony were playing nicely with some other kids, taking turns going down the slide. She recognized a few of the mothers but they looked so deep in conversation that maybe they would not walk over to chat, Kyla secretly hoped. She could not wait to get to Sam's and confide in her about her fight with Freddie. Sam had a way of saying the right thing and giving good advice. Kyla always had a blast when she went over there too. Kyla did not have to worry about her kids because Sam's daughter and niece adored them and kept them occupied. Kyla could actually sit down with Sam to talk, laugh, and have a cup of coffee, even if Sal was home. He usually left them alone anyhow. He couldn't be bothered with girl talk, Unlike Freddie who would be up their asses, listening to every word they spoke. He was always either criticizing or volunteering his unwanted advice. That did not happen too often though. Freddie pissed Sam off so much in the past, that she rarely came over to Kyla's.

"Hello, Kyla. How are you?" *Great,* Kyla thought as she smiled back at Jordan Stevens, Queen of the gossip. She was also extremely conceited and annoying. Never mind the fact that Kyla was busy reading and had earphones in. This woman was down right rude and as inconsiderate as they come. Jordan was wealthy and let everyone around her know it. She often bragged about her kid's grades and about how they won the game for the ten thousand teams they played on. She was the typical annoying neighbor that you could not stand but waved and smiled at to be polite and keep the peace. Her kids always sold the most products for the school's fundraisers whether it was holiday wrapping paper, chocolate, plants or any other shit parents don't need but buy so their kid can get the cheap ass prize. Rumor was Jordan brought all the stuff herself just so her kids could be the winner. She always brought baked goods to every town and school event. But those who knew her were on to her. Jordan could not bake to save her life! Her cookies were like hockey pucks and tasted like ass. It was her housekeeper who baked. Jordan just passed it off as her own. "Hi, Jordan. I am good, thanks." Kyla forced herself to say. "Glad to hear it. My Ethan just loves Francesca. He talks about her all the time. I would like to set up a playdate at my house sometime." *Why me?* Kyla said to herself as she continued smiling at Jordan. *So Francesca will go to their house, see all that she does not have, be treated horribly by that rotten spoiled brat, Ethan and then I will get to pick her up and hear all about the latest chandelier that is all pure crystal and is one of a kind and how it cost a fortune to have it sent to the Stevens Household. Or it will be about the month-long vacation around Europe with their butlers tagging along. I would rather cut myself and then jump straight into a shark pool!* "Sure, anytime, Jordan. Just let me know what is convenient for you." Kyla replied with the utmost phoniness. "Great! Oh, and maybe you could come for tea as well Kyla. I hired a new housekeeper from "Por-toe" Rico but she does not speak English that well. Spanish is her native language. I thought maybe you could help out with the language barrier and teach her a few words in English." Kyla cringed as she stared back at Jordan. She lied as best she could, trying to keep a straight face. "Um, I can try but I am not fluent in Spanish. Although my parents are both Puerto Rican, (emphasizing pronouncing Puerto correctly) *It's Puuuuuerto Bitch! Not Pooooortoe!* Kyla angrily thought. They were born here and only spoke in English to me and my siblings. "Oh, ok, then, I will be in touch!" Kyla watched as the snooty bitch walked back over to her other Cunt friends. *I'm sure I won't be hearing from her now, knowing I can't give her something she needs. Thank God for small miracles.* Kyla chuckled to herself. *She doesn't need to know that I am bilingual. Besides, Sé más español de lo que piensas.* She put her earphones back in her ears and decided to blast Daddy Yankee.

As Kyla listened to music and watched her kids chase each other on the jungle gym, she wondered if she would hear back from Tina. Kyla sent her a text earlier, to see if she wanted to get together for drinks. Seeing Tina brought back many memories and before Tina had done what she had done, they shared a lot of good times. Kyla knew that she would have to try to keep that quiet when she saw Sam later. From the way Sam had reacted to seeing Tina and the thought of Kyla getting together with her, Kyla thought it would be best to not mention it. She was not about to get into that whole thing again. Sam got all pissy and once she got that way, there was no reasoning with her. As if Kyla were psychic, her phone went off. It was a text from Tina, stating how she would love to get together and to name the date and place.

Sam did a once-over of the house to check for anything out of place or dirty. Kyla was due to arrive a little bit with the kids from the park. Sam knew the house would be turned upside down once the kids came, but she at least wanted it to look presentable at first. "Damn kids," Sam said out loud as she scooped up cupcake crumbs from the kitchen counter and off the floor. "Did they get any into their mouths?" Sam heard a noise and turned around. Bobby and Joey came into the kitchen. "I didn't know you two were here." Joey was Sam's son and Bobby was Kristen's. "Yeah, Ma. We just stopped by to grab some food, then we're off to shoot some hoops. Bobby is staying tonight." "Hi Aunt Sam," Bobby said as he kissed Sam on the cheek. "Oh, ok. Bobby, your sister is here too. She is in Natalia's room. She is spending the night also." Bobby made a face. "Just think, when I finally get some peace, my little sister has to come. I can't escape!" "Oh hush!" Sam said as she smacked him with a dish towel. The boys then proceeded to open the refrigerator and start making sandwiches. Sam continued cleaning the kitchen around them. The doorbell rang. "Girls!" Sam yelled. "Kyla and the kids are here!" Sam quickly washed her hands in the sink, dried them on her pants, and opened the door.

"Hey!" Sam shouted at Kyla, Francesca & Anthony. Anthony walked right in while Francesca hid behind her mother's legs. "I bet, she will be up Natalia and Nikki's butts in no time", laughed Kyla.

"C'mon in," Sam said as she shut the door behind them. "Ohh, Kiddos?" Natalia and Nikki came running down the stairs to greet everyone. "Look who's here? What a surprise!" Bobby sarcastically said out loud as he looked at his sister. "Oh shut up loser." Nikki barked back. "Now now, children," Sam scolded. Kyla couldn't help but laugh. "Oh, I can't wait for mine to be that age! "Les patearé el Culo!" Nikki was puzzled. "Not sure what that means but we're stealing your kids, so I hope you don't mind," she told Kyla as she grabbed Francesca by the hand and proceeded to go back upstairs. Anthony smiled at Natalia and proceeded to follow the girls upstairs. "Just make sure you keep an eye on Francesca!" Sam yelled as the kids went into Natalia's room. The boys threw out their plates, kissed Sam on the cheek, and opened the door. "Bye, Aunt Ky yelled Joey. "Bye baby," Kyla yelled back. "Bye Bobby". Kyla smiled at Sam. "I love that he refers to me as his aunt. It's so cute." "Sit down and relax, Ky. I'll pour the wine, Sam winked at Kyla. She then retrieved two glasses from the bar in their family room. Kyla sat down at the kitchen table and sighed. "Whew. I love my children but it feels good to get them out of my hair for a bit. Especially when I know that they are having a great time. Francesca is probably all smiles now." Sam laughed. "You may not get them back." She placed two glasses of wine on the table and sat across from Kyla. "So what's up? You know you're welcome here anytime but when you ask to come over and I know Freddie's at home, something's up."

Kyla stopped smiling and began to cry into her wine. "Freddie and I had a big fight this morning." I kind of told him in a roundabout way that I am bored with our sex life. "Ouch" Sam replied as she grabbed Kyla's hand. "So I take it he did not appreciate that....no man would." Kyla looked at Sam through her tears. "No, and to make matters worse, Francesca heard some of it. I am not too worried though because we both covered it up." Sam chuckled. "Sorry Ky, I don't mean to laugh, but she is too young to even realize what you were talking about so you can make anything up. I wouldn't worry about that." Kyla wiped her face with a napkin on the table. "I'm not. It was just some salt added to the wound. Anyway, Freddie ran to the gym to release his anger since I pissed him off. What do I do now? What do I say to him? Kyla started to cry again. Sam felt bad for Kyla. *Damn you, Freddie. You're a poor excuse for a man and husband. You make her cry more than you make her smile.* She thought to herself. Sam picked up Kyla's chin and looked straight into her eyes. "Now is your opportunity to speak up and tell him what you have been feeling. Tell him you love him very much but some things need to change. You're a good wife and mother, Ky. Tell him he needs to realize that and start listening to your concerns before it's too late." Kyla nodded. "There's something else too, Sam."

Kyla put her head back down. "What is it? Your vibrator broke?" Sam started laughing again. "No, you jerk. I wasn't going to mention this to you because I know how you'll react and get pissed off. However, we're best friends and I can't hold anything from you." Sam stopped laughing at this point. "Just tell me, Kyla." Kyla turned her head so she wouldn't have to look at Sam's face once she told her. "I sent Tina a text to see if she wanted to meet up and she replied. We are getting together, Sam." Sam guzzled the rest of her wine down and stood up from the table. She walked over to the counter and leaned on it. "Kyla, While there's no denying I have no love loss for Tina, it is not for me to say you should feel the same. It isn't my place to tell you, you cannot see her. I can only give you advice and what I would do in that situation. I told you yesterday how I felt. You do what you feel is right for you. No need for us to rehash this. The last thing I want is for our friendship to be in jeopardy. Especially because of her." Sam walked over and hugged Kyla. "Thanks, Sam. I love you." "I love you too." Just then, they heard a bunch of footsteps running down the steps. The kids returned to the kitchen. "We're bored."

Kristen was smiling from ear to ear as the car drove along the highway. After Sam dropped her off, Peter called and said he wanted to see her. Nikki was at Sam's hanging with Natalia and Bobby was hanging out with his older cousin, Joey, doing whatever it is that young men do nowadays. He decided to spend the night over as well. Little did he know that Nikki would be there too. Kristen couldn't help but chuckle at that. Those two had a love-hate relationship with one another. But truth be told, after what their father did, they grew a little bit closer. They had each other's backs when it came down to it.

Since both kids would be gone for the rest of the day and night, Kristen was free. Peter was delighted to hear this when he called. He picked her up and they drove up the highway, with the top down, listening to the radio. It was a gorgeous day and Peter was taking her to a place he knew where they served drinks on the water. She couldn't remember the last time she felt this good. It had been a long time. Not since Chris went to prison had Kristen felt like this. It was like being a teenager and having your first crush. She was elated.

Peter noticed it too. He saw how happy Kristen was in the moment. He truly liked her. Her family was pretty awesome also. She had great parents who would give anything to see their daughter happy. Her sister was down to earth too. Both women had great kids. If things kept going well with Kristen, he planned on introducing them to his daughter, Rachel. He knew Rachel would mesh well with Natalia and Nikki. They were all around the same age and had similar interests. *Don't get too much ahead of yourself with Kristen, man,* he thought. *You just met the girl. Let's not forget what a psycho your ex turned out to be. History cannot repeat itself! Lauren,* his ex was nuts. Even Rachel wanted no part of her. Her mother became a loose cannon with a temper and he had to get him and his daughter away fast! Living in the same house as that woman was toxic! His ex drank too much. She would get violent when she drank which was often. She'd smack Peter and constantly put her daughter down with insult after insult. Rachel had gone through so much anxiety about leaving her mother, however. But those therapy sessions did help her to understand that it was for her good and sanity. But rushing her into something else would not be wise right now. So far, Kristen seemed to be the whole package, nevertheless and Peter planned on holding on. She was too good to lose. She was beautiful, had brains, and was a great mother to her children. *Her ex-husband must be a real douchebag to screw up his marriage with her. Why cheat on her and commit crimes that screw up your life and your family's? He must be a real piece of work. Kristen was not the materialistic type. She didn't crave more than she had in life.* "Hello, Earth to Peter?" Kristen was waving her hand on the side of his face so as not to block his view. "What? oh sorry." "I asked if we were almost there? What were you thinking about just now?" Peter smiled at Kristen and picked up her hand to kiss it. "I was just thinking of how beautiful you are and how lucky I am to have this opportunity to spend time with you." Kristen blushed.

"We are almost there, my lady," Peter said in a poor British accent. "Great. I am in the mood for a dirty martini", Kristen replied, staring at everything they passed. She loved the Victorian houses, the little shops, and the gorgeous view of the river. Kristen began to envision what it would be like, living here, married to Peter. *What an adorable town. I wouldn't mind having a house somewhere over here. And Sam is not that far away! But before any of that happens, I need to get my shit together. Moving out of my parent's house will be number one. Bobby will be off to college soon and as long as Nikki can get to Natalia, she won't have an issue! But Peter does have a daughter himself. He's told me she is not close to her mother but when it comes to a parent being involved with someone else, sometimes shit hits the fan. For now, I'll just take it slow. I definitely do not need any more dramatic relationships or stress! Dealing with Chris was draining and exhausting. The kids and I went through so much emotional hurt.*

Slut, Serial Killer or Lesbians?

Tina called Brielle from the gym to find out who the guy she banged into was. "All City Gym," some guy answered. "Um, is Brielle there?" "Yeah, she's on the floor, Who should I say is calling?" Tina hesitated to give her name. She knew it might be announced over the loudspeaker to alert Brielle that she was calling, plus Brielle might not recognize it. *Damn. Why couldn't Brielle be at the front desk at this time and the one that answered the phone? Oh, what the hell,* "It's Tina Santiago." "Ok, hang on." From there, Tina heard this guy announce that Brielle had a phone call. He didn't mention her name. Thank goodness. She could hear background noise and then heard that guy tell Brielle that Tina was on the phone. Brielle picked up. "Um, hello, this is Brielle." "Brielle, hi. It's Tina." She heard silence on the other end. "From the gym, Tina Santiago." "Oh hi", Brielle replied. "Sorry, it took me a second." "That's ok, I know it's strange, me calling you at the gym." Truth was, they hardly spoke, except for when they discussed Tina's gym membership of course. "I am so sorry to bother you at work." Tina felt embarrassed now. "I just had a quick question and I'm hoping you can help me." Brielle was floored. *Tina Santiago never says two words to me, but now she wants my help? She walks around the gym like she owns the place, teasing men and shooting dirty looks at other women. But, it's not worth losing my job over being rude to her. I have to maintain a professional and friendly attitude to all of the members, even if I can't stand them!* "Sure, Tina, what's up?" Brielle answered in the fakest voice she could muster. "Thank you." Tina smiled as she looked in the mirror to check out her reflection. "I met a guy in the gym today.

We chatted for a bit and then he ended up asking me out to dinner, Tina lied. "I was just hoping you can give me some background info on him. I wanna make sure he's not weird or anything. God forbid he's a rapist or serial killer. You can never be too careful, you know?" Tina let out a fake laugh. Brielle rolled her eyes. Luckily Tina was on the phone with her and not in person so she couldn't see the look of disgust on Brielle's face. She took a deep breath before replying. "Oh, well, I can try to help you. However, to protect our members and their privacy, I cannot reveal too much info." Now it was Tina's turn to roll her eyes. It was her turn to be fake. "I understand completely. I don't know anything about him, so anything you can give me will help." Tina crossed her fingers. "Ok, do you have his name?" Brielle now annoyed asked. "He said his name is Freddie. He is probably in his thirties and has piercing blue eyes." Again, Brielle rolled her eyes. "Was he with another guy with a lot of tattoos? Tim Pinto is his name." "His friend has tattoos but I am not sure what his name is either." Tina replied. "You're probably talking about Freddie Lovazzo. He's a great guy from what I know about seeing him here, but Tina, he is married. His wife comes to the gym sometimes as well. "Oh, he is?" Tina smirked and tried to sound shocked. *Not that that matters,* she thought. *but now I made him look bad. Brielle thinks he asked another woman out while being married. Oh well. It's just Brielle. She's not anyone special or important. But, I don't want him* *to get into trouble with his wife.* " Well, thanks for letting me know, Brielle. I appreciate it, This information certainly helped. It doesn't matter whether he's a rapist or not. Not that that's ok either. But being married is a no-no." For the third time, Brielle rolled her eyes. *You lying slut. Like that even matters to a whore like you. Now I will have to keep my eyes on both of you. His wife is a good person."* I can't see that guy cheating on his wife though. He seems so quiet and timid. If anything, it's his loud, obnoxious friend, Timothy Pinto that would do that. That man is a pig!*"Ok, glad I could help. Do you need anything else?" Brielle asked, hoping to get this conversation over with. "Nope, that's it. You've been very helpful. Thank you so much, Brielle," Tina replied. "Ok, well have a good day, Tina." Brielle hung up the phone. "I hope that whore gets what's coming to her," she said out loud. She turned around and saw Ryan, her co-worker staring at her. " Was that Tina the Tina that was here earlier? he asked. "She's a fine piece of ass." Brielle whacked him with a gym towel. "You guys are all the same. Dogs! And it's not even worth discussing," she told Ryan. "I gotta get back to work." Brielle walked away from the front desk and back to what she was doing before Tina called. *That was such a waste of my time. The nerve of that slut to call here and ask me about another member. It would serve her right to tell the wife and watch her beat Tina's ass."Just stay out of it. Mind your own business.* Brielle sighed.

Tina hung up the phone. She was excited, to say the least. Not only was this guy hot, but he was married, fitting her type. But she didn't even know how much he made or what he did for a living. Yet, that didn't bother Tina. What did bother her was that it didn't bother her. *What was it about this guy?*, She wondered. Now, I will just have to figure out his workout schedule and go to the gym when he does. Wifely better not tag along. It's bad for business.

Freddie returned home after the gym to an empty house. Shit, *Kyla and the kids are not here. She probably told that bitch Sam about our fight this morning and Sam convinced her to not go home for a while. I guess we're not doing much today. Oh well. She'll get over it. At least I have some time to myself. I should call her though to see where she is and to feel her out. She might still be angry and upset with me.*

Kyla's phone rang. "It's Freddie," she told Sam. "What should I do?" "Um, pick it up," Sam said sarcastically. She then went outside to join the kids in an intense game of dodgeball while Francesca and Anthony kept score. *Kyla should have some privacy on the phone, even if it's with that douchebag.* "Hi, Freddie." Kyla winced as she answered his call. "Hi, Kyla. Where are you? Kyla. She knew Freddie would be upset to hear that she was Sam's. *He'd say "Of course you are. You always run there when we fight, seeking advice from the great Samatha Dimartino.* But she got,"Oh, ok. Do you know how long you'll be? I'll eat something here for lunch and then we can take the kids out somewhere tonight for dinner." Kyla was shocked. Why didn't he react to her being at Sam's? And did he forget they argued this morning? "No I am not sure, I just got here. I took the kids to the park earlier. I'm gonna stay for a bit. The kids are having fun playing with Natalia. Nikki is here also. But, I'll only be here an hour or so, then I'll head home. "Ok, see ya later." Freddie hung up. Kyla was dumbfounded. *What the hell just happened? Who was that on the phone now? It certainly wasn't my husband!* Sam walked back into the house and the kitchen for some drinks for the kids. It was hot outside and they were sweating. "The kids are having a blast, even in this heat, she told Kyla. She got no response. Sam turned around and looked at Kyla, realizing she wasn't paying attention. Kyla was staring into space. "Kyla, did you hear me? What happened with Freddie? Is everything ok? Hello, Earth to Kyla." Kyla snapped out of her trance and stared at Sam. "Sorry Sam, what did you say?" Sam frowned. "I said the kids were having fun. Where were you just now? How'd it go with Freddie? Is everything ok?" Kyla looked at Sam. "I...I think so. He asked where I was. I told him, thinking he would freak out and he said, "ok, see ya later, let's take the kids to dinner tonight," Sam smiled at Kyla. "See? Maybe he is starting to realize what he has and he better start doing the right thing before he loses you. If I were you, I'd stay here for a bit, just to show him that you just don't come running when he says what you want to hear. I wouldn't stay here too long either, to show you're willing to patch things up. Of course, I'm not kicking you out. You can stay as long as you like."

Sam put her hand on Kyla's shoulder. Kyla covered it with her hand. "Thank you so much, Sam. You always know what to say and do. You're a great friend....my best friend." Kyla kissed Sam on the cheek. They turned around and saw Bobby and Joey staring at them. Joey smirked. "Are you two lesbian lovers now?" Sam whipped a water bottle at him.

Freddie put down the phone after he hung up with his wife. He was proud of the way he conducted himself with Kyla on the phone. He didn't tell her to come home or sound upset when Kyla told him she was at Sam's. He probably blew her mind. He walked into the bathroom to take a shower. He was full of sweat from working out. As he stepped into the shower, he found himself thinking of the woman he banged into at the gym. *"Tina, she said her name was. She was beautiful, from head to toe. Not that Kyla isn't. This woman just had a way about her that was so sexy and intriguing. I was attracted to her. The way she spoke, she moved, her physique.... I felt myself starting to sweat again and was nervous. I haven't had a reaction like that since Kyla and I started dating. What was it about this woman I liked so much? Kyla is my everything. We built a beautiful life together, raising two awesome kids. But this woman made me feel powerful, manly. I could tell she was attracted to me too. Kyla doesn't look at me that way anymore. Over the years, it has gotten worse. She seems less and less interested. And judging from this morning, it confirmed how she felt. As if I snapped my fingers, however, that woman Tina made me feel like the man I once was, as short as that moment was. It was nice to feel that way again.*

Freddie finished washing and stepped out of the shower. *Snap out of it man. You're a married man and Kyla is a good woman. You'd be stupid to jeopardize that.* He knew he was right but he still couldn't stop thinking about Tina. The way he was feeling was too good to pass up. *What could be so harmful if I see this woman at the gym again and do a little flirting? I won't cross the line with it. Besides, it may even improve my marriage a little. I heard that men who have sex with another woman outside their marriage end up having a better sex life with their wives. Not that I would go there, but having someone to flirt with and get attention from might lift my spirit. It may very well result in a better relationship with my wife, both emotionally and physically.*

Kristen and Peter walked into the restaurant, holding hands, and asked for the table in the corner on the patio. It had a beautiful view of the Hudson River and the Bear Mountain Bridge. They were seated at the requested table and the waiter took their drink order. Kristen was trying so hard to curb her excitement. Moments before when they arrived and parked, Peter got out of the car and walked over to her side. Peter held the door open for Kristen to get out. Once she was out of the car, he pulled her into his arms and kissed her passionately. Now, they were here, at this beautiful, serene place. It had been a long time since Kristen did anything like this. It felt good...right. *Could this possibly be a second chance for me? It is too good to be true. He doesn't know the whole story though. Will he stick around once he knows?* She realized Peter was staring at her. "I'm sorry Peter. Did you say something?" Kristen asked him. Peter grinned. "I asked if this place was ok." Kristen smiled at him. "It's more than ok." They chatted away, each enjoying each other's company. The drinks came and were finished as quickly as they took to come. They ordered another round. Kristen began working on her second dirty martini while Peter enjoyed his second gin and tonic. They were both taking in the atmosphere and the view around them in beautiful Coldspring, NY. It was a beautiful day to be on the water, soaking up the sun and just relaxing. Kristen was so relaxed and was on cloud nine.

"It sure is beautiful here," Kristen told Peter. "I love the city and all it offers, but there's something to be said about getting away from it all and coming here. I can hear myself think. No horns are blowing, people shouting obscenities and the people!...they are so polite and kind. It certainly isn't what I am used to. And I'm not even that far away! Who knew you could be so close to the jungle but paradise was just on the side of the door!" Peter smiled. He loved seeing Kristen so happy. He wanted her to enjoy herself. If they pursued a relationship together, she needed to enjoy being with him. "I have other plans for us today around this area as well." He told her. "I want to take you on a hike, on a trail that leads to Anthony's nose. It's in a cute town not too far from here." Kristen coughed. "Nose, hike? That doesn't sound appealing. Why would I want to hike up someone's nose?" Peter laughed. "Not a real nose, silly. The trail is named after the poet, Cyrano de Bergerac. The peak of the mountain resembles his nose structure. The views are astounding. Or! We can take a cruise over to Bannerman Island and tour the castle there. The tour includes walking around the garden, the ruins, and the residence. It's about 2 ½ hours long. It will take us about 10-15 minutes to get there from here. Do either of those interest you? We can find a quaint little restaurant for dinner afterward. Kristen was excited. "Wow! There are so many fun things to do around here! I can't believe I haven't visited this town or any other town close by that has all these amazing features, before. I never even heard of it. Sam isn't too far from here either. I wonder if she knows about any of this. She has never mentioned these places. But then again, unless shopping is involved, she probably doesn't know anything about it," Kristen and Peter both chuckled. "Being I am not wearing sneakers, can we save the hike for next time? I already broke one pair of shoes this week.". Peter loved it when she laughed and he was the reason for it. Her ex-husband made her cry so much in the past, Peter just wanted to bring her joy. *I will never hurt you, Kristen. You don't deserve that.* "There's a great ice cream shop on the next block that the kids would love. Maybe next time we can get our girls together and take them on the hike too and then come here for ice cream." Kristen stopped smiling and gulped down the last of her martini. This made Peter nervous. "Did I overstep? Am I moving too quickly? I am sorry. I didn't mean to suggest that we should introduce our girls to each other or that you should even meet my daughter." Peter had already met Kristen's daughter, Nikki, but that was only because he had picked up Kristen from her home on a previous date. Sam and her daughter happened to be there as well, picking up Nikki for the movies. "Oh no, please don't apologize, you did nothing wrong." Kristen twirled the olives around in her glass. " I am the one that should be apologizing. I didn't mean to give the impression I was opposed to the idea. It's just that I'd like to see what comes of this first before we start introducing our families, especially our kids. Nikki has been through so much over everything with her father. I don't wanna cause any more pain or confuse her. I have to protect her. Whereas my son, Bobby, is older and probably won't even care." Kristen felt bad. She did not mean to offend Peter. She was starting to like him. She wanted to take it slow so nothing could screw it up. But what if her reaction just scared him off because he thought she had trust and relationship issues now? Peter grabbed her hand. "I completely understand. My daughter is still going through a lot of emotions over the separation from her mother. I would never introduce her to something she is not ready for, or make her or you, for that matter, feel uncomfortable. As parents, we have to have our children's best interests at heart. We'll take this slow. And, it turns out that we are better just as friends, so be it. I hope not though. I like you, Kristen." Peter said sincerely. "However, if this does progress into something more when we're all ready, we can get them together." Peter leaned back in his chair. "Besides, that just means, I get to have you all to myself for a little while longer." He raised his almost empty glass. "To us, the start of new endeavors." Kristen smiled and raised her empty glass. "Cin Cin!" The waiter, who had been patiently watching them and waiting for the right moment, came over to their table. He did not want to disturb them. Their conversation looked intense. Plus, he needed a good tip! "Shall I bring another round of drinks for you two?" "Yes please!" Kristen and Peter both said in unison.

Everyone Likes a Little Ass

"I'm gonna get to going," Kyla told Sam as she put her wine glass in the sink and began to wash it. Sam tried to stop her. "Leave it Ky. I'll wash it later. Besides, that's what dishwashers are for." "It's one glass, Sam. I can manage it and the dishwasher? Are you that lazy? Kyla asked sarcastically. "Smartass.

Everyone likes a little ass, no one likes a smartass," Sam winked. Kyla laughed. "Ok, well, I've been here for over two hours. Freddie is waiting for me and as you know, we have certain things to discuss, just as long as the kids are out of earshot. That fiasco involving Fransceca this morning was uncalled for. Not to mention, I have to buy eggs now. I think he learned his lesson from me not being there when he came home from the gym. I also didn't come rushing home when he called me. Do you think he knows his days of trying to control me are over? I have hit my breaking point! Besides, if I have any more wine, I won't be able to drive the kids or myself home. It's also probably not a good idea to confront my husband when I've been drinking. I may put my foot in my mouth again." Kyla laughed. "You didn't do anything wrong, Ky, " Sam replied. "You were being honest. Your statement may have crushed his ego and hurt his feelings, but it's for the better. Maybe bringing it into the open, will result in new concepts both in your marriage and your sex life. As much as I can't believe I am saying this, Freddie is a good man. He sucks at being a husband sometimes, no doubt, especially when it comes to his neediness and wanting to control you. He can be a little too nosey in your business at times. Sometimes it doesn't even have anything to do with him and you're not hurting him in any way. Needless to say, there are a lot of things Freddie is, that are not the greatest qualities. However, there are a lot of things, Freddie projects, and it's good stuff. Your marriage is very important to you as it should be. Don't say or do anything that may threaten that. What you have with each other is golden. When you look beyond all this bullshit, anyone, even you can see that. I am here for you always." Sam kissed Kyla on the cheek and gave her a big hug. "I love you, Samantha Dimartino. What would I ever do without you?" Kyla had tears in her eyes. "Hopefully, we'll never find out!" It was Sam's turn to have her eyes swell up. "Francesca, Anthony, vamos! It's time to get going. Daddy is waiting for us," Kyla yelled to her kids. All the kids came running down the stairs with Francesca in Natalia's arms "I don't want to leave, cried Francesca as she held on to Natalia for dear life. "I told you, she'd be this way, Kyla laughed, as she tried to pry her daughter from Natalia's arms. Francesca wrapped her whole body around Natalia for a firm hold. Natalia started whining. "I love you Ceski, but you're pinching me!" Sam looked at Francesca as she managed to pull her off of Natalia. "You are welcome here anytime, little lady. You'll be back real soon, and we'll plan the entire day filled with fun stuff, ok?" Francesca began to squirm. "You promise Aunt Sam?" "Yes, yes, Cescki. Sam bent down to give Francesca a hug and a kiss. "Drive safe, Aunt Kyla." Natalia kissed Kyla bye, grabbed Nikki's hand and they ran back upstairs. "Hurry, before Francesca runs back up the stairs to catch us," she whispered to Nikki. They flew up the stairs before Francesca could even flinch. "Come on, I'll walk you to your car," Sam told Kyla as she picked up Francesca. Kyla grabbed her bag and followed. Sam helped Kyla put Francesca into her car seat and shut the car doors. As Kyla reached to open the driver's door, Sam placed her hand on Kyla's arm. "Remember what I said. Listen to what he has to say. Make sure he listens to what you have to say. Don't give in and don't take his crap but don't be a bitch either. You won't have to yell to get your point across. Don't say anything you'll regret, even if that's what you are feeling then. Once you say something, it can't be undone. " Kyla hugged Sam once more. "I am going to follow your advice, promise. She crossed her fingers and held them up. I'll call you tomorrow and let you know how I made it out. That is of course unless I show up on your doorstep later with a bunch of suitcases and the kids; mascara running down my cheeks." Sam rolled her eyes. "Don't even talk like that. That's not gonna happen. You'll work it out. And by chance you don't, then it's not meant to be." Kyla got in the car, and looked at Sam, "I hope Sal realizes what a great woman HE has!" With that, she blew Sam a kiss and turned around to face her kids. "Kids, let's go see your Daddy!" She pulled out of Sam's driveway.

Sam walked back into the house and started to clean for the second time today. *It was so much fun having Kyla and the kids come over but they definitely can make a mess!* Sam thought as she wiped down the stainless steel refrigerator from all the tiny fingerprints. She then cleaned up the crumbs that left a trail from the kitchen up the stairs to Natalia's room. Once the kids found the cupcakes that Sam made that morning, they devoured them. Chocolate, Vanilla, and all the fixins, including tiny sprinkles, chocolate chips, and more. *Did they get any of the actual cupcakes in their mouths or just on the counter and the floor? Sweeping and vacuuming it is! But not for me alone!* "Natalia and Nikki, get your butts down here!" Natalia swung open the door to her bedroom. "What do you want, Mom, we're kinda busy, trying on what we got at the mall today." "You wanna play? You must pay." Sam yelled. "The two of you come down here and help clean up from yourselves and the little minions." Moaning could be heard followed by "Ok, we have to get dressed and we'll be down. Sam sighed. *They must think I'm a maid and will clean up after them. Not!* A few minutes later, heavy steps came down the stairs. The girls walked into the kitchen. Natalia grabbed the vacuum from the closet while Nikki grabbed a broom. "Have fun, girls", Sam said with a smirk as she began to walk over to the couch to sit and read a magazine. "Thanks for the help," Natalia yelled at her mother as she walked out of the kitchen.

The front door opened and in walked Sal. "Daddy!", Natalia yelled as she dropped the plug for the vacuum and ran over to her dad to hug him. "I missed you!" "I missed you too, Baby," Sal said as he kissed her on top of her head. He stopped hugging her and looked at his daughter. "They just came out with a new version of your phone and I believe someone is due for an upgrade. Wanna go to the store to check it out?" Natalia squealed. "Can Nikki come too?" "Of course!" "Ok, let's go now and I'll take a shower when we get back." Sal caught Sam glaring at them. "Oh Hi, Babe. I didn't see you there." He walked over to kiss Sam who was pissed. "The girls were just starting to clean. Ky and the kids were over. They left a big mess." Sal turned and looked at Natalia who had a frown on her face. "Please Daddy?" Sal turned back to Sam. "Aww, they can clean later. Come on girls, get your shoes on." The girls ran upstairs to grab their shoes. "Sam, We'll be back by dinnertime. Decide where you want to go." Sam rolled her eyes at Sal. "They can clean later? Says the man who always bitches about the house being a mess and no one cleans but you? Sal started to respond, "Sam," "I'm not done", Sam barked back. "You are spoiling our daughter Sal. She will never learn to appreciate things if you keep doing this. Besides, think about how that makes Nikki feel. Her mother cannot provide those things for her. I'm sure it makes her feel bad." Sam was pissed. But, Sal just smiled at his wife's bitchy expression on her face. With a sarcastic tone, Sal answered her. "Then I guess I'll have to buy one for Nikki too." Sam let out a deep breath. She didn't know whether to smack him or kiss him. "That is very generous Sal, but that's not the point. Natalia bats her eyelashes or puts on a sad face and you cave. What is that teaching her?" Sal laughed. "How to pick a husband that will support her love of materialistic things? Man, good luck to that guy!" He faced the staircase. "Girls let's go! Andiamo! See ya later Sam. Please tell the girls that I am in the car." He walked out and Sam just sat there, not sure how to feel. On one hand, he spoils their daughter and now Nikki. He is a good provider and supported them all, but he dismissed Sam's feelings as a parent. That wasn't cool. He made light of Sam's feelings. *We should be discussing anything that involves our children together and both be in agreement.* The girls came bouncing down the stairs. "Bye Mom." Natalia could see her mother was annoyed. "We'll clean up when we get back. Promise." "Yeah, yeah. Dad's in the car. Good luck getting a phone. Make sure you get a case. We won't be replacing it for a while," Sam mumbled. She didn't mention Nikki getting one too. Let Sal surprise her. Out the door, the girls went. Sam sighed. *I guess it could be worse. Natalia could be asking for a new phone and we couldn't afford to get her one. And besides, at least I don't have to deal with the issues Kyla has. It's a constant battle between her and Freddie. According to what Kyla told me about the phone call with him, he was surprisingly pleasant, however. Good for her! I hope she sticks to her guns and lets him know how she feels. I should talk. Even though our situations are very different, I am doing no better with Sal!"* Sam stood up and started to vacuum, knowing the girls would not do it when they got home.

They'd be too excited to play with their new phones. And Sal will complain that the house is a mess. "Oh Kyla, why did you have to leave? It's my turn to vent!"

Tina sat down at her kitchen table and opened her laptop. *Lets just see if this Freddie Lovazzo guy has any info on social media.* She was determined to find out more about him. All Brielle could tell her was that he was married. "And?" Tina asked out loudly. *Like that matters,* Tina chuckled. *Brielle sounded like a bitch on the phone too. Sorry, you don't have it going on girl. Just because you work in the gym, doesn't mean you belong there. Newsflash Bitch, gym members walking into the gym to better themselves, want to see hot, firm, good-looking people behind the counter. They are looking for inspiration and support. What was the manager thinking when he hired you? You obviously don't maintain yourself. With you being the first thing they see when they walk into the gym, I'm surprised they don't lose their willpower to better themselves. Or maybe it has the opposite effect. They see you and are like, "Oh damn! I better workout before I end up looking like the hot mess she is." You must clean the gym pretty well. I should work there. They need me behind the counter.* Tina moved on to another website as she had no luck with this one. *"Damn! He has a profile page but it's private. His profile photo was a picture of a blue Bugatti Chiron. Hmm, I wonder if that's his car,* Tina thought as she tapped a perfectly manicured, red Stiletto nail on her tabletop. She found nothing else as she stalked all the social media sites looking for information. *Maybe he already cheats, and his profile photo is of a car instead of his wife. I bet she's an ugly one too. He probably tells her he goes to the gym but sees other women. He only tells the truth sometimes when he is really at the gym.* Tina felt sorry for the Mrs. now. *Oh well. If she's dumb enough to believe him, she deserves it. I bet she probably isn't giving him the attention he craves. Well, Mr. Freddie Lovazzo, you're in luck. Tina's here now Baby. I'll do whatever you ask.* Tina closed her laptop and started a bubble bath. Once it was full of water and bubbles, Tina slid herself in, closed her eyes, and pictured Freddie in the tub with her.

"Hey, we just left Sam's. We should be home in a bit," Kyla told Freddie when she called him from the car. "Ok, see you soon." Freddie hung up, grabbed a beer from the refrigerator, and sat on the couch. *Ahh, a little time to myself to just relax before the rugrats return. I don't know if Kyla will forget about this morning's argument or be ready to go to war. It was hard to read her from the phone call. Let's hope she forgets or at least feels it's not worth rehashing, especially if the kids are around.* He turned on the tv, looking for the game that was on now but found himself thinking about the woman from the gym again. He shut the television off as he wasn't paying attention to it. His mind was focused on Tina. *Damn man, why can't I get this chick outta my head? "Cuz she's hot that's why. Not to mention, the attention she gave me. I definitely needed that after Kyla's remark this morning.* Freddie felt confident in himself. *I can still attract other females. Hot as fuck too! Maybe Kyla is the one feeling insecure.* Freddie got up and walked into the den. He sat at his desk and turned on his computer. *Social media rocks when you wanna find out about a person. I can probably find out some info on that chick. A girl like that is probably so vain and wants to flaunt herself to the world.* He began pulling up social media websites to see if he could find anything on Tina. All he had was her first name and knew what she looked like. He could pinpoint the location somewhat since she had to either live in the area or work there. *Why else would she go to that gym? The gym! Yes, that's the answer. The gym has a social media page where members can join. They post closings, photos, and more. Even members can upload photos. Maybe Tina has some.* He belonged to it as well, unlike his wife who preferred to stay anonymous. She didn't care that he joined it as long as he didn't show his face in any photos. Freddie agreed. Why invite trouble? As soon as Freddie began searching for Tina by her first name on the gym's page, she popped right up. *She is definitely gorgeous. Just look at the body on her.* It listed her last name. "Santiago," Freddie said out loud in a Spanish accent. He then searched for any Tina Santiagos' in the area, looking for her personal page. He found her based on her profile pic. The page itself wasn't too private and he could access some parts of it. From looking through it, he was able to get some basic info on her. *She is listed as single which is probably a bad thing for me,* laughed Freddie. *With no husband, she has nothing to be concerned about or hold her back. She can flirt and come on to me as much as she wants without having to be sneaky. I can do the same if I want to, being totally innocent, but she may run with it, enticing me to want more. That would be dangerous. Kyla would be angry regardless.* He continued looking through her page. *She lives near the gym and loves shopping. Of course!* He moved on to the photos. They consisted mostly of her in some sexy outfit. *This chick loves selfies and herself for that matter, Freddie chuckled again. There were a lot of photos of designer outfits, shoes, and handbags. Not to mention the backgrounds.* He recognized some of the fine dining establishments in the background of her photos. He had been to company parties at some of them. *Man, she has a lot of guy friends. But yet she wasn't in any photos with them. Strange,* Freddie thought as he scrolled through them. *Are there any women on here? Oh, wait, a mom, a sister, and a niece.* Freddie laughed. *I guess she isn't too popular with the females.* He must have been looking at Tina's page for a while because the next thing he knew, his beer was finished and Kyla was opening the front door and yelling, "Freddie?" Freddie quickly shut the computer down and walked into the hallway to greet his wife and kids.

"This day has been so amazing", Kristen exclaimed as she and Peter walked around Bannerman Island. "First, a delicious lunch, surrounded by a beautiful and serene atmosphere. Not to mention the delicious drinks! Now, here we are, in this beautiful place. I'm having a great time!" Peter grabbed Kristen's hand. "I'm so glad you are enjoying it. I am too. I wanted to do something where we could concentrate on getting to know one another more and spend quality time together." Peter was delighted he was pleasing Kristen. It would only make her want to spend more time together. He knew he had screwed up with the whole getting our girls together thing by suggesting they all go on a hike and for ice cream. The look on Kristen's face had said it all. He made her uncomfortable. Even though they talked through it, he could sense that her guard was still up. *Maybe she will put that behind her and focus on us.* He brought his attention back to what Kristen was saying. "Dinners and bars are such clichés for the first few dates. And in the movies, you can't talk to one another, so why bother? You get so much more out of meeting for a cup of coffee. "So when we went to the movies and out to dinner, you got nothing out of it and it was awkward for you?" Peter was confused. "Oh no! That's not what I meant. Please don't get me wrong, I like going out to eat, in fact, I love it. It's just awkward when you don't know someone yet. They may as well be a stranger that sits next to you on the subway. And bars? I'll save that for a girls' night out or happy hour. But we started out meeting for a cup of coffee so by the time we went out to eat and to the movies, I already felt comfortable and like I knew you. Peter smiled and felt his mind ease a little. He then chuckled at what Kristen said, "No, you're not from NYC are you?" Kristen laughed back. "A city girl who can also appreciate the trees and the trails, not streets or blocks. And! Let's not forget the subway! It's nice knowing that you can walk around and not have to worry about getting mugged or stabbed. Now they both were laughing.

They continued walking around Bannerman Island, enjoying the sights. Peter spotted an advertisement on the walkway. "Would you be interested in seeing a play? They are having one today in about a ½ hour here on the island. We can see if there is any availability. Plays weren't really Kristen's thing. But she felt compelled to give it a shot. *Maybe I should broaden my horizons. Peter seems to be an intelligent, classy guy who appreciates the finer things in life. He has a passion for the arts too. It's a refreshing change from the guys I usually meet. They think they can buy you dinner and a few drinks and then you'll sleep with them.* Kristen had quite a few of those relationships in the past, never lasting more than a few weeks. "Sure, sounds like fun, " she said, smiling at Peter. "Great! Let's walk over and see if there are any tickets left. Holding hands, they walked over to the ticket booth. "You're in luck! the lady at the booth told them. "We have just a few tickets left. The show will begin in about twenty minutes. We have a cash champagne bar located on the far left of the venue if interested. Enjoy the show!" Peter grabbed the tickets from the lady. "Thank you." In one hand, he held the tickets and held Kristen's hand in the other. He led her to the entrance of the venue. "Would you like a glass of champagne, my lady? Peter pretended to tip his nonexistent hat at Kristen. Kristen grinned. *Sure it's corny, but it's also cute.* "I'd love some." She knew she had to be careful though. She already had a few drinks earlier and champagne always went right to her head. *I'll be nursing that drink for sure!* The last thing she wanted was to get tipsy and have Peter think she was lush or even try to take advantage of her. *Not that I think he would ever do such a thing. Plus he might be obligated to buy me another one if I finish it too quickly,* "Two champagne's coming right up!" Peter did his tip the imaginary hat thing again and walked over to the bar. Kristen watched him as he went. *I don't want this day to end. I am having such a good time and haven't felt this way in a long time. It's like I am in a fairytale. Peter is treating me so well, that I feel like a princess. I can't even remember the last time Chris took the initiative. energy, or money to splurge on me when we were together. Not since we were silly teenagers anyhow. Maybe it or even I was never worth it to him. He took me for granted. All those infidelities, lies, and secrets. He hurt not only me but the kids too. I don't think Nikki will ever forgive him. And Bobby being such a vulnerable age having to deal with all of this. How dare Chris! Like my sister says, "You wanna play, you must pay." I hope being divorced and incarcerated is what you were aiming for, Christopher Michael Lapis. Was our whole relationship a lie? Sam doesn't like many people, but she isn't wrong about this one. Oh well, everything happens for a reason. It took some time, and many frogs to find a prince, but I may have just found him and I'm in a better place now.* Peter finished paying for the drinks as he walked back over to her, one champagne flute in each hand. "Here you are, my lady," Peter said as he handed her the flute. "Let's go find our seats."

She Made it Itch

Freddie greeted his wife and kids at the door. "Hey everybody! I missed you guys! Francesca yelled "Daddy" and ran into his arms. Anthony followed. Freddie scooped up both kids in his arms, leaned over, and kissed Kyla. She kissed him back. *Well, that's a good sign at least.* Freddie felt a sigh of relief. *I*

 "How was your day? He asked her as he put the kids down. Before Kyla could reply, Francesca spoke. "It was great, Daddy. First, Mommy cleaned up the mess you made in the kitchen this morning with the eggs. Then I told Mommy that it's not nice to not do your laundry when you're too tired. Then, we went to the park. Mommy talked to Ethan's mommy there. I think Mommy was upset with Ethan's mommy though, probably because she hurt mommy's finger. I think she said she made it itch because mommy held up her finger up to Ethan's mommy when she walked away." "Racist bitch," Kyla whispered in Freddie's ear. "Then, this is the best part, Daddy. Daddy, are you listening?" Francesca grabbed her father's face. Freddie was trying so hard not to laugh at what was coming out of his daughter's mouth. He had to keep his head down so Francesca wouldn't see him laughing. "Yes, Cheski, I'm listening. So what was the best part?" "Ok. After we left the park, we went to Aunt Sam's house. Tali and Nikki were there. So were Joey and Bobby. We had cupcakes that Aunt Sam made. They were so yummy! Franscesca rubbed her little belly. We played dodgeball outside with everyone, and went to Tali's room. They gave me crazy hair-dos!" Francesca was laughing. "Tali told me not to tell Aunt Sam that her room was messy. I didn't Daddy, I didn't! Maybe Tali needs Mommy to clean her room too like she cleans up my messes and now yours too!

Francesca was just rambling on and on while her parents looked at her, smirking at one another. "Oh yeah. Aunt Sam brought us cold drinks too. I was sweating! "It was the best day!" Freddie smiled at his daughter. "What about you, Anthony? Did you have fun too?" Anthony just nodded at his dad and left to go play video games. Kyla picked up her daughter. "Ceski, why don't you pick out a movie for you and your brother to watch and when it's over, we'll go get dinner. Daddy and I need to talk about some stuff, ok? Kyla patted Francesca on the head. "Ok, Mommy. I hope your finger feels better." Their daughter ran into the living room to join her brother. "And, how was your day, Mommy? Freddie smirked. "You dare ask that after the mouthful that Francesca gave you?" Kyla asked her husband, laughing. "That wasn't enough?" "Well, it sounds like you had quite the adventure. "Not really," Kyla replied. "We just went to the park and paid a visit to Sam's afterward. Nothing exciting or crazy. But then again, I'm not four years old!" Freddie laughed. "I am curious though. What was the whole "racist bitch" part about then and your finger too?" Kyla sighed. "Jordan came over to me. I clearly had my headphones in and was reading a book but that mujer is so rude and obnoxious, it didn't phase her. Anyhow, she wanted to know if Francesca would be interested in having a playdate with Ethan. Freddie was confused. "So, what's wrong with that? Aside from, barging in on your space? Should she have called or texted you instead even though she saw you at the park? "No. Any other person, I wouldn't care if they walked over to talk, knowing I was preoccupied. But her, she's always rude and inconsiderate. She has no respect or boundaries for anyone but herself. Anyway, what that Cabrona was really getting at, is that she wanted the kids to have a playdate at her house so I would have to take Francesca over to their house. When I dropped her off, Jordan could nonchalantly ask me to help with the language barrier between that Twat and her newly hired Hispanic maid. Freddie started laughing. "I'm sorry Babe. It just sounds funny. Seriously tho, what did you tell her? That she can kiss your beautiful Boriqua ass? Usted tiene un buen culo!" Freddie's Spanish pronunciation was terrible. "Just like I say to Sam, you should stick to English and Italian. You would suck as a Latin man. Besides, it doesn't matter what I told that asshole. Our daughter, nor I, are not stepping foot in her house. Miss soy mejor que el resto! She will brag about her nice furnishings or the pictures on the walls of their latest trip to "The most exquisite and EXPENSIVE place in the world. Vete pal carajo! Thanks, but, I'd rather hang out in a NYC subway, begging for change." Freddie stared at his wife. *Jordan must have really hit some nerve! Kyla only flips back and forth between Spanish and English like this when she's pissed off at someone. And the subway reference?* "You have been hanging around Sam I see." Kyla couldn't help but laugh. *Sam does have a deep hatred for the NYC* *subway system. She'd rather drive to the city, pay $100 to park, and deal with the traffic on the Westside Highway than take the train. But the woman loves to shop and not everything is available in the suburbs or they don't have a big enough selection. If Amazon doesn't have it, Sam is forced to go into the city. She drags Kyla along for the ride and company.* "Yes! And the smell of her cupcakes made me hungry." Kyla rubbed her stomach. "Where to for dinner?" I was thinking of either doing Mexican or Chinese. I'd like to pick up a bottle of wine for later too. We can have a glass or two after we put the kids to bed. I think we could use some relaxation and quiet time together. What do you think? Freddie smiled. *Clearly, Kyla has chosen to let our argument go. She is willing to move on, therefore I am too. She didn't apologize but she's not letting it escalate either. I'll take it. I just wanted to forget the whole thing anyhow.* He pulled his wife into his arms and smiled at her. She kissed him on his lips, then pulled her face away. "Speaking of cupcakes, I didn't have any because I'm trying to watch what I eat. I need to work out. I was so busy bitching about that pendeja, Jordan,I forgot to ask, how was the gym?"

Even though she wanted to desperately call Kyla and vent, Sam knew she would have to wait. Kyla needed to go home and hash things out with her husband. As much as the ladies committed themselves to being the best friend they could be to each other, they both agreed that their marriages and children will always take priority.

Sam spent the next few hours, cleaning and meal prepping for the always hectic week ahead. She pushed herself to make weekly meals. Otherwise, she'd lose sight of her goals and possibly her husband! She chose to do her workouts at home. Going to the gym was not an option for her. Too many muscle heads being obnoxious and too many women comparing themselves to one another. Not to mention the gossip! No thanks. With all the exercise videos on the streaming networks, she didn't need to leave the house in order to be fit. Today, however, Sam decided to forgo her daily workout. She was just too exhausted from cleaning the house, and leaving early this morning to go clothes shopping with two teenagers. She sat on her couch to read, but quickly dozed off. She awoke to the front door opening and Sal coming in with two very happy girls. "Mom, take a look at my new phone!" Natalia blurted out and shoved the phone in Sam's face even before Sam had a chance to fully open her eyes. "Very nice Tali. I hear that you got one too, Nik." Nikki whipped out her phone from the bag she was holding to show her aunt. "Yes, Uncle Sal got me one too! He is the best Aunt Sam! Tali, let's go to your room and take photos of us with our new phones. Everyone will be soooo jealous!" Up the stairs the first went and slammed shut Natalia's door a few moments later.

"Congrats on being Father/Uncle of the Year," Sam sarcastically said to Sal. They both look like they're over the moon." "Aww, it was nothing. Both of them are good kids. They deserve it. My parents had to struggle a lot to just make ends meet so if I have the chance to give my kids something they want, I'm gonna do it." "And your niece." Sam reminded Sal. "And my niece. Maybe it will make up a little for that piece of shit father she has." "Who is getting out by the way," Sam said as she flipped through a magazine. "Wait. What? When did this happen?" Sal sat down next to his wife on the couch. Sam rolled her eyes. *Wow. He hears something juicy and suddenly I have his attention.* "Kristen got a letter in the mail yesterday. It was from the State Penitentiary. Chris is being released in three weeks." Sal was mad. "Oh my God. Poor Nikki. She just got used to him being in there and her life how it is now. Wait until she finds this out, poor thing." Sam looked at Sal. "She knows. Apparently, she did some detective work on the internet and found out." "Kids are so smart these days." Sal stood up."Well, if I cross paths with that Pezzo di Merda, I'm gonna kill him!" Sam rolled her eyes once more. "Relax Salvatore. Noone is killing anyone. It won't do anybody any good to harm Chris and have you arrested." Sal looked like a dog with his tail between his legs. "Well, what about your sister? Surely, she's not taking this so well." "Obviously Kristen is upset but it is what it is. She knew this day would come. She may very well run straight back into his arms and forgive him for all that he's done. He is still her husband and father to her children. She is seeing someone else though. I am not sure how that is working out yet.

"Good luck to that guy!" Sal said walking into the kitchen. Sam followed. "And, what does that mean, exactly?" "Nothing Babe." Sam grew agitated. "No, you said it. Now tell me what you meant by it!" Sal could tell his wife was pissed. Unless he wanted to spend his Saturday night without speaking to one another, he better explain. "All I meant was that she is about to go through a divorce, her soon to be ex-husband is being released from prison, she has two kids, one being a teenage boy who will compare this guy to his dad in every way. On top of it all, Kristen and both of her children live with your parents! If this guy doesn't think she thinks he is her meal ticket, then he's a saint!" Sam had to admit, Sal had a point. "Well, I met this guy, Peter and he seems like a decent man with morals. He is divorced himself and shares a daughter with his ex. From what Kristen tells me, he has his own issues with a psycho ex." Sal let out a chuckle. "Great! They're meant for each other then! Woohoo!" Sam sucked her teeth. "You can be such an asshole at times, Mr. Dimartino!" Sal smacked his wife on the ass with a dish towel. "Thanks Babe. Now where do you want to go for dinner?"

Tina fluttered around her apartment for the next few hours doing small tasks. As busy as she was, she couldn't keep her mind off of Freddie. She needed to know more about the man from the gym. Brielle wasn't very helpful. Tina had questions, dammit! What does he do for a living, how long has he been married and more, but she really wanted to know where his next whereabouts would be so she could see him again. If it was at the gym, would he be there with his wife? Brielle did say that she was a member. Tina couldn't make her move with wifey around. Tina huffed. *Get your head out of your ass, Bitch. You need to stop this bullshit.* Tina was annoyed with herself for feeling this way. It made her weak, vulnerable and the type of woman she hated. . She decided to jump in the shower and get ready for her usual Saturday night out. *Maybe going out will take my mind off this Freddie Dude.* "I need to re-focus!," she yelled at Diamond.

Just as she was getting out of the shower and grabbing a towel to wrap around her body, her phone rang. Judging by the ring tone, it was her Mama. She quickly put on her bathrobe and ran to pick up the phone. "Hey Ma." "Hola mija. ¿Cómo estás tú? " "I'm fine Ma. Went to the gym today, ran some errands, then came back here and did some stuff around the house. Now, I'm getting ready to go out." Her mother took a deep breath. "I see. And are you meeting anyone special I should know about or is this another one of your nights acting like a puta sucia?" Her mother did not approve of her daughter's lifestyle. She was very religious and conservative. Tina once told her mother that she should have been a nun. Her mother had simply replied, "Then you would never have been born, Tina dear." That made shut Tina up. "Mother! Por favor! I don't need this from you!" Tina was appalled at her mother's response but her mother meant it. "Tina, I think it's time you start settling down with someone and give me some grandchildren. You're too old to be hanging around bars and clubs like some mujerzuela or floozy. Your niece needs some cousins in her life. Where I come from, familia lo es todo, Stop acting so cheap. Leave the married men alone! Tina decided to end the conversation before she said something to her mother that she would regret. "Ok, I gotta go now Mama. My Uber will be here soon. Call you tomorrow. Te quiero." Tina blew a kiss into the phone and hung up. She loved her mother but seriously? Did her mother just refer to her as a dirty whore?

She pinned her hair back while she applied her makeup. As the minutes passed on by, Tina felt less and less like going out. She was thinking about what her mother said. *I can't believe that I am actually contemplating this, but maybe it is time for me to start settling down. I am not getting any younger and don't want to be alone forever. One day, Mama won't be here and my sister has her own life, her own family now.* Tina imagined herself married to Freddie and having children with him. "This is crazy." she yelled to Diamond. "I don't even know the man, yet I am imagining my entire life right now....with him!." With that, Tina got up and washed the makeup off her face. She looked at her cat who was staring back at her from his bed. "So Diamond, what movie shall we watch tonight?

Once the show was over, Peter grabbed Kristen's hand and led her out of the theater. It was still light out with a beautiful sunset over the Hudson River. "It is so beautiful and I love it here." Kristen said as she squeezed Peter's hand. He was still holding on to it, even though they left the theater a few minutes ago. "Like you." With his other hand, Peter grabbed Kristen's chin and brought her lips up to his. They kissed softly. Kristen pulled away first even though she didn't want to. *This is happening so fast. I am falling for him but it's not the right time yet.* Peter noticed the expression on Kristen's face. "Did I overstep again? I am so sorry. I am just really enjoying being with you. I like you Kristen and I am having a hard time controlling my emotions." Peter turned and looked away. Kristen felt bad. "No, you're fine Peter. I am the one that should be apologizing. While I am enjoying every moment of this day and dreading it when it comes to an end. I must confess. It is happening too quickly for me." Peter turned back around to face her and opened his mouth to speak. Kristen placed her hand over Peter's lips. "Please, let me finish. For years, it was Chris and I. In fact, that's all I have ever known. We met in high school and were with each other up until he went away. All I know is how to be around Chris. I don't know anything else. How to act, speak, etc. I finally have come to accept how things have turned out. This is a chance for me to find out who I am and who I want to be. I need to find out what I like, what I don't, both in myself and a partner. I also can't bring another person into my kid's lives until they're ready. That said, I think you are truly amazing. I really like you too. But I need for this to happen one step at a time. I am not sure if that is something you're willing to do or wait for. I don't know when I will be able to move past this and be free from all of it. It may be next month, it may take a year. To make matters worse, Chris is being released. We are still legally married. I am going to have to deal with all of that once he's out. What if he wants joint custody? I thought Chris was a reasonable man but after all this, I am not so sure. I am still going to pursue a divorce regardless. I want you to know that. There's no chance of us rekindling anything. I don't have an ounce of love left for that man. I may even go as far as saying, I hate him. But he is still the father of my children and for their sake, I have to be civil." Kristen's eyes started to swell up. She turned away from Peter and walked down the path towards the water. Peter just watched her as she walked. *Wow! That was a lot to take in. Now it's up to me to decide on what to do. I thought I had at least a year or two before her ex was released. I am not sure if I want to get involved in all of that. On the other hand, Kristen is one special lady. I may not have another opportunity to meet someone like her again. What if she's the one? After what I went through with Lauren, I didn't think it was in the cards for me to find happiness and have a stable relationship. Our marriage and all its drama is enough to last a lifetime and then some. And the emotional and mental strain that Rachel experienced. I'd rather spend the rest of my days alone then go through that again. But I have to go with my gut on this one. She's it man.* He took a deep breath and walked down the path over to Kristen. He looked into her eyes. "Please tell me that this isn't the last sunset we will watch together. She smiled at him. "It won't be for me if it isn't for you." Peter felt the grin appear on his face. And with that he wrapped his arms around Kristen and kissed her deeply.

Sundays Are For Eating with Family

Sunday mornings were glorious in Kyla's eyes. She worshiped every hour of it each week. She could sleep in and enjoy a cup of coffee in peace, without having to rush to get the kids ready for school or to take Anthony to practice. Freddie would be patient waiting for his breakfast as he also had nowhere special to be. They'd read the newspaper together at the kitchen table and make their plans for the day. Kyla had decided to go along with whatever Freddie wished to do today. *No sense in arguing again, especially after the way things turned out last night.* And what a night it was. They took the kids out to eat, and had a blast with them. It was a lot of fun, not only for the kids, but Freddie and Kyla too. Afterwards, they came back home and played some games before putting the kids to sleep. Freddie played a video game in Anthony's room with his son before tucking him in. Kyla read a fairy tale to Francesca in her room and then tucked her in. Once the kids were asleep, Freddie and Kyla shared a bottle of wine in their bedroom while listening to a fabulous playlist of the latest romantic R & B songs. The sex was empowering and Freddie was invigorating. Yes! Last night was memorable. One that Kyla hoped there would be more of.

She rolled over in bed to stare at Freddie. She began to stroke his hair. He looked so quiet and innocent, lying next to her. He was making soft sounds in his sleep. *Wonder what he's dreaming about?* Kyla pondered as she watched her husband smile and make those noises. She thought about last night again. It gave her goosebumps just thinking about how well it had gone. She and Freddie got along with no arguments. They had let go of their feelings from that morning's fiasco. Even though Kyla knew it would and should come up again for discussion, she was satisfied that she brought it out into the open and Freddie was aware now. *Had I known that my little comment would make things turn out this way, I would have said it sooner!* In fact, when they made love last night, Freddie was different. He had been passionate and freaky at the same time, exciting Kyla. I can't *remember the last time I enjoyed him or our love making so much!* Kyla smiled as she rose out of bed and put her rob on. She pulled the comforter up higher on Freddie and tip-toed out of the bedroom. She found Anthony and Francesca sitting at the kitchen table, eating bowls of cereal and watching a show on the kitchen tv. "Hi Mommy" Francesca yelled out as milk spilled from the corners of her mouth. "Anthony said we should let you sleep but I was hungry! Anthony made me cereal." Kyla smiled at her daughter and then her son. "Thanks Ant." "Sure thing Mom. Is Dad still sleeping?" "Yes, so the two of you keep it down please." She then started the coffee pot and began making pancakes. She tried hiding the smile across her face but she was grinning from side to side.

Ten minutes later, Freddie walked into the kitchen wearing his gym clothes. "Good morning my people," he chanted as he kissed Kyla. "You were great last night," he whispered in her ear, looking over at his children. They were mesmerized by some show on television. Freddie could have screamed it out loud and they probably wouldn't have heard it. They did not even realize he was in the kitchen now. "Good morning, Kyla said back, eyeballing her husband. "And are you going somewhere? The gym maybe, hmm?" Freddie turned red in the face and grabbed a water bottle out of the refrigerator. "Well, after our little spat yesterday, I thought I might work on improving things both physically and emotionally." Kyla frowned. "Freddie dear, I have absolutely no issues with your physique. In fact it's better than most guys I know. She grabbed his ass. "Me encanta tu cuerpo caliente!" Freddie removed her hand and sighed. "I know but if I am going to work on myself, I need to work on it all. Not just mentally." Kyla felt bad. She really must have hurt his ego yesterday. "I don't expect you, on your day off, to hit the gym. Working out can wait until tomorrow. Besides, If you still want to look at shelf paper, we can go out and do that. Then maybe take the kids for lunch somewhere." "And we can still do that, he said as he kissed her again. "I am going to the gym for a quick workout and will be back before you're even finished getting ready. See you later Babe." Out the door Freddie went. Kyla stood there dumbfounded while Freddie got into his car and thought about possibly running into Tina at the gym, especially after the dream he just had with her in it.

"Guys C'mon!" Sam yelled at all the kids plus her husband. It was Sunday which meant the weekly family get together for the Marinos. Every Sunday, Sam, Sal and the kids would go over to Sam's parents house. Kristen and her kids would also be there. They played cards, ate a meal that could feed a whole state and Nonna and Nonno would grill their grandchildren about their love life. This particular Sunday, Sam had agreed to drive her mother across town to the salumeria for "The best imported Italian ingredients." Nevermind that there was a perfectly good store up the block from the house. Her mother refused to go there, saying the owner was a "Bacciagalupe."

She also had to bring Bobby and Nikki back so two cars were needed. Sam did not like that. This meant driving her own car over there so she would have to drive back home later. No vino for her! Or at least not as much as she would of liked to have. "Guys! Andiamo! I don't wanna have to hear Nonna!" Natalia opened the door to her room and looked at Sam with one eye open. "Mom, you're at a 10, I need you at a two." Sam rolled her eyes at her daughter. "I'm guessing someone stayed up late with their new phone." Now it was Natalia's turn to roll her eyes. Sam ignored it. "Get your cousin up, take showers and get dressed. We are leaving here in forty minutes. " "Forty minutes! Natalia cried. It takes me at least that to do my hair." Sam stared at her daughter. "Forty minutes

Tali. Or you can deal with the wrath of Nonna." Sam moved on to Joey's room.. "Boys, let's go! Nonna is waiting!" "Ok mom" Joey said on the other side of the door. Just then Sal walked out of their bedroom, dressed and smelling like the cologne counter in the department store. "Wow! Are you trying to asphyxiate us with all that cologne?" Sal smirked. "Just trying to smell good for you Babe. Maybe my scent will turn you on so much that you ravish me." Joey opened the door to his room just then. "Ew, gross. You two should get a room. Oh wait. You have one. Go use it. There are innocent children around. Sam smacked Joey in the head and Sal laughed. "No time Joey. Nonna is waiting. Your mother will just have to keep her hands to herself for a little while longer." "You guys are disgusting. I am going to shower." Joey went into the bathroom and closed the door. "Could you refrain from being nasty around the kids, Salvatore?" Sam was embarrassed, talking like that in front of her son. "Oh please! Like he doesn't talk that way!" Sal shook his head and went downstairs, leaving the hallway smelling like straight up dude. "But not to his parents," Sam yelled after him. She walked back to her bedroom but not before she yelled, "The bus leaves in a half an hour!"

Sam sat down on her bed and thought about her best friend. *I wonder how everything went yesterday when she got home. It will be awhile before everyone is ready, so I think I will call that crazy chick and see what's up.* Sam picked up her phone and dialed. "Hola mi mejor amiga! ¿Cómo estás?"Kyla answered on the first ring with. Sam paused as she wasn't sure how to answer that. "Um I think bien and sounds like you're ok." "Why wouldn't I be? Kyla asked, puzzled. "Because you and Freddie had a fight and you weren't sure how things were gonna turn out." "Oh right. I am so used to talking to you every night, I forgot we didn't speak again after I left your house." Kyla continued. "Everything is fine. We didn't talk about it per se, we just let it go and moved on. We took the kids out for dinner, then came back here. We ended with a bottle of wine and some great sex!" Sam could sense the enthusiasm coming from Kyla. "Well, I certainly wasn't expecting you to say that, but I am happy for you. Maybe even a little bit jealous." Both women laughed. "Oh please, Sam. Like you have something to be upset about. Puh-leeze!" "So what's on the agenda today then? That's if you can walk!" Sam laughed again. "Very funny Samantha. I don't know yet. Freddie went to the gym. He is trying to build a better body for me to keep me interested. I tried telling him that his physique isn't the problem, but he insisted. " "At least he gives a shit about what you said and didn't dismiss you." "So what are your plans for the day?" Kyla asked as she visioned Freddie in the gym lifting extra weight just for her. "Same old Sunday. We Italians like to focus on food as the main event. We will stuff our faces until we puke or as Natalia says, "barf" and then we'll eat some more. Only this time, I get to drive my mother to the Salumeria across town so she can go back and forth with the butcher over the freshest meats he has. My darling husband will hang out with the boys, watching football, while my father tries to understand the game. He will ask Sal in Italian to explain it to him. Sal will and my father still won't get it. He thinks because we call it "football," it should be more like soccer. Kyla laughed. "I love your Dad! He is the cutest!" "Thanks. I hate to cut you off but if I don't light the fire under these kid's asses, we'll never leave. Mrs. Marino will drown us all in her tomato sauce!" Kyla laughed once more. "Uh, good luck with that. Have fun with the famiglia. Talk to you tomorrow. Love you." Sam hung up the phone, smoothed over the bed where she was sitting and checked her reflection in the dresser mirror. She looked at her watch. "Let's go! Before Nonna stuffs us into her braciole!"

Tina woke up to Diamond kneading his paws into her stomach. "You won't find much cushion there, silly kitty. My tummy is as flat as they come." She realized she was on the couch in her living room and not in her bed. Did I fall asleep here? She heard a song playing. Tina looked over and saw that her TV was on. "Diamond, did we fall asleep here last night," asking her cat as if he was going to answer her. "I can't remember the last time I just stayed home on a Saturday night. And there's no guy in my bed to kick out either!" Tina didn't know what to do with herself. Since she fell asleep early, she woke up early. Normally, she doesn't wake up before noon on the weekend and it's always with some man she met the night before. They usually end up having sex again, followed by showers and if she likes him, he can stay for breakfast. But that's it! Tina kicks him to the curb whether he wants to leave or not. "Never get involved," she often reminded herself. By the time that's all done, it's mid afternoon and Tina runs her errands. As much as she felt joy in not having someone in her apartment that she had to entertain for once, she was used to having someone around. It was less lonely. She loved Diamond, but a cat isn't the same as having a human to be with. She jumped off the couch and turned off the tv. She walked into her kitchen followed by Diamond who was hungry.

"Would you like some breakfast, Di," as she bent down to pet her fur baby. Diamond purred and rubbed his body along her legs. "So what to now? First things first, coffee!" Tina proceeded to put on the coffee pot and make egg whites for herself. She rubbed noses with Diamond while her eggs cooked. "I bet that Freddie guy eats egg whites. Now there's someone I'd like to have breakfast with, Di!" *Since I am up early for a change, maybe I will hit the gym and by some chance, he's there too. But before any of that, I should call my mother and tell her that I took her advice and stayed home. Won't she be thrilled!*

Tina dialed her mother. It rang a few times before her mother picked up. "Hola Christina Alana. You're up early. You called to apologize for abruptly hanging up the phone on me yesterday, I hope." Tina sighed. Her mother just knew the right buttons to push and how to provoke her. Her mother often asked her why she couldn't be more like her sister, which Tina hated and her mother knew it. Today, however, Tina decided to stand her ground but bite her tongue when her mother lashed back at her. "Yes Ma. I am very sorry. You just hit a nerve. I am a grown woman who is responsible for her own actions and behavior. I know that. I don't see anything wrong with how I conduct myself as long as I am not hurting anyone, however. Tina braced herself, ready for her mother to unload on her. "Tina, your father and I just want what's best for you, mija. One day, you're going to wake up and regret your past actions. You're going to find yourself with many should of, could of, would of. We don't want that for you. Forget that, what if you cross paths with someone who doesn't have your best interest at heart or even worse, ill intent? Dios no lo quiera!" Tina was in shock. Her mother was so calm. Maybe she felt bad about how she spoke to Tina last night. Tina felt bad herself. Her mother could be a pain in the ass at times, but Tina loved her and knew her mother had her best interest. "I hear what you're saying, Mami. I appreciate it, I really do. But the last thing I want is to settle for something or someone less than what I want. This person has to be someone I want to spend the rest of my life with, maybe even have children with if I meet him within the next few years. So you see? I can't just choose anyone. " Tina felt a lump in her throat and her eyes swelled up with tears. "I know, Christina, but at your age, it should have happened by now. You're too picky. You must look beyond looks and his salary. There's much more to a relationship. Love a man who loves you for you, not for your looks alone. In fact, we are going to church in an hour. Why don't you come with us? Maybe you will meet someone from the church or someone that knows someone who is available." Thank God, her mother could only hear Tina and not see her. She stuck her finger in her throat as if she were gagging. "I appreciate the invitation Mami, but no thank you. Going to church is pushing it. I gotta take baby steps if I am on a road to becoming a better version of myself. but I do understand and get what you are saying. I will try to do better. In fact, I have already started. I stayed in last night, just like you wanted me to." "What? How are you ever going to meet someone that way, Tina Dear?"

The sunlight was shining right in Kristen's eyes as she woke up. Not even the thickness of Peter's bedroom curtains could keep out today's sun. She turned away from the light to see Peter peacefully sleeping beside her. *What have I done? This seemed like the perfect thing to do last night but now I am not so sure. I got caught up in the moment.* She had poured her heart out to Peter yesterday, being totally honest with him. Now Kristen thought Peter wouldn't take any of that seriously as she went home with him and slept in his bed. Peter opened his eyes, saw that Kristen was awake. "Good morning Beautiful. Sleep well? I apologize for being so bright in here. I've been meaning to buy new curtains. "No, it's fine, Kristen squeaked out.

Kristen struggled to get out of the bed but realized she was naked underneath the covers so she just laid there with the sheet up to her neck. Peter, eh, I think I made a mistake coming back here with you." Peter was frowning at her. "Do you regret coming here? You feel it's a mistake?" Peter looked like a lost puppy and turned away from Kristen. "No, it's just that after I spilled my whole heart and soul to you, I ended up going against it and came here. I don't want you to think less of me or that I'm weak." Peter turned to face her. "Kristen, we both wanted this. Even if it was just in the moment, although I must admit, I hope it will be the first of many. We are both adults here. I don't feel any different about you now then I afternoon. I am happy you are here. Just because you are, doesn't mean that this is the way it has to be from now on. You said to me yesterday, that I may not want to get involved or willing to wait for you to sort out everything going on in your world. The truth is, I want to wait for you, for as long or as little as it takes. You are worth waiting for. We can take this as slow as you want. No one in our lives has to be a part of this for now. We can introduce our families whenever."

Kristen's face dropped. "Oh my God! Peter! Your daughter! I gotta get out of here before she sees me!" Peter laughed. "Relax Kristen. Rachel spent the night over at her friend's house. They are going hiking with her friend's parents so she won't be back until much later. I never would have brought you back here if she was around." Kristen felt stupid. *He is probably wondering why I didn't question it last night before coming.* Then as if he read her mind, Peter picked up her chin. "You asked me last night if Rachel would be home. Kristen felt a sigh of relief. The last thing she wanted was for Peter to think she didn't care about his situation or respect it. Now, I have a very important question for you. This made Kristen nervous again."How do you like your eggs?"

Peter left to go start breakfast in the kitchen. When he was out of sight, Kristen jumped out of the bed and quickly got dressed. She reached for her phone. Shit! Four missed calls from Sam. Kristen crept open the bedroom door. She could hear Peter whistling in the kitchen and banging pots. She closed the door and dialed her sister's number.

"Thank God, you're alive! Are you hurt or in trouble Kristen?" Sam was screaming into the phone. "Calm down. It's nothing like that. " "Then why the hell didn't you come home last night? Ma is worried sick." "I am sorry. I..I spent the night at Peter's." "Go Kristen!" Now Sam sounded overwhelmingly pleased. "I am happy for you, dear sister of mine, but what the fuck were you thinking, not calling your mother? She's probably envisioning you lying in a ditch somewhere, bleeding with no one around." I know I have your kids and they're older, so no need to check in with me, but c'mon!" Kristen closed her eyes. "I know. That was stupid of me. The time just got away from me and apparently the champagne went to my head. Please call mom. For me. Tell her that I called you and I'm fine but I really can't talk. I am with someone. And after yesterday when she scolded me and told me I should be staying home, well....good luck Sam. You're just better at handling our mother than I am. She bites your head off, you bite back. Me? It's like I am five years old again when it comes to that woman." Sam smirked. "Ok, but you owe me for this. It won't be easy. And don't forget. It's Sunday. You know what that means, La Festa di Marino. "Nope, how could I forget? I live with the woman, remember? Sam laughed. "Hey! I have a great idea! Why don't you bring that guy of yours to dinner? If he can survive through a family gathering, he's the real deal!

When the Cookie Crumbles

Kyla hung up with Sam. She smiled thinking about Sam's plans for the day imagining Sam patiently waiting while her mother took forever in the store trying to decide which cut of meat she wanted. Kyla felt a pang in her heart. It made her think of her own mother and how much she missed her. They used to have family get-togethers and celebrations when her mother was alive. Their events were something! Over the years, since her mother's passing, it hasn't gotten any easier for Kyla, losing her mother. Oh *how much Mama would have loved Anthony Francesca! I wish she could have met them and seen how much Francesca looks like her.* Kyla spoke to Freddie's mother often and occasionally got together with her, but it wasn't the same. His mom could be nice and all, but the elder Mrs. Lovazzo lacked personality and the little she did have, was given to her daughter's children. She often came off as cold and fake. Truth was, Kyla had a better relationship with her mother in law on social media than she did with her in person. The kissing emojis, hearts and hugs were a substitute for the real thing. Freddie on the other hand was too mushy and needy. *He certainly did not get those traits from his mother!* Kyla sighed and walked back downstairs and into the kitchen. The kids left the kitchen a mess with their cereal bowls on the table along with spilled milk. Cereal crumbs were all over the counter and floor. Kyla sighed once more. *At least they let me sleep in,* she thought as she grabbed the broom from the closet to start cleaning the mess on the floor.. She took a deep breath. *I guess I shouldn't complain. Just think how big of a mess the Marino kitchen will be today! There will be 9 people eating! If I know Sam's mother, it will be enough food for 19 people! Plus she makes everything from scratch. There will be tomatoes and even more tomatoes everywhere!* Kyla laughed to herself and began thinking that maybe she should start holding her own family get togethers on Sundays just like the Marino Family. *I can continue my mama's own family traditions and maybe it will bring Freddie and I closer. I could invite my brothers, their wives and kids. I could do something like my mama used to do with making a big pot of rice for everyone. Maybe I could also invite family on Freddie's side. His sisters can teach me some of their Italian specialties.* Kyla got along with his sisters. They had a much nicer personality than that of their mother. *Yes! I am going to ask Freddie what he thinks about it when he gets home from the gym.* "Whatcha thinking about Mommy?" Francesca had walked into the kitchen unbeknownst to her mother and grabbed a cookie from the jar on the counter. Now cookie crumbs added to the mess on the counter and floor that Kyla just swept moments before. Not to mention the many that left a trail down Francesca's nightgown. "Francesca, honey, you have a funny way of just showing up in the kitchen without a peep. You're like a little mouse. A cute mouse that is!" Kyla bent down and tickled Franscesca in her tummy. Francesca squealed and ran behind the chair for cover. "Now Ceski, I told you to ask first before you grab a cookie." "I'm sorry Mommy. But you did tell me that I cannot have snacks before a meal or it will ruin my appe-something. I already had my breakfast, remember Mommy, Anthony made me cereal because you were sleeping." *These kids get smarter everyday.* "True, but ask me anyway when you want a snack, ok?" Francesca frowned but agreed. "Ok, Mommy. The cookie reminded Kyla of when her mother would bring out a huge tray of homemade cookies for the kids. Hey Cheski, what do you think about having a family dinner here with your aunts, uncles and cousins? Would you like that? Francesca began jumping up and down. "Yes! They can play in my room! I can show them the doll you got me last week. Can Tali and Nikki come too? I like them." Kyla could see the excitement in Francesca's eyes. *You would have thought I asked her is she wanted to go to Disney World!* "No Baby. They will be with their family, having dinner too." Francesca made a face. "If they're not family, why does Tali call you Aunt then?" "It's just because her mommy and I are close. We're always over at their house right?" "Well, then you're family Mommy. Just like Olive Garden says, when you're here, you're family. If we go to Aunt Sam's, we're family. If you invite her over here for dinner, then she's our family. Get it Mommy? I have to go now. I am going to watch the Funny Fruits show now. Byeee!" Kyla watched her daughter skip from the kitchen into the living room. Kyla just shook her head. Note to self, check the parental controls on the tv and move the cookie jar to a higher shelf.

Sam did the sign of the cross as she dialed her mother. "Please God. Let this go over well." Her mother picked up on the first ring.

"Hello...Samantha? Have you heard from a your sister yet?" Sam braced herself. "Yes Ma. She's fine. She just stayed over a friend's house last night and forgot to call you." Sam pulled the phone away from her ear as she could hear her mother seething, waiting to unleash her anger. She didn't need to have the phone to her ear to hear her mother clearly. The entire car heard Mrs. Marino loud and clear. "Samantha Rose, you forgeta to picka up an item at the grocery store, you forget to set your alarm, what YOU don't forgeta is to call your mother when you're gonna be late!" Sam could vision her mother foaming at the mouth. "I know Ma, but..." More anger came through the phone. "Buta nothing Samantha! There is a no excuse! She was irresponsible and hada complete disregard for you father and I! We were worried a sick! Our home isa not a hotel where you cana just come and go asa you please! And furthermore, I am guessing she a just called you now, but you've had her a kids since yesterday afternoon! "Ma, calm down,..please, before you give yourself a stroke. First of all, her kids are not babies. There is no need to check on them. Besides, if she wants to check on them, she can call them directly, on their own phones. Secondly, my sister may be a lot of things, but she definitely is not irresponsible. She also has nothing but respect, love and gratitude for what you and Pop have done for her and the rest of the family. She respects you guys and your house wholeheartedly. I don't think it's fair to say those things about her. "

Sam winced. She knew her mother was not going to appreciate being scolded by her daughter. "Fine Samantha. You're right. I still wisha she woulda have called. Your father anda I worry. Look at what Chris has puta her through. She's nota thinking clearly. Would you? By the way, did she tella you that the stronzo di merda is getting out in a few weeks?" Sam looked in the rear view mirror and glanced at Nikki in the backseat of the car. "We can talk about this later Ma. I'm about to leave for your house with Natalia and Nikki. They can hang out with Pop. They don't want to come shopping with us. Picking out fine cuts of meat just isn't their thing." Natalia giggled. Sam hung up with her mother and imagined the Italian obscenities coming out of her mother's mouth at that moment. She looked at Nikki through the mirror again. She looked upset. "Are you ok?" Sam knew that Nikki heard the entire conversation between her aunt and grandmother. "Yeah, but, I am guessing mom stayed out last night and that Nonna is pissed off at her? And she has it out for my father?" Nikki was about to cry. "Aunt Sam, is my mom really ok though? Why didn't she come home last night? Where was she?" Sam was annoyed with herself for speaking to her mother through the bluetooth in the car, rather than the handheld. "Nik, she's just concerned for you guys, that's all. And your mother is fine. She had a few drinks and decided to stay over at her friend's house, rather than drive. I think she did the responsible thing, don't you agree?

And as for Nonna, She wouldn't be Nonna if she didn't scream and holler at us." Sam started the car and motioned to Sal that she will follow behind him for the forty minute drive.

"Yeah right, Mom. Aunt Kristen shacked up with some dude and Nonna is going to kick the shit out of all of you," Natalia blurted out. "Natalia Daniela Dimartino! Watch your mouth!" If Sam hadn't started driving already, she'd turn around and wack Natalia for her filthy mouth. "Sorry Mom." Natalia put her head down while Nikki just laughed and responded to her aunt. "Well, if my mom spent the night with some guy and is ok, then good for her. It's about time, she found some joy after everything that's happened. She deserves to be happy." *Is she really only fourteen?* Sam thought when Nikki said that. She was brought out of thought when the phone rang in the car. It was Sal calling to say he needed gas and was stopping at the gas station on the next block. When they pulled into the station, Sam sent her sister a text. "You owe me big time!"

Tina passed Brielle as she was walking by the treadmills in the gym. *God! She is here today too? Girl, are you that hard up for money that you work here everyday?* Tina said good morning to her, but Brielle just gave her what Tina took as a fake smile. *She's probably sore over our phone conversation yesterday and upset that someone in the gym took notice of me while no one pays any attention to her, ever!* Tina laughed to herself as she headed towards the locker room. As she walked through the gym, she nonchalantly looked for Mr. Blue eyes from yesterday's encounter. Tina frowned when she got to the locker room and didn't see him. *Oh well. If it's meant to be, we'll just bump into each other at another time.* She found a locker and hung up her jacket and put her bag down. Tina looked in the mirror and put her long hair into a ponytail. She glanced at her reflection and liked what she saw. "Damn! I'm cute!" She then selected a playlist from her phone and adjusted her sports bra so that she revealed more cleavage. A few women walked past her in the locker room. They rolled their eyes when they saw Tina adjusting herself. Tina just chuckled and winked at them. She walked out of the locker room and onto the main gym floor. It was leg day, her favorite muscle group to work on. It included the gluteus maximus so Tina always enjoyed this type of workout. Not only did she get to work on her ass to become bigger and rounder but she also got a kick out of the men who drooled at the site of her flexing her ass muscles in each exercise. Tina walked over to the leg machines. The lying leg curl machine was just as much of an attention grabber as the hip abduction machine was. Much to Tina's dismay, the gym owners had moved both machines to the back corner. The abductor machine even faced the wall now. *I bet some ugly ass chick complained that men were gawking at her,* Tina thought. *Now what am I gonna look at? The dirt on the wall?* She thought about the conversation she had with her mother this morning. It made her smirk. *To think my mother wanted me to go to church with them today instead of coming here. This is much more fun than sitting in a pew and praying for my sins. Who knows? The church may burn to the ground if I'm in it! What type of man did my mother think I'd meet and be interested in for that matter? I doubt single guys don't even go to church and if they do, it's probably to pray they get a girlfriend!* Tina shook her head and laid down on the leg curl machine. She liked starting off with her legs, doing curls, extension and calf raises. Next, she moved on to working her butt. Tina did some kickbacks and a few lunges around the gym while she waited for a squat machine to become available. Eventually one did become available and Tina adjusted the weight to what she wanted. The first and second sets went off without a hitch. The third set was a bit of a struggle however. She had put a little more weight on than her usual. Tina was trying to impress all the onlookers, both male and female. On her eighth rep, she struggled to lift up. She started to lose her balance and beads of sweat formed on her forehead. "Here, let me help you." Tina looked up and was staring back at Freddie. He lifted the bar and placed it back on the rack. Tina smiled but was embarrassed that he witnessed her struggling. "Um, thank you, Freddie, right? I...I don't know what happened. I was fine and then my knee started to give out." Tina knew she had put more weight on the bar than she could handle, but she wasn't letting Freddie know that. Much to Tina's liking, Freddie looked concerned. "You know, you really should have someone spot you when you do those. It can be dangerous. You might have kissed the gym floor if I hadn't grabbed the bar." Freddie was smiling at her. "Well, you're my hero then so I should kiss you instead." Tina gave him a peck on his cheek. She noticed he smelled really good as she leaned in. Now it was Freddie's turn to be embarrassed however. "I was joking about kissing the floor, but thank you. I'd spot you anytime by the way when we're both here." Tina was elated. "My name's Tina by the way and I am going to hold you to that spotting offer. I have certain days that I work on my legs and glutes. I may need you for when I lift weight for the chest exercises also. What days are you here?"

Kristen got dressed and went downstairs to join Peter in the kitchen. He was busy cooking eggs, while bacon was sizzling in the pan next to him. Hot coffee was brewing and toast was heating up in the toaster oven. Orange juice sat in a pitcher on the kitchen table. The whole kitchen smelled amazing and Kristen felt like she just walked into a breakfast buffet at some beach getaway. "Wow! You certainly have been busy I see!" Kristen exclaimed. "I hope you're not going through all this trouble on my account. I feel like the hooker in the movie Pretty Woman when the guy orders everything off the menu for room service because he didn't know what she liked." "Trouble? What trouble? And you feel like a hooker?" Peter asked jokingly as he flipped an omelet in the pan. "Besides, I gotta eat breakfast myself. And as a bonus, now I get to stare at a beautiful woman while enjoying my meal instead of the usual...staring out the window, wondering what I should do for the day." Kristen blushed. Peter pointed to the table. "Have a seat, my lady. Your breakfast is coming right up!" Peter flipped the bacon over and went back to the omlet. Kristen started to protest. "No, where I come from, everyone has a job in the kitchen. Then in a true Italian accent, she mimicked her mother. "You no help, you no eat." Peter laughed. "Spoken like a true, Italiana. Well, let me impress you. "Amore mio siediti e goditi la tua colazione." Kristen was stunned. "I thought you were Irish!" Peter smiled. "I am Irish silly. But I studied abroad in Italy when I was in college. I picked up a word or two from my paisans. I may or may not have had a romance or two while there as well." Peter winked at Kristen. "That's so awesome! And romances? Good for you, you sexy uomo!" Kristen exclaimed! "You have the ability to communicate with my parents now!" Kristen blurted it out before she had the chance to catch herself. She felt her face getting hot. Peter could tell that she didn't mean to say that. Kristen turned away from him. "I...I am sorry. I didn't mean to suggest that you should meet them anytime soon. I spoke too soon. I'm sorry." Peter pulled her into his arms. He kissed her and made love right in the kitchen. When they were done, Peter looked at the stove. "I owe you another omlet.

This one is a hockey puck. Kristen laughed. Peter stopped smiling. "Seriously though, I would love to meet the people responsible for bringing you into this world for me to meet. Whether that's today or a year from now, we can all sit, speak Italian and enjoy each other's company. Kristen looked him in the eyes. "Funny, you should mention that."

Rice, Meatballs, Eggs and a Little Beer

"Where is Freddie," Kyla asked out loud. Freddie went to the gym this morning and should have been home a while ago. *Maybe the gym is packed*

and he has to wait to use every machine. It is Sunday. Kyla whipped out her phone and dialed Freddie's number. It went straight to voicemail. "Great, that means he's still in the gym then. Otherwise, he would have picked up." The gym did not allow cell phones on the gym floor. Anyone could easily take a photo of someone or could slip one one if it's on the floor. Besides, you wouldn't be able to hear anything on a call. The music in the gym is set at a high volume. She sent him a text asking him to call her when he got out of the gym. *At least he'll see my text when he gets back to the locker room. He also has an activity tracker that supports texting so if he's wearing it, he'll see my text that way too.* Kyla decided to call her brother, Eddie and see how he felt about getting the family together. *I don't need Freddie's permission anyhow. This is my home too.*

Her brother's machine picked up. Kyla left a message asking him to call her back. Five minutes later, Diana, her brother's wife, called her back. "Hey Kyla! Sorry, we were outside. Well, Eddie still is. He's washing his car. What else is new? God forbid, it has any dust." Kyla laughed, Her brother was obsessed with his car, keeping it immaculate and pimped out. Her sister in law complained to her once about her husband loving the car more than her, Kyla tried her best to explain to Diana that they didn't have much growing up, so now that he can afford a nice car, he was a little obsessive that's all. Diana told her that she understood but Kyla wasn't convinced.

Kyla went on to tell her sister in law that she was thinking about starting a family tradition of Sunday get togethers or if the whole day was too much, then get together for dinner. "I think that's a great idea! There may be a Sunday here and there where we can't make it or be a little late but other than that, I think we should do it!" Kyla was happy. "Of course! Understandable. There will probably be some Sundays where we can't either." We can alternate too. "Like you have the first Sunday of the month, I have the second and Jess has the third. Oh wait, were you including Jess also?" Jessica was married to Kyla's other brother, Tony. "Sure! I know Tony works on Saturdays though so I am not sure that he will want to commit to something on his only day off. But I'll check with them. Kyla made a mental note to call her other brother next. "We can always leave the 4th Sunday in a month for a Sunday where we need a day to do stuff. Or an extra Sunday if we have other plans on one of the first three." Diana said. Kyla was shocked. She didn't think Diana would be so enthusiastic about her idea. *Wow! She is really on board with this. She is a busy mom herself, running after four kids and all but my brother gives her whatever she wants, so I know they're in. Freddie though? He'll want to know if his side is included. I just can't see his mother interacting with my side of the family. They're warm, sincere and outgoing. She's...well..unless she can benefit from them somehow, she won't bother being decent. I wouldn't want to put my poor brother and his wife through that anyhow. It's bad enough when we have to see her and I am tortured by listening to all her me, me, me stories. But ask my brother to? After one night with that woman, he'll never speak to me again!* "Ok Di, let me talk to Freddie and come up with a plan. Mention it to Eddie to get his thoughts." "Oh, you know that brother of yours. He goes with the flow." *And whatever his wife says too,* Kyla thought. But, Kyla really did like Diana and didn't care that she wore the pants in her brother's marriage. Her brother was no pushover. He was just a man who made his wife happy and took care of his family....and his car!

As soon as she hung up with Diana, Kyla went back to thinking about where Freddie was. He really should be home by now. I'm getting worried. She tried calling his cell phone again. No answer. It went straight to voicemail Kyla paced back and forth for another five minutes. Then she couldn't stand it any longer. "Fuck it. I'm calling the gym and having his ass paged.

Sam pulled up behind her husband's car in her parent's driveway. Both girls jumped out of her car while the boys jumped out of Sals. Sam saw Sal grab a six pack from his trunk. She rolled down her window. "Excuse me sir. But just where did you get that beer?" Sal turned around and smirked at Sam. "Duh! The gas station." Sam frowned. "You plan on drinking a six pack and then having a glass of wine with dinner? Holy calories. Not to mention you gotta drive home later. Remember, we took both cars." "Relax, O worried one." Sal said, teasing his wife. I am sharing the beer with your father. We are going to watch the game and he wants to play bocce in the yard after." "Oh boy. You better not let my mother see you. You know my father is diabetic and has to watch his blood sugar. It's gonna spike with her food alone. She will murder you, Salvatore." Sal laughed. "I guess I will have to hide it then." "Maybe you should leave them in the car until after we drive away so she doesn't see it." Sam suggested. "Good idea. See? I knew I married a smart woman." Sal smirked again as he opened his trunk again and put the beer inside. He closed the hood just in time as Mrs. Marino was coming outside.

"Buon pomeriggio! Salvatore, mio marito ti sta aspettando." Mrs. Marino gave her son in law a kiss. "Hello Ma. Good to see you. You look beautiful as always." He opened the car door for his mother in law. "You crazy kids have fun. Don't be flirting with them butchers now." Sal chuckled as he walked inside. Mrs. Marino turned and looked at her daughter. "Tuo marito è pazzo!" She shook her head. "Sì, lo so." Sam laughed. Unbeknownst to Mrs. Marino, Sal was patiently waiting for his wife to back out of the driveway and out of sight before returning to his car to fetch the beer.

Mom, are you sure you want to go to the butcher across town and not up the block? Sam asked her mother before she jumped on the highway. "Samantha Rose, do youa not want to drive your mother over there? Am I not wortha the extra time?" Sam rolled her eyes. "Of course you are, Ma. All I'm saying is that there is not much difference in the salumeria here as the one that's in the next town over." Her mother made a face. "The owners of the one we are a going to, are from the sama village I am from. We taka care of each other." "Whatever you say Ma." Sam braced herself for what was coming. As if her mother could read her mind, "Samantha, dida Kristen say what time she'd be home? I am sure the children miss their mother." "Ma, per favore! Kristen's kids are no longer babies. Do you really think either one of them cares what time their mother shows up? No having to hear, clean up your mess, do this, do that. They are with my kids, hanging out, doing what people their age do." Her mother frowned again. "That's a terrible Samantha. Is that howa kids today feel about their parents? Is that how youa and your sister feel abouta your father...me? All I do is a naga you? Non sarebbe meglio per tutti se io sparissi dalla faccia della terra?" Now it was Sam who frowned this time. "Ma, are you sure you weren't an actress in Italy? The drama! Her mother was confused. "Scusi?" " Sam took a deep breath. "Noone is saying anything about you being a nag, Ma. We all love and appreciate you, dearly, con tutto il nostro cuore." Sam pulled over and gave her mother a hug. Her mother had tears in her eyes and Sam felt bad. Her mother was aging and becoming more sensitive by the day. Sam made a mental note to have more patience with both her mother and father from now on. Sam started the car again. "Basta! Enough! Andiamo! Let's hurry and get to the store before all the good meat is sold out. Bad meat equals bad meat a balls!"

"I really have to get going now." Freddie told Tina. He had been standing there talking to Tina for over an hour. They were comparing their workout routines and schedules. Both of them asked many questions to get to know one another. Freddie didn't divulge in the fact that he was married with children. He was enjoying being flirtatious for once. Why ruin it? Freddie was offering to show Tina some training tips next time they are in the gym together as well as give her a spot. Tina was all too eager to oblige. "Oh, am I keeping you from something? I'm sorry, I didn't mean to. " Tina batted her lashes at Freddie and made sure her chest was sticking out in his face as she said it. "Um, no...I...I just have to get home to my wife and kids". *Shit asshole. Why'd you say that for? She doesn't need to know you're married. But, you're wearing a wedding ring Dick, so I'm pretty sure she already knows you're a married man.* "Oh, ok, I understand. Your wife is one lucky lady to have such a gentleman for a husband. A good looking one at that!" Tina winked at Freddie. "I hope she appreciates what she has. Us single women crave to be with a guy, any guy who is half way decent looking and knows how to treat a lady, Enjoying each other's company and having similar interests is a plus. If you know of any, please send him my way." Freddie felt weak in the knees. *Was this girl flirting right back...with me? Clearly she doesn't care that I just mentioned going home to my wife and kids. She's still hanging around and pursuing me.* "I will definitely keep you...uh, I mean...a guy in mind for you." Freddie paused. "I don't mean to be nosy but can you tell me why a beautiful woman such as yourself is still single? I'm just curious." *God, she is beautiful.* Tina smiled. *He's staring, good.* She leaned in a little closer. His aftershave was so enticing. Her voice became low and sexy as she spoke. "I mean, I don't want to settle for just anything. I've had offers but they just weren't what I was looking for. You know? I go after what I want and when I find it... we'll both know." Freddie swallowed hard. He was pretty sure this Tina chick was referring to him. Her body language said it all. Freddie didn't want to leave but he knew he had to. Besides, someone may recognize him and it will get back to Kyla. He certainly didn't need that. "Well, Tina, I hate to run, but I really gotta go now. Meet you here after work tomorrow for our first session together." Tina smiled at him. "The first of many, I hope. I look forward to it. Oh and by the way, I hope I am not taking you away from your gym buddy. I noticed you were with another guy here the other day." *She did? She was actually paying attention to me?* Tina continued talking. "Or anyone else for that matter." She let out a fake laugh. *Meaning your wife!* "Nope, no one is coming here with me tomorrow. I'm heading here, straight after work. "Why don't you give me your number so I can text you when I get here and we can meet up?" Tina was ready to burst with excitement. "Sure!" She gave him her cell phone number and gazed at him while he created a contact for her in his phone. "See you tomorrow Tina. It was nice formally meeting and getting to know you."Tina winked at Freddie as he grabbed his water bottle and started walking away. "Nice to meet you too!" she yelled. *And hopefully, I'll get to know you even better as the days go by.* "Damn! He is fine!" Out of the corner of her eye, she saw Brielle staring at her with a puss on her face. Tina smiled and returned to working out.

Tina finished doing a set of leg curls and walked over to a cleaning station to wipe down the machine. The intercom came over the loudspeaker. "Will Freddie Lovazzo please come to the service desk for a phone call please. Freddie Lovazzo, thank you." Tina stopped what she was doing and looked up at the speaker. *Freddie Lovazzo? I was just talking to him. Who would be calling him at the gym and not on his cell? Maybe someone is waiting for him here?* Tina cranked her neck to look for Freddie and see any signs of a wife or any other female by him. *He sure was in a hurry. Could that be his wife stalking his whereabouts and questioning him when she doesn't have eyes on him? If that's true, this just might be easier than I thought. He is probably dying to get away from her!*

"What do you mean, now that I mention it? Peter asked Kristen. Kristen buttoned her shirt back up from their little rendezvous in the kitchen and turned off the stove that was still on. The eggs looked more like a burnt steak now and the bacon had disintegrated in the pan. Peter glanced at what was left of their meal. "I think maybe we should go out for breakfast, no?" chuckled Peter. "Only the toast survived." Kristen looked at him and laughed. "Well, that depends." "On what?"

Kristen sat down in a chair at the kitchen table and fiddled with her coffee mug. "On how you feel about coming with me to my parents house for our weekly festa and if you're coming, you need to save room in your stomach. My mother is a food bully." Peter didn't know what to say. He wasn't expecting Kristen to ask him this after what she had said yesterday and again this morning.

She looked out the window. "I know, stupid right? After everything I said?" It's just that when you came down here to start breakfast, I called my sister and she suggested I bring you. Sam always has these crazy ideas." Kristen bit her lip. "Do you want me to come or your sister?" Peter sat in the other chair across from Kristen. "I...I am not sure. On one hand, I think my family will love you and I don't want to leave you." "But?" Kristen got up and walked to the other side of the kitchen. "My parents are old school, Peter. Not to mention protective. It does not matter to them that I am forty. I am still their little girl. They will grill you and grill you. They will have us married by next week if they can get away with it. Plus my mother is afraid with Chris getting out, that I will run right back into his arms. She will latch onto anyone for me so that I can't go to him. I don't want to make you uncomfortable. My family is very loving and caring but they can be overbearing. It might be too much for anyone to handle. Also, from what Sam tells me, my mom is pretty annoyed that I stayed here last night. "Does she think you're a virgin or can't sleep with someone unless you're married?" Kristen threw a dish towel at him. "No silly. I never called her to say I was staying out. My parents were worried. "Well that was dumb on your part. Cattiva figlia!" Kristen laughed. "However, the fact that you're not of Italian descent but took the initiative to learn her native language, lei lo amerà!" They both laughed. Peter got up from the table and pulled Kristen into his arms. "As long as you're comfortable with it, I would love to accompany you to your parent's house. I hear your mom kicks ass in the cucina and I'm starving!"

All About the Balls

Kyla heard the key in the door. "Freddie walked in and put his gym bag down. "Where were you? What took you so long?" She integrated her husband before he took another step inside their house. *Lie man, lie,* Freddie thought. "The gym was packed. I had to wait five to ten minutes for each machine.

Too many people probably indulged too much on Saturday night, eating out. There was that food truck festival. Maybe everyone ate too many tacos!" Freddie laughed at his own humor while Kyla just nodded. "Oh and I ran into a buddy. We got to talking and I lost track of time. Sorry Babe. Miss me?" Freddie grabbed Kyla around the waist. She pulled away. "What buddy?" she asked. "Uh, Greg. Yeah, Greg Parsons. You remember Greg right? The guy I went to school with?" Kyla just shrugged her shoulders and went into the kitchen. *Can she tell I am lying? God, I hope not.*

"Freddie?" Kyla called him from the kitchen. *Either she believes me or she is waiting for me in the kitchen with a butcher knife behind her back.* He hesitated to answer her. "Um...yeah Ky?" "Can you come in here for a minute?" Freddie got goosebumps and started to sweat. *This is it man, she knows. Now she is gonna cut my balls off for betraying her even though I really didn't do anything but be a little flirtatious.* Freddie walked into the kitchen hesitatingly. "I'm sorry Ky. I didn't mean to..." Kyla was sitting at the kitchen table, writing out a grocery list. There was no knife in her hand, only a pen.

"Sorry for what?" Kyla looked up from what she was writing and looked at Freddie. "Uh...for taking so long at the gym. I didn't mean to worry you and I'm sure you want to go out. We have things to do, right?" Kyla smiled. "Oh, that's ok. I'm not even dressed yet. Sit down. I want to get your thoughts on something. Freddie eased himself into the chair, relieved that his wife was not about to murder him. "Freddie, are you sweating?" "What, oh I guess so. It's a little warm in here, don't you think?" Kyla frowned."I hope you're not getting sick. I think it's fine in here. "No, I'm fine. Just probably overheated. I worked out hard today." Kyla nodded.

"So! You know how Sam goes over to her parents on Sundays for their family dinner?" Kyla asked Freddie, ready to tell him she wanted to start having their own family dinners. "Yeah, I guess so. Why?' Freddie was never so happy to hear Kyla mention Sam's name. *As long as it's not Tina!* I spoke to Sam today and she was getting ready to go over to her parent's house with Sal and the kids. Her sister would also be there with her kids. I got to thinking that it would be nice to do the same thing with our family, like my mama used to. She'd make a big pot of arroz con gandules, pollo guisado, and other dishes. She always baked cookies for the kids. I spoke to Diana earlier and she thinks it's a great idea. I have to call Jessica and ask her." "I think that's a great idea. Anthony and Francesca should be around their cousins more. Besides, you're a great cook. A sexy one too!" Freddie grabbed one of Kyla's breasts. She pushed his hand away. "Knock it off, Frederico Antonio Lovazzo!" Your kids are in the next room! Freddie laughed and backed away from Kyla. "Like I said Ky, it's a great idea but can I ask if you plan on asking my side too? I am sure my sisters would love to. My mom, ehh...you can ask her. Good luck with that!" Kyla rolled her eyes. *At least Freddie knows his mother is a pain in the ass too.* "Freddie, I have every intention of inviting your sisters. Your mother as well. I am sure your sisters would love to attend, they'd probably offer to cook as well. Your mother, on the other hand, will feel obligated to attend and will only do so for the sake of showing face and to see her grandkids. She does care more about what my family would think if she's not there, than actually spending time with her own children and grandchildren, however." Freddie felt embarrassed. He knew his wife was right though. His mother was obnoxious, vain and really did not give a shit about anyone or anything unless she benefited from it. His sisters knew it too and just called her every now and then to keep the peace.

"You're right, Ky. So we invite her and let her decide. At least we will know we did our part. If she comes, great. If not, then that's on her. She's the one that will miss out on being with the adorable little munchkins, both on your side and my side." Kyla loved when her husband took her side over his mother. It just made things easier. Freddie didn't deserve to be put in the middle. His mother will try to make him feel guilty no matter what he says anyhow. "What if she does come, and hates what I make? She will have the balls to push her plate away and ask you to order take out for her. Either that, or she may only eat your sister's Italian food because the recipes were hers. You know your mother thinks only her food tastes good and everyone else's sucks.. She will intentionally try to make me feel bad. Kyla scowled. Freddie looked at his wife and grabbed her hand. "Then Kyla, honey, kindly ask her if she wants the plátanos or maduros shoved up her ass first."

Two hours later after Sam left her husband, she pulled in behind his car again. She and her mother had returned to the house from shopping. Sam was exhausted. It was bad enough having to deal with all the drama her mother had spewed out about Kristen and being a nag to everyone before they even left, but then they spent another hour in the salumeria., unnecessarily. Her mother argued over and over with the butcher about which cut of meat was the best . When her mother had finally decided on the cut of meat she wanted, the price became an issue. It cost more than what her mother thought it should be. Mrs. Marino tried so hard to talk the store manager into lowering the price for her. She even brought up that they come from the same village in Italy. *As if that would persuade him!* Sam huffed. *So much for taking care of each other!* She was floored. In the end, her mother refused to pay the asking price and the manager ended up giving it to them at a discount that was acceptable to her mother. He probably just wanted them to leave! In fact, the entire store probably wanted them to. A line of customers had formed at the meat counter since too much time was being spent on one customer. Some of them even showed signs of being pissed off. Sam was humiliated. Thank

God, they were not anywhere near where she lived. Imagine if someone had seen her. Being frugal is not something Sam wanted to be known as.

What had already been a bad situation became worse when they got back to the car. Her mother could see the frustration on Sam's face. Once they were inside, her mother started her shit. "What's the matter for you? Don't looka at me like that. We will eat good in this family. Sometimes we have to stick up for ourselves and fight. Your father and I comma with nothing to thisa country. We broka our backs to provide for you anda your sister. Avere un certo rispetto per ciò che è giusto!" "Here we go again Ma. No one is doubting or even saying you and Pop didn't do what you had to, to take care of Kristen and myself or survive. Paying the exact price for something that the store is selling, has nothing to do with coming to this country to make a life. I am sure the store owners have dreams as well and work hard themselves to provide for their family while keep the store afloat." Sam started the car, annoyed. Her mother had this look of disgust on her face as she stared at her daughter. "So you thinka I was wrong? Did I not get it for cheaper?" Sam shook her head at her mother. "Really Ma? They probably wanted to just get rid of you. You gave them such a hard time over everything! What meat looks like it's going bad. Which cut looks flimsy. Which one is too fatty. God forbid the meat isn't perfect for your meatballs! And then you argued about the price! Good grief Ma! This wasn't some tag sale we went to where you can make an offer. The prices are set! You either pay it in full or you don't get it. It was sooo embarassing! Capisci?" If looks could kill, Sam would be dead. Her mother threw her pocketbook in the backseat, while looking daggers at Sam. "I ama sorry I embarrassed you, Samantha. But what's right is right. Thata man should be honored that we drive far justa to come to his astore. How dare he take advantage of hisa customers. Non ho capito. Farla franca. Bastardo! We should have wenta to the store in town. I bet they don'ta rob their customers." With that, her mother shut her eyes and went to sleep. Sam loved her mother, but never wanted to slap her so much ever before. Instead, she turned up the music and drove back across town.

She helped her mother carry in the bags from the store. Sam could hear the beer bottles clinking together. Her husband hurried past them with a garbage bag. ""Excuse me please." He ran outside. Sam smiled to herself. *I guess he and Pop had a few. My mother needs a drink herself!* When Sal returned, his mother in law was waiting for him. "Whatsa matta for you?" Sal had to think quickly. "Oh, something in the garbage smelled awful. I had to get rid of it. The whole house stunk." Mrs. Marino made a face. "My house no stink, Salvatore. I puta a new bag in before I left. Maybe you had a cigar and that's whata stinks." She pushed past him and went to see her grandkids. Sal shrugged his shoulders and looked at Sam. She threw her hands in the air. "Look out. My mother's in rare form." Sal laughed. "How was shopping?" Sam rolled her eyes. "Do you remember the scene in Christmas Vacation where Chevy Chase gets locked in the attic instead of going shopping with the family and then falls through the floor?" Sal, confused, just glared at his wife. "Um yeah. Why?" Sam grunted. "I would have preferred being Chevy Chase."

"Well, well, well. We meet again." Tina was walking out of the gym and into the parking lot when she ran right into Mike from the other night. "Are you following me? Did you change your mind about me? Maybe you thought about it and want to get to know Mike a little better now, hmm?" Mike stood inches away from Tina's face. "First of all, jackass, move back. I can smell your bad breath. Secondly, I happen to be a member of this gym for several years now. So obviously, I am not following you. In your wildest dreams, maybe. You know where I live and the gym is pretty damn close, so it would make sense that I come here, no? Or are you to stupid to realize that?" Tina could feel her heart coming out of her chest. Who the hell did this guy think he was, approaching her like this. He had some set of balls. She felt like kicking them. "Are you a member? Are you following me? Shithead, I have friends that work there so I can get your info very easily. Maybe I should ask my friends for your phone number so I can call the little wifey and tell her all about your little adventure the other night. What the fuck do I care? I got nothing to lose." "You Bitch! You stay away from my wife! Mike was beat red in the face now. "Oh but, I thought you're separated Boo. Does she know that? Should I ask her?" Mike leaned toward Tina as if to choke her but then two guys came walking out of the gym at that moment. They were looking at the two of them as if they sensed something was wrong. Mike moved a few steps back. Tina used this to her advantage as she knew Mike wouldn't do anything with people around. "Approach me again, and see what happens. Take this as a warning, Loser." Tina unlocked her car and got in. Mike just stood there, gawking at her. Tina waved as she drove away. "Fucking asshole!" she screamed. "The nerve of that mother fucker, coming up to me like that. Me!!! Tina was so enraged that she wasn't paying attention and blew a red light. A second later, she saw the red and blue lights in her rear view mirror. Fuck my life, she yelled as she pulled over.

Peter pulled up to the house. Every spot was taken in the driveway so he parked on the street. Kristen saw her sister's car and silently thanked God. It would have been so awkward for all of them if she got here before her sister got back from shopping with their mother. Especially for Kristen's kids. They had met Peter before, but that was different. He had been picking Kristen up for a date, not coming here for the family get together. Her parents had not been home last time so this was the first time meeting Peter. Kristen was nervous. "You ok?" Peter asked Kristen as she fiddled with the zipper on her pocket book. It was taking her forever to get out of the car and Peter was getting anxious. "What...yeah, I'm fine...No, I take that back...I'm not. " Kristen looked like she was going to burst out crying at any second. "Why? What's wrong?" Peter was concerned that maybe they moved too fast and Kristen wasn't ready to take this leap yet. "I'm just worried about how my parents will react, my kids." Kristen put her hand over her face. "Kristen, listen to me. All they need to know is that we are seeing each other. We are not getting married tomorrow. Just pull whomever you're worried about to the side and explain. You just wanted a friend to accompany you. That's all. Besides, I picked you up yesterday. You needed a ride home. Tell your mother you did not want to be rude and just send me on my way without getting to taste the delicious feast she made. Kristen laughed. "Wow! My mother is gonna love you!" As she was facing Peter, she heard a bang on the window. Kristen nearly jumped out of her skull. It was her nephew Joey . He and Kristen's son, Bobby, were shooting hoops in the driveway and the ball got away. "Hey Aunt K." She rolled down the window. Joey leaned in for a kiss. He looked at Peter. "Who's this?" Kristen stammered. "Ah...this is..." Peter leaned over Kristen. "My name is Peter. I am a friend of your aunt's. She tells me your Nonna is one hell of a cook and I need to try it. So here I am!" Kristen turned to face Peter. "Thank you" she whispered. Joey stood back up. "The best! You won't be disappointed. He tapped the car. "See you inside." He walked back to the house. Unbeknownst to Kristen and Peter, Joey was whispering to Bobby who had been waiting for him to return. "Yo! Your mom is here and she brought some dude with her. Definitely different from your dad. This guy looks like a school teacher. Wait till Nonno and my dad see him. They are gonna eat him alive!"

"You ready now?" Peter was asking Kristen. She nodded and opened the car door. She grabbed the pastries they picked up from the local panetteria. As well as fresh Pana di Casa. Her mother loved the one that came from Il Forno. That was sure to score some brownie points with her mother. Hopefully this will make amends with Mom for not calling her last night.

Even though she had the key to the house, Kristen chose to ring the bell. She thought the more she looked like a guest there, the less obtrusive her mother would be towards her and even Peter. She did a quick, "Please God...." as she knocked on the door. She could hear footsteps on the other side of the door. "Here we go!" Kristen squeezed Peter's hand. He smiled at her. "It's gonna be fine. You'll see." She instantly felt better. Peter had a way of reassuring her when she was nervous or concerned.

Sam opened the door. "Ciao mi sorella! Yay! You brought Peter too! Welcome, thank you for coming!" Sam was thrilled that her sister decided to bring Peter. It was good for Kristen to finally move past Chris. It also ensured that Nonna would be on her best behavior in front of the company! "Piacere!" Peter said to Sam. Sam was impressed. "Kris, I thought you said he was Irish." Kristen looked at Peter and laughed. "He is Irish and can we go inside now please? I am starting to get nervous again standing here." "Of course. I'm sorry." Sam moved out of the way so they could pass and then shut the door behind them. She pointed to Peter's coat. "Here Peter, give me your coat. I'll hang it up. You can follow Kristen into the living room where everybody is. I hope you like football." Peter nodded and followed Kristen.

In the living room, sat Kristen and Sam's father, Sal and the boys who had come in from their basketball game. Nonna was in the kitchen cooking and the girls were upstairs, hanging out in the bedroom that had been converted into Nikki's room.

All the guys turned around and stared at both Kristen and Peter. Kristen felt her face flush and felt awkward. Peter smiled and said hello. He walked over to Kristen's Dad and shook his hand. Sal stood up and shook Peter's hand. "Peter, I'd like you to meet Sal, Sam's husband. That's my Dad, Enzo, my son, Robert and you've already met my nephew, Giuseppe. "Aunt K.....?" Kristen laughed. "Sorry,

Joe or Joey. Her son spoke. "Same for me....Bobby." "Got it," Peter replied. "Nice to meet you all." "Wanna sit? We're watching the game." Sal offered. "In a moment Sal, thanks. But first I gotta introduce him to you know who." Kristen winked. "Ok, good luck with that." "Thanks, I will need it." Kristen helped up praying hands. Now Peter was getting nervous. "Is she that bad?" Enzo shook his head and laughed. "My wife...she a pain in da ass. Quella donna mi fa impazzire." Kristen's father had no idea Peter spoke and understood Italian. So when Peter nodded and laughed, Enzo was confused. Once Peter and Kristen went into the kitchen, Sal began to mock Peter. "He's so feminine. Kristen might break him. Where'd she find this nerd?"

"Mom, I'd like you to meet my friend Peter." Kristen and Peter walked into the kitchen and over to her mother who was leaning over a pot of sauce, stirring it slowly. Her mother turned around, wiped her hands on her apron and shook Peter's hand. "It's a pleasure to meet you, Mrs. Marino and it smells amazing in here!" Peter exclaimed. Kristen's mother smiled. "Nice to meet you too and please, call me Rosemarie. You musta try one of my meatballs. They are fantastico! I maka them with love and the besta meat I can find!" Mrs. Marino shot Sam a look who just rolled her eyes. "Yes, Kristen told me they are amazing. I can't wait to taste one. Oh, and we brought some pastries and Pana Di Casa for you." Kristen handed the bag to her mother and gave her a hug. "Thank you Kristen. It wasa very thoughtful of you but that doesn't excuse you from nota calling last night. "You're right. I am sorry, Ma. I just forgot." Her mother gave her a disapproving look and then turned to Peter who was eyeing the sauce on the stove. "Anda you, you were wita my daughter last night?" Peter looked at Kristen's mother, went to open his mouth but Kristen spoke before he had a chance to. "Oh marone a mi! Ma!" Peter smiled. "That's ok Kristen. She wouldn't be a mother if she did not inquire. Our babies are our babies, whether they're four or forty. Mrs. Marino, Rosemarie, ci dispiace."

Sitting at the kitchen table, Sam was texting her husband. "This guy is good!" Mrs. Marino smiled at Peter. "Is ok, Pietro. No do again though!" She shook a bony finger at them. Kristen kissed her mother on the cheek. "Peter, go inside and relax. Ma, what can I do?"

Inlaws

Kyla hung up with her brother's wife, Jessica. They would be coming for dinner the following Sunday. So was her other brother's family. Both sister in laws, offered to make dishes. They were stoked about getting the family together and even cooperative when Kyla told them she was also inviting Freddie's side as well. Sisters from both sides knew each other and got along. Even the kids played nice together. Both Diana and Jessica also knew the elder Mrs. Lovazzo. They weren't exactly fans of her, but tolerated her in their presence for Kyla's sake.

"Now for the hard part." Kyla asked God for guidance as she dialed. His sisters shouldn't be a problem though. They are normal and actually like getting together with family. They think it's fun, not an obligation. Even they know how difficult their mother is when it comes to these things. Imagine them growing up with that kind of woman for a mother! They didn't get to escape the attitude and criticism of her either. It was just a bit less than the people that came in contact with Mrs. Lovazzo. Kyla felt bad for them. She called Freddie's older sister, Olivia first. Olivia was ecstatic about getting together and agreed to help keep her mother at bay if she attended. Olivia knew how rude her mother could be with someone else's cuisine, so she offered to make one of her mother's classic dishes just in case she decided to be her usual self. Kyla argued that it wasn't necessary and could handle any criticism thrown at her, but Olivia insisted. "She can be a real bitch, Ky. Especially towards you. This may help a little. It's ok. I know you will refrain from saying anything because she is my mother, but I get it. Danny's mother is no prize either. Danny was married to Olivia. "Thanks, Liv. I'll see you next Sunday."

Next, Kyla called Freddie's younger sister, Isabella. Isabella accepted the invite as well but told Kyla she would be late since her son had a game that afternoon. She was also a little more sensitive and compassionate to her mother. Isabella frequently made excuses for her and defended her many times. She knew how others perceived her mother, but she was still her daughter. So when Kyla told Isabella that she was inviting their mother and asked Isabella for prayers, Isabella wasn't amused. "She is just getting old, Ky. She is set in her ways. Let's keep the peace. One day, she won't be here anymore and we'll be sorry for how we treated her." *How about how she treated all of us? And I'm sorry. I may not shed even one tear when that woman goes. Ella es un bruja!* Kyla decided to bite her tongue. She truly did like Isabella and it was her mother so she should be defending her, rightfully so. "I understand Isabella. I'm sorry. I just feel like your mother has a vendetta against me. "No, no. She loves you. She just has a funny way of showing it." Kyla rolled her eyes. Yeah ok, whatever you say, Isabella. Isabella also loved her mother in law so couldn't relate. "Bye Bella. See you next Sunday."

"Ok Freddie. Your sisters are on board for next Sunday. " Kyla looked over at Freddie who wasn't even paying attention. He was looking at something on his phone. Kyla sighed. "Now to call my favorite mother in law!". Kyla held up praying hands. "Good luck, Babe." Freddie heard that one. He got up, kissed Kyla on the head and walked out of the room. "Thanks for sticking around for support!" Kyla yelled. *He can be such an asshole!* Kyla let out a huge sigh as she dialed her mother in law's number. *Maybe the machine will pick up and I can just leave a message. Wouldn't that be wonderful?*

Helloooooo?" *Great, she picked up*, Kyla was disappointed. *She really did nor want to talk to her mother in law.* "Hi... Mama Lovazzo...it's Kyla. Kyla's mother in law never suggested Kyla call her just "Mom", so Kyla refrained from doing so. *She would never consider her, her mother anyhow. There's no comparison. She could never be hold a candle to my own mother.*" Kyla would think that every time she spoke to her. "Oh Kyla dear, do you need something?" *Why on Earth, did the woman think I only called when I needed something? Maybe that's because that's how she operates? Funny, when she calls us, she's so cheery and pleasant. It's usually because she wants something. But if we call her, she answers like she lost lost her best friend. Unreal, Bruja.* "No, Mama Lovazzo. I was just calling to invite you over to the house next Sunday. I'm having my family over as well as your daughter's Olivia and Isabella." Kyla cringed as she waited for a response. "Oh I see. Next week you say? " "Yes, I'm cooking some of my family recipes and Olivia and Isabella are also. Kyla knew that if her mother in law knows that her daughter's are cooking, she'd agree to come. "Besides, Francesca and Anthony miss you." Truth was, Anthony could care less and Francesca barely knew her since she'd seen her just a few times here and there during her short life. "I miss them! Of course I'll come. "Fabulous." Kyla responded, lying through her teeth. I was hoping she had prior plans. "Thank you for inviting me Dear. What time shall I be there?" Kyla, now exasperated, "Is 2 ok?" "Fine Dear. See you then." Her mother in Law hung up and Kyla stood there, staring at the phone in disbelief. "No, Can I bring anything or a thank you? Cabrona!" Freddie walked back into the room. "How'd it go?" Kyla threw her hairbrush at him.

Sam was so thrilled to see that her sister decided to bring Peter along to their Sunday family gathering. It had been awhile since Kristen had a companion to do fun stuff with, offer a shoulder to cry on...anything. She was truly happy for her sister and hoped that her soon to be ex- husband being released from prison was not going to get in the way of her sister's happiness. She also hoped Peter knew and understood where Kristen stood on that. As far as her sister was concerned, Chris was no longer a husband or anybody she cared about. She didn't love him or even think about him anymore. The only thing Kristen was grateful for anything when it came to Chris nowadays, was Bobby and Nikki. He was just a sperm donor.

Was Peter up for the challenge? *I sure hope so,* Sam thought. I like him and could see him as a future brother in law. Kristen appears infatuated with him. He is a good match for her, especially what came her way soon after Chris went away. Kristen had been on several dates since Chris's incarceration, but nothing ever came from any of them. They were either too cocky, boring, ugly or something else Kristen would make an excuse for. Sam told her sister that she was just looking for a way out when things were getting serious and afraid to actually find someone that she liked. It made her scared. Kristen told Sam she was correct to an extent. She invested her whole life in Chris. The thought of making that same mistake again shook Kristen to the core. Sam wasn't buying it however. "You gotta have faith, Kristen. Jump in with both feet. Good finds good. Sometimes, we have to kiss a lot of frogs to meet a prince."

Sam left Kristen with their mother in the kitchen. She wanted things to go as smoothly as possible for everyone. Kristen needed some time with their mother to make amends for last night and Sam didn't want Peter to feel awkward going into the living room by himself to join the rest of the fellas. Sal can come across as a tough guy at times and she was concerned that Sal might pick on Peter, unintentionally embarrassing him. Sal always thought his jokes and teasing were funny but to the rest of the population, they just weren't.

"Peter? Did Kristen introduce you to the rest of the squad?" Peter turned to Sam and smiled. Yes she did! Glad to meet all of you and thanks for having me. Sam shot Sal a look that meant, "You better behave," but Sal just smiled and told Peter how nice it was to finally meet him after hearing the two sister's mentioning him in previous conversations. Sal even got up and offered a beer or a glass of wine to him. Peter was more of a wine guy rather than beer, but the guys in this family looked like the manly type. He didn't want to come across as meek so he opted for a beer. "My preference for great Italian food is some vino so maybe later for that also, if that's cool." Sal laughed. "You got it. Besides, you think you can get away with having a beer instead of a merlot or chianti at Rosemarie's table? You gotta better chance of seeing Jesus!" They all laughed, even Enzo. "You knowa my wife eh too wella, Salvatore. She no lika anything ona the table but what she think will go wit her food. She thinka she the besta cook in all of Italia." Peter smiled. "Well it definitely smells good. Che fame che ho!" Enzo looked at Peter. "Parla Italiana?" "Sì, sono andato a scuola lì." "Molto bene!" Enzo was pleased with whom Kristen chose to bring home. He thought he was smart, charming and witty. He was a perfect match for his older daughter.

Kristen walked into the living room unbeknownst to the rest of the family. She was delighted to see Peter conversing with her father and getting along so well with everyone. Her father was not an easy man to please so Kristen was elated. Seeing Peter at ease, without even having her presence in the room, put her own mind at ease.

Maybe this can really work afterall. She smiled. Sam noticed her sister standing in the corner. She stood up quietly and walked over to her. Sam put her arm around Kristen and kissed her cheek. She whispered in Kristen's ear. "See? I told you, you had nothing to worry about. Vogliamo a bene Peter." Kristen put her head on Sam's shoulder. "Thank you. I needed this."

Mrs. Marino came into the living room with her hands on her hips. Her apron was covered in tomato sauce. "Are you alla deaf? I said dinner isa ready! Go sit in the dining room. Salvatore, open a bottle of vino please." "Sure thing, Ma." Sal walked toward the wine rack but not before winking at Peter.

The family all piled into the Marino dining room, one by one. They each took their seats and Kristen motioned Peter to the seat next to hers. Sam was on the side of him, so he was relieved. Sam, I can deal with. Her mother, not so much! She may throw the spaghetti at me if I do something wrong! Once everyone was seated, Rosemarie took her seat. She always sat last so she could admire the looks on people's faces when they saw their feast. She raised her glass of wine. "Here's to another lovely Sunday together. We celebrate mia famiglia as well as Kristen's friend, Pietro. Benvenuto Pietro. Buon appetito!

I don't think this day could have gone any better if I planned it ahead of time! Ok, minus being pulled over and running into that dick, Mike. " Tina exclaimed to Diamond. "But! The cop didn't give me a ticket. He let me go with a warning. I'm sure my cleavage through my sports bra helped with that and as for Mike, well, I'm pretty sure he won't be bothering me again. Too risky to have the little woman find out. It can be hard work to keep these guys in check!" Tina was back home from the gym and excited about what transpired earlier. "Can you believe it Diamond? I saw Freddie in the gym this morning and it was awesome!" Diamond just sniffed Tina's hand and walked away. "Thanks for being excited for me, Di." Tina laughed as she watched her cat stroll away.

Tina replayed the incident back in her mind. Freddie saw me struggle though. I would have preferred to not have him catch me like that but then he may not have approached me and our conversation wouldn't have happened. Besides, I think men like it when they come to the rescue of a damsel in distress. Tina snickered. Judging by the look on his face, he was pleased to oblige. He probably enjoyed coming to my rescue. It made him feel powerful, manly. Guys like women who make them feel that way. Well, I'm your woman, Freddie boy! You can spot me any time! She yelled out loud. Diamond took off running.

Tina turned on the shower and stepped in. As she began to wash her hair, she continued to think of Freddie. This is the second time I've seen him now. Both times, his wife wasn't with him. I am starting to wonder if he's the one that's really separated and not that douchebag Mike from the other night. Brielle said his wife is a member at the gym also. Maybe she just told me that so I'd leave Freddie alone? Or maybe Brielle wants Freddie too! Ha! Like you have a chance, Ella es muy fea!

When she was done with her shower, Tina decided to give Kyla a call. Let's see how serious Kyla is about meeting up with me. I actually could use someone to talk to that's not my critical mother or a clueless cat! My sister never has time for me since she's busy all the time, too. Maybe Kyla and I can become close again like we used to be and she can distance herself from that pendeja, Samantha. Tina looked at her cat. "Whata say Di, shall we call Kyla?" She dialed Kyla's cellphone. After four rings, much to Tina's dismay, it went to voicemail. She decided to leave a message. "Hey Lady! It's Tina. I am just calling to see if we can pick a date and time to get together and catch up. I know you're busy, me too, but I'd love it if we could take a breath and meet up. Call or text me back. Adiós bonita." Tina hung up and threw her phone on the bed. As she started walking away, it started to ring. Kyla was calling her back. Tina picked up. "Well that certainly was quick!" Kyla let out a huge sigh. "Sorry. I was taking a minute to slow my heart rate down. I was on the phone with my mother in law. You know how that goes. Or maybe you don't." Kyla laughed. "Tina, you may be single but at least you don't have a mother in law to worry about. She is only out for herself. Esa mujer loca hace lo que le dé la gana. She doesn't care, even if she hurts us or inconveniences us along the way. Maldita!" Tina pulled the phone from her ear and stared at it. I remember Kyla as sweet and innocent. This doesn't sound like her at all. "Tell me how you really feel!" Tina blurted out. "I apologize again. That woman just irritates me and everytime I talk to her, my blood starts to boil. Her son, my husband, is no help. He knows how his mother is, but he chooses to let me deal with it by myself. Sometimes I just wanna say fuck you all and leave! His sisters are normal at least. Otherwise I'd tell that bitch where to go!" Tina felt bad for Kyla. "I am sorry Kyla. But this is even more of a reason why I think we should get together. I think you and I need some catching up and girly time. Not to mention to vent!" Both women laughed. "I want to hear all about your marriage, your kids....your life. Do you think we can meet up?"

Kyla shut the door to her bedroom. The last thing she wanted was for Freddie to hear her making plans with Tina. If he knew Tina's history, he would definitely have a problem with her hanging out with his wife. "I would really like that. It's been a long time, Tina. We used to be so close. I don't know if we could ever get that back again, but I am certainly willing to try. Tina smiled. "Me too, Ky. I've missed you over the years. Who knows? Maybe one day, I'll get to meet your kids and that husband of yours!"

Peter was busy shaking hands with Kristen's parents and thanking them for a wonderful meal. Kristen pulled her sister to the side. "Sam, I can't thank you enough for suggesting I bring him here and then going above and beyond to make him feel welcome and comfortable. Kristen had tears in her eyes. "Hey. What are sisters for? It wasn't just for you, you know. Seeing you happy makes me happy. I watched what Chris put you through and how it almost destroyed your spirit. But, the women in this family are fighters and I knew you'd be strong. You just needed a little push from your little sister." Sam hugged Kristen. "My little sister who has a very BIG heart." Sam rolled her eyes. "Don't go getting mushy on me now Girl." They laughed, then Sam frowned. She whispered in Kristen's ear. "Does Mom know you are going back with Peter?" Kristen smiled at her sister. "Are you kidding? She doesn't care. She is already referring to him as her son-in-law, her Pietro. She even packed us food to take back for Peter's daughter." Sam laughed. "What about the kids? Do they care?" " Both Bobby and Nikki told both me and Mom that they didn't care if I went back with Peter. They like seeing me happy too. Besides, I'm sure Nikki loves it when I'm not up her ass!

Lips, Sips, and Hips

Kyla finished talking to Tina on the phone and hung up. She slowly and quietly opened her bedroom door so Freddie wouldn't hear it creaking and wonder why she closed it in the first place. She glanced out the bedroom window and saw Freddie sitting in his car, staring into space. *Great, he went*

outside and didn't hear my conversation with Tina. Both ladies agreed to meet during the week for lunch to hang out and catch up. It turns out that they still had so much in common (besides marriage,) and didn't live too far from one another. Kyla didn't like keeping her meeting with Tina a secret from Freddie but she knew that he would disapprove of her friendship with Tina. *He will think she is a bad influence just like he thinks Sam is. Some things are just better off unsaid. It's not like I am cheating or doing anything bad anyhow. Although I don't plan on telling him, it still feels like I am lying though. If he knew about Tina's past he would have a problem with it and her being around me. However, he should trust me and know me well enough to know that I don't follow the leader. Maybe once I see Tina a few times and can decipher for myself that she is a decent woman and not a threat to our marriage, I can bring her around and introduce her to Freddie and the kids. But according to Sam, she's still the same ol' Tina. Sam quickly informed an opinion of her that night in five minutes! I think she deserves a chance. Just about everybody speaks highly of themselves when they run into someone they haven't seen in awhile. It's your ego that does the talking! Nevertheless, it felt really good to talk to her. She's an old friend. Sometimes I feel that I can't tell Sam certain things for fear that she'll be too critical or judgemental. I never got that with Tina and I don't see it happening now.* Kyla sighed. *At least I should feel lucky that not only do I have* one close friend already but I'm about to probably have another one as well!

While Kyla was on the phone in their bedroom, Freddie took advantage of that time to run out to his car and change his Tina's contact info to Tony. *If she ever saw some female's phone number in my phone that she didn't recognize, she would turn into the Queen of Hearts. "Off with his head!"* Freddie laughed to himself. *Kyla actually dressed like that for Halloween once. I was the Mad Hatter and Anthony was the White Rabbit. Things were much simpler then. Kyla looked at me differently.* Freddie let out a huge breath. *When did things get so complicated? I love her and our life together. But seeing and talking to Tina again today, brought out feelings inside of me that I haven't felt in awhile. Is it wrong to feel this way? Noone can help the way they feel.*

Just as he was locking the car and about to go back in the house, his phone rang. It was Kyla. "Hello? Ky? You do know I am in the driveway right?" Freddie asked his wife jokingly. Kyla was not amused. "Yes, Freddie. But what is it that you are doing out there exactly? I saw you out the window and through your windshield. You looked perplexed. Is everything ok? What were you thinking about?" Freddie walked back inside the house looking to come up with a quick response again. "Yes Babe, everything is fine. I was just trying to figure out what tools and material I needed to bring to the job tomorrow. It might be late when we get back and I may not be in the mood to pack the car then." "Oh, ok. I am just about ready. Are you ready to go out? I wanna stop at the store to pick up some stuff I will need for next week's family meal. Your mother is coming so I gotta be on point." "Don't stress, Ky. She will bitch no matter what. Make it easy on yourself. Anyway, I gotta take a leak, then we can go." Freddie was relieved he came up with an answer so quickly and Kyla was satisfied with it. He threw his phone on the kitchen counter and went into the hall bathroom. Kyla put her grocery list as well as some coupons in her bag. Freddie's phone began to vibrate. Kyla picked it up off the counter. "Freddie? She walked over to the bathroom and knocked on the door. "Yeah?" Freddie yelled as he flushed the toilet. "Your phone rang. Some guy named Tony just tried to call you."

"Thanks Ma. Everything was great, especially the meatballs!" Sam winked at her mother as she put her shoes and coat on. Her mother shot her a look and pointed her finger at Sam. "Non sei divertente Samantha Rose! No geta smart! Sal let out a little laugh. "Sam get smart? Oh no! Not my wife!" Now it was Sam who shot her husband a look. "Shut up Sal and mind your business!" Sal frowned and walked to the steps to put on his shoes. "Goodbye Nonna. Thank you for another delicious meal and good time. As always, you do too much! We love you!" Natalia kissed her grandmother on the cheek and headed to the car, extra meatballs in hand. Joey was right behind her. "Ciao my beautiful Nonna," he said as he kissed his grandmother goodbye. "Bye Papa," he yelled to Enzo who had returned to his favorite chair in the living room to read the paper. Since they came in two cars, Joey was riding back with his father, while Natalia was going back home with her mother. She wanted to stay and spend another night with her cousin, but she had school tomorrow. She wasn't in the same school district and could not ride the bus to school. She was forced to go to bed earlier than her cousin anyhow, since she was younger.

After he put his shoes on, Sal kissed his mother-in-law goodbye. " Rosemarie. Tutto delizioso, grazie!" He walked out the door and headed for his car. Sam started to follow him, but her father motioned for her to come to him in the living room. "Vieni qua per favore." Sam walked over to her father. He proceeded to tell his daughter how her husband made fun of Peter and maybe she should speak to him before there is trouble in the family. Sam assured her father she would speak with Sal and kissed her father goodbye. She tried to keep a smile on, but she was angry and embarrassed now. She kissed her mother goodbye on the way out, but now her mother was looking to speak to her." "Samantha, aspetta....per favore." Sam was concerned from the worried look her mother gave her. Her mother couldn't possibly know about Sal's behavior too, no? She was in the kitchen the whole time. *Better act like I don't know what it could be to be safe!* "Mom, what is it? If this is about the store earlier, I'm sorry. Mi dispiace." "No, that was nothing. Forget about that. It's concerning tua sorella, Kristen. Is she ok? I mean is shea happy with this guy, Pietro?" "Mom, it's Peter. He's not Italian. And yes, she really likes him and I can tell, he likes her too. I think he's good for her. This is what she needs now. Sono felice per lei." Her mother looked relieved. She put her hand over her heart. "Anche io. I want what'sa best for her and my grandchildren. PETER seems lika he suits her. Ifa she lika him and he doa right by her, then is ok." Her mother then did the Sign of the Cross, like the devoted Catholic she was. Although it bothered her that her daughter was spending nights with a man she wasn't married to. She mentioned that to Sam earlier.. "Oh Ma! Marone a mi! She's forty years old, has two kids and this is the year 2023!" Sam had responded. Her mother didn't care what Sam had said. "That doesn't make ita right, Samantha. Nota for this Catholic woman anyway! People...they talk." Sam was frustrated. Here her mother was scolding her yet once again for the second time today but now Sal was growing impatient, waiting. Even though they came in more than one car, he still wanted to follow behind his wife for several reasons. First, to make sure Sam and his daughter would be ok. There had been several attempts of carjacking near the Marino home. Secondly, he needed Sam to pull in the driveway first so she wouldn't block him in. He left for work before anyone in his house did and needed to get out. "Sam, lets go! Andiamo!" he yelled from his car. Even though she could of cared less what Sal wanted at that moment, she chose to keep the peace. "Ma, I gotta go. I love you. And who gives a shit if people gossip about what Kristen is doing? Tell them to mind their own fucking business. Worry more about what people say about your frigin meatballs then Kristen's love life, ok?" Sam leaned in to give her mother a hug, but Rosemarie pushed her away. "Watcha you mouth, Samantha Rose!

Tina put down the phone when Freddie didn't answer. She didn't leave a message. *Shit! I hope he's ok.* She was concerned since the gym paged him. She also hoped his phone wasn't near his wife so she could see her calling. *Maybe it was a mistake calling him,* she thought. *He was probably staring at his phone, seeing my name pop up and thinking, I just met her and left her moments before. Why would this crazy mujer be calling me? Later for this psychopath!* Tina got nervous. "Diamond? What should I do?" She looked at her cat as if he would give her an answer. "Fuck it. He can have friends right? If his wife is that controlling and insecure, he needs to get away from her anyhow. She decided to send Freddie a text. "Hey! I hope you don't mind that I called you. When you left the gym, they paged you. I just wanted to let you know in case someone was looking for you or you left something behind. Talk soon." Tina hit send and put her phone down. She let out a huge breath. Diamond rubbed against her legs. "If he is smart, Di, and his wife saw the phone call, he should just tell her that he is working on becoming a physical trainer and he exchanged info with a potential client. Good one, right Di?" "They don't call me Tina the schema for nothing!" She wasn't sure if that was something to be proud of but she laughed anyway.

"In other news, Diamond, Kyla and I are getting together this week for lunch. I want to catch up and hear all about her life. What's she been up to, what she does for fun, etc. Maybe I'll even meet the little rugrats and that husband of hers. Speaking of husband, she sounded upset on the phone. It seems like she has issues with her mother in law and gets no support from her man. And that's one of the many reasons I don't want to get married. Dealing with a husband is hard enough. But throw a mother in law plus anyone else on his side into the mix, Oh hell no! No thanks! I'll stay single until they put me in the ground, thanks." Tina walked into her bathroom, ready to take a shower. *Now, that guy Freddie though, if he were to propose, I just may have to reconsider.*

Once she was done showering, Tina walked back into her bedroom and picked up her phone. She had a text from Freddie. "Hey sorry, I missed your call. I was in the shower. I am ok. I don't know why the gym paged me. Maybe I dropped something. Thanks for your concern, Tina. See you tomorrow!" The text was followed by a happy face emoji. Tina was thrilled. "He responded!" she shouted. Once again, she scared the daylight out of her cat, Diamond. He took off, scratching the floor with his claws as he scurried away. "You're such a scaredy cat, Diamond. Ha! I made a joke, scaredy cat. Get it? You're a cat!" Tina laughed at her own amusement. She was in a good mood. She got to see Freddie earlier and they now progressed to texting each other.

Tomorrow seems so far away. And I even have to go to work before that! How will I ever make it through the day, anxiously waiting until I see him again? She went over to her dresser and decided to pick out a gym outfit for tomorrow. "Let's see. I think these pants make my ass look best." Next, she selected the matching sports bra that accentuated her chest perfectly. "If Freddie doesn't get turned on from this ensemble, then there's something wrong with his libido!" Tina thought about the conversation she had with Freddie earlier. *He said he will be alone.* She squealed. *I get him all to myself! Not to mention it will be one on one too! We're gonna be gym partners. I can hardly contain myself. Maybe he'll want to grab a drink or something to eat afterwards. Wouldn't that be awesome?*

The phone started ringing. Tina jumped up. Maybe that's him and he found a minute alone to call me! She raced over to the phone to pick it up. Much to her dismay, it was John Benecasa. "Great, just what I need." Tina decided to answer it so she wouldn't have to go back and forth with this guy. "Hello?" "Tina babe. How are you? It's John." Tina rolled her eyes. "Hi John. What's up?" John was silent for a second then spoke. "I thought....I thought after you had a day or two to think about it, you would reconsider us not seeing each other anymore. Tina frowned. *Can you believe this asshole?* "No, I haven't changed my mind." "Come on Tina. We've been seeing each other for eight months now. We had a lot of great times together. Can you let what I said the other night about going home to my wife, just go? I made a mistake. I miss you and your beautiful face." John sounded like he was about to cry. Tina however, felt like she was gonna puke. *Yeah right. What you miss is my beautiful ass.* "That was one mistake too many, Mr. Benecasa. In those eight months, you should have learned that I am not some toy that you can just take off the shelf when you want to play with it and put it back when you're done. Nor, will I be treated like one. You fucked up, John...you! And now you are paying the price. Maybe your wife accepts your bullshit and willingly takes it, but I sir, definitely do not! Let this be a lesson to you. Many women out there refuse to settle or let a man control them and call the shots. John...baby....I am one of those women. You enjoy the rest of your fucking life and don't ever call me again. Adiós!" Tina hung up and flung her phone back down on the bed. "Fucking asshole!" Diamond took off....again.

"Kristen, are you ok? You're so quiet." Peter looked over at her as he drove. They had been driving for a little while now and Kristen hardly said two words. "Yes, I'm fine. I'm sorry Peter. I'm happy, actually. I'm just thinking about how everything went. My whole family adores you, my parents, my sister...my KIDS!" Peter looked confused. "And this makes you quiet? Usually when people are upset, they're quiet, not happy or in a good mood." Kristen looked at him. "I am a big believer in 'If it's too good to be true, it probably is.' That frightens me. I like where we are headed and the fact that there are no flaws, not even a small one, scares me." Peter smiled. "Unless you counting my real name not being Pietro." Kristen couldn't help but laugh. "You'll have to excuse my mother. She can be very laid back and goes with the flow most of the time, but when it comes to her heritage, she's proud. Don't ever attempt to change or modify it. " "Like how she uses raisins and pignoli nuts to make her meatballs and the rest of the family wants her to just make them with the spices alone?" Kristen laughed again. "Exactly! She is Sicilian and my father is Italian. My mother likes to remind him constantly about the difference. The only thing she bends a little on, is the dialect. It can even vary among the different villages in Sicily. When she speaks, sometimes my dad will yell, 'No capisco, no capisco!' This infuriates my mother. But she picked up on his dialect through all these years together so she talks in a way, he'll understand.

As long as it's a form of Italian, so be it." "Ah, then maybe she does care for me so much since I am not an Italian." Peter made a face. "Oh please. My soon to be ex is Italian but my mother swears that unless his last name ends in A, E, I or O, he really isn't." They both laughed. Chris used to get so mad when he would mention something of Italian nature and she'd say, 'What do you know? You're not a real Italian." She will think of you more as an Italian than him anyhow since you've actually been to Italy and lived there." Peter nodded. It's important to me that your family approves of us being together if we pursue a more serious relationship. "Me too, Peter, me too." They continued talking for the rest of the ride back to Peter's but Kristen still felt worried inside.

Once they got back to Peter's, Kristen relaxed a little. She took off her coat and sat down on the couch. Peter poured them a glass of wine. He asked Kristen if she wanted anything to snack on. "Are you kidding? I ate so much of my mother's food. I can't eat anymore. I'm stuffed and on a calorie overload! Once on your lips, forever on your hips!" Plus, I've had so much wine already! Ok, you twisted my arm, just a few more sips. Kristen willingly accepted the wine glass from Peter who was nodding in agreement. "And that was some feast! Your mother is an amazing cook. No wonder you guys have a weekly dinner together. Where did she learn to cook like that?" "Her mother, who was taught by her mother and so on. Or as the story goes." Peter was intrigued. "Can you cook like that? If so, let's get married right now." He blurted it out before he had a chance to catch himself. *Oh no, she's gonna freak out.* Kristen just laughed however. "I may know a thing or two. My sister on the other hand, could care less if she eats Italian, Spanish, Chinese or any other cuisine. She's a professional when it comes to take-out. Sam hates cooking. She thinks it's ridiculous to spend hours wasting in the kitchen for everyone to eat it in 10 minutes. And then to have to clean up? No way! Sam rather pay to have someone else cook it and eat it out of everything disposable. My mother just shakes her head at her."

"Dad, I'm home!" The front door slammed and Rachel walked in. Kristen felt her face get red and her palms sweaty. She knew Rachel was coming home tonight and that made her nervous. Rachel walked into the living room and glared at Kristen. Kristen stood up, wiped her hand on her pants and extended her hand to Rachel. Peter spoke up. "Rachel honey, I'd like you to meet a good friend of mine, Kristen." Rachel shook Kristen's hand. "It's nice to meet you. My dad has mentioned you to me. He told me you were pretty. He was right." Kristen looked at Peter who winked at her. "What a nice thing to say! I think you're pretty too Rachel." Rachel smiled. "My dad told me you have a daughter about my age. Maybe I can meet her one day." Kristen nodded. "Yes, her name is Nikki. She is very nice. I'm sure you two would get along great." Rachel smiled back at Kristen and Peter. "Well, I have an assignment due for school tomorrow. I was busy all weekend so I have to work on it now. It was nice meeting you, Kristen. Goodnight Dad." Rachel kissed her father on the cheek and headed upstairs to her room. Once she shut the door, Kristen let out a huge breath. Peter's eyes widened. "Are you ok?" "Yes...no...I don't know...I anticipated this moment. I know how judgemental my own daughter can be. I hope Rachel approves of me being with her father. " Peter grabbed Kristen's hand and led her to the couch. "Kristen, Rachel has been through a lot with the divorce and her mother's temperaments so right now, she is just looking for some normalcy, for herself....and me. Unless you turn out to be batshit crazy, I think we're good. Kristen laughed. "Let's hope not. Now, because we didn't think this through, am I sneaking out a window tomorrow morning?"

Get Over Yourselves!

It took forever getting out of the house, but they finally did. The sun had even started to make its way down. Kyla buckled Franscesca in her carseat while Anthony buckled himself in. Freddie started the car and soon they were on their way to another ordinary Sunday, being lazy all day and then running some errands.

Kyla was a little bit annoyed that Freddie had taken so long in the gym. She wanted to get out of the house early so she could take her time and not rush to the supermarket. She had to get everything she needed for next Sunday's feast. What was he doing there for so long anyhow? He claimed the gym was crowded. *I have been there on several occasions when it was a Sunday. It's always practically empty. He also mentioned that he ran into Greg Parsons. I thought he lived an hour away. Why would he be in the gym down here? And who is Tony? I've never heard him mention him before but Freddie's getting calls from him?* Something was eating at Kyla, she just didn't know what. "Where do you want to go first? Ky?....Kyla? Um hello, Kyla Lovazzo?"Kyla snapped out of her thoughts. "Wha...what did you say?" Freddie grinned. "I said, 'Where do you want to go first? Where were you just now? Care to share your thoughts?" Kyla looked down at the floor. "Nothing. I was just trying to think of what I needed at the store." "Talk about boring. I thought you had some juicy thoughts there, and I thought I saw you making a list? Weren't you in the kitchen writing stuff down?" "Yeah but I want to make sure I thought of everything." "Oh, ok, gotcha." *Whew. I dodged that one. I don't want him thinking that I'm questioning his trust with me. Things are going smoothly right now.* Kyla watched the cars pass by while Freddie continued driving, lost in his own thoughts. *Thank God, I changed Tina's name in my phone to Tony.*

She called and Kyla saw! Why would she call? She knows I'm married and it's a Sunday afternoon. I'm obviously with my wife right now. And then she texts me. Kyla is probably wondering who this "Tony" is since I've never mentioned him before. Here I go lying again, man. Clearly, Kyla is thinking about something. I hope she was really thinking about groceries and the phone call went over her head.

First, the Lovazzo family ran errands, shopping for materials they needed for some home improvement projects. They then headed for the grocery store. "Ky, are you buying perishable items now? I'd thought we take the kids out to dinner but I don't know how long the foo will keep in the car. It's not that cold out." Kyla thought of her lunch date with Tina that week. *That's the perfect excuse to tell Freddie why I have to run out! This way I don't have to even mention meeting Tina. I don't even have to lie.*" She smiled at her husband. "Let's take the kids to dinner. I'll run out during the week and pick up what we need. I like buying the meat fresh anyhow and not having to freeze it." "Sounds good. Where to?" They opted for a little Trattoria in town that had reasonable prices and a kids menu.

Sam pulled into her driveway right behind Sal. She was exhausted from the day's drama with her mother and didn't even want to look at Sal. She longed for a hot bath, silky pjs, a glass of wino and her bed. Maybe there would be some good movies she could stream. She turned around to stare at her daughter who had passed out on the ride home. "Too many of Nonna's meatballs, " she chuckled. "Natalia wake up, we're home." Natalia groaned and rolled her head to the side. "Natalia Daniela! Andiamo! I'm tired. C'mon!" Natalia groaned again but this time, she reluctantly grabbed the car door handle and got out of the car. She stumbled across the driveway and into the house. The door was already opened from Sal and Joey. Both guys had raced into the house, ready to give back Nonna's cooking.

Once she was in the house, Sam locked the door and hung up her coat. Natalia, already in her pajamas, kissed her mother. "Goodnight Mom. I have studying to do, see you in the morning." "Goodnight Tali. Sweet dreams. I'll send Dad in once he comes out of the bathroom." Natalia smirked. "I'll be asleep by then." Sam laughed. "True but I'll tell him to say goodnight anyhow." Natalia shrugged her shoulders and went back upstairs and into her room.

Sal came out of the downstairs bathroom. "Now I know how you felt giving birth," he told Sam. Sam just looked at him with disgust. "You are so disgusting, Sal. She squeezed past him and walked into the living room. "What's your problem now, Samantha?" Sal glared at Sam. "There's nothing wrong with me, Sal. Tali is in her room studying and then going to bed.. She is waiting for you to say goodnight." "Whatever you say Samantha" Sal shrugged his shoulders and shook his head at Sam. He went up the stairs to say goodnight to his daughter. Sam waited until he was in Natalia's room before she went up the stairs into her own bedroom.

While the tub was filling up, Sam undressed and took off her makeup. She put on a soft jazz playlist. Once the tub was finished filling up, she slid in with her wine glass and placed her head on the towels perched up on the rim of the tub. She turned on the jets of the jacuzzi. Sam closed her eyes and tried to release the tension she was feeling. *I just need to unwind for a bit.*

Sal came in a few minutes later, opening the bedroom door so much that it bounced off the wall mount and slammed shut again. Sam jumped and water spilled out of the tub and onto the floor. "Holy shit Sal! Are you a fucking barbarian? Can't you open the door like a normal person?, she barked. Sal stared at his wife in the tub, completely ignoring what she just said. "Hey now. Our daughter has fallen asleep. Joey is in his room with his headset on, talking to his minions. Wanna fool around? Is there room in that tub for one more?" Sam let out a huge sigh. She threw her hands up. "So much for Tali studying!" She looked at Sal. "Not now Sal. I have a headache and just want to de-stress from today." Sal huffed. "De-stress? What do you have to de-stress about? We spent the day with your mother. Your mother did all the work. So you helped her clean the kitchen a little. That overwhelmed you?" Sam rolled her eyes at her husband. "Of course not Sal. And I would have gladly helped my mother with anything she needed, cooking, cleaning or otherwise for that matter. Don't get smart. I meant the mental and emotional aspect of it all. It drained me. From my mother's bullshit antics at the Salumeria with the butcher today to my sister's anxiety over having Peter accompany her to my parent's house for a family dinner. It was just a lot to take in."

Sal walked over to the bed and sat down. "Weren't you the one that just suggested to Kristen that she bring Peter? Isn't that what you told me or am I imagining things?" Sam stood up in the tub and reached for a towel. Clearly, this was not going to be an enjoyable and relaxing moment for her like she had hoped before Sal began interrogating her about today's events.

"Yes, Sal. I did suggest to Kristen that she invite Peter. And I am glad that she did. She needed to get past the whole first introduction stage. I knew she was worried about my parent's impression of him, plus him engaging with the whole family, not to mention her KIDS! I just had to lean my shoulder for a bit. Sam took a huge gulp of her wine. Sal shook his head again. "You women, worry too much. Why do you care what other people think? You all need to get over yourselves." Sam could feel herself turning beat red. "Need to get over ourselves? Just what the fuck does that mean? And yes, we women do worry. For instance, being worried that my husband, who is an adult physically, would not act like he was five years old for a change and make fun of Peter! Just what were you thinking Salvatore? My dad saw you motion to the boys how weak and meek Peter is. I'm just glad you had the decency to wait until he went to the bathroom before your dumbass reacted. Thank God my sister didn't see either. That would have been so embarrassing and humiliating. Just how old are you and what makes YOU God's gift? Have you looked in the mirror lately? I am guessing you haven't or maybe you would of kept your mouth shut about Peter!" Now it was Sal's turn to get mad. It was a joke, Sam. What he didn't hear or see, won't hurt him. I would never be disrespectful to him and in your mother's house no less, either. And is what you just said what you think and feel about me?" Sam rolled her eyes. "I said it didn't I?" "Well fuck you Samantha Dimartino." Sal flung open the bedroom door, once again, sending it to bounce off the wall mount and slam shut. Sam put her head in her hands and sobbed.

An hour later, Tina was still feeling pissed off from the phone call she had with John earlier. *The nerve of that man thinking he could just come crawling back to me after he basically threw me away, like I was a piece of garbage. Who the hell did these men think they were, John and Mike? They need to get over themselves and slow their role. They both must be married to some pretty gullible and naive women. Do they really believe they can pull their same shit with me? If that's the case, they are in for one rude awakening !* Tina decided to find something to do that would take her mind off these stupid men. She opened her laptop and began searching for Freddie on social media again. "Let's see if there are any new developments, shall we?" It was the same as before, however. Car photos and that's it. *What are you hiding sir?* Tina thought for a minute. When she called Brielle yesterday, Brielle mentioned Freddie having a friend named Tim Pinto. *Maybe I will find something if I search for this guy.* Tina spent the next half an hour trying to find a guy named Tim Pinto. She came across a Timothy Pintor, a Timmy Pintaro and more. There was one that had the exact name but it was a female profile. Next, she tried the gym's social media page. There was a photo of both Freddie and Tim in it. Several people we tagged in the photo. One being Freddie, but Tina already had his personal media page and just stalked it moments before. But there was another one labeled "Inkman87. Tina decided to look up that one since this Tim had tattoos.

Low and behold, clicking on that name brought her to a new page. She was staring at a photo of Tim Pinto showing off his abs and the ink that covered them. Tina searched his whole page for the next hour. She found out that he had a wife named Lisa, who Tina thought was pretty mousy looking. *I am guessing she doesn't accompany her man to the gym.* They didn't appear to have any kids as there weren't any photos of any children or mention of. She managed to find one album titled, "Gym." Tina got excited. *Freddie has to be in here!* To her dismay, most of the photos were of Tim posing in his gym outfit with the weights in the background. *This guy sure likes to show off his guns!*

Just as she was about to give up her quest for finding anything on Freddie, she decided to look at one last photo in Tim's gallery. This one also had Freddie in it and Tina thought he looked damn good! She was ecstatic. The photo showed both guys standing sideways, flexing their biceps. They both had a tough expression on their faces. Tina felt herself getting turned on by the sight of Freddie, his body and the face he was making. She looked at the date it was posted. It was recent, which pleased her even more. She saved it to her computer and from there, sent it to her printer. "Now I can look at him whenever I want", she told Diamond. "It will be my little secret." When the photo was printed, Tina cut Tim out of it and cut the rest of the photo into a heart shape. She placed the photo on top of her nightstand. *Now Freddie will be the first thing I see in the morning and the last thing I see before I close my eyes every night. Although one day very soon, if I play my cards right, I will have the real thing at my bedside.* She looked over at Diamond, who clearly could care less about what Tina was saying. He had curled up into a ball in his bed and went to sleep. "Gee, thanks Di." *I hope Freddie likes cats.*

Peter wanted Kristen to stay the night and although she was skeptical, Kristen agreed. She did not want to leave Peter's side. But if she was staying, they would have to wait until Peter's daughter fell asleep, then sneak into his bedroom. Kristen also would have to call her office in the morning and tell them she was running late. She'd have to wait for Rachel to leave for school, then creep out of Peter's bedroom. Rachel could not not find out that Kristen spent the night with her father. *Thank God for small miracles,* Kristen laughed to herself when she thought of her shower earlier that morning. Peter's bedroom had a bathroom in it so she was safe in the likely event she had to pee. "You couldn't leave anyhow, Kristen, Darling. You see, you have no car. And I have been drinking, therefore I cannot drive." Peter smirked. "That sounded creepy didn't it? Saying you can't leave. Like I kidnapped you or something." Peter laughed at himself. *Someone's had a little too much vino, I see.* Kristen thought to herself. She found it intriguing though. Usually Peter was on his best behavior and so proper. It was nice to see another side. Even if he was a bit tipsy. "Me having no car here is even better to hide me from Rachel. If my car was in your driveway in the morning, it would be a dead giveaway. But as soon as the coast is clear, I will need you to take me back. I can't go to work too late. I have deadlines to meet." "Whatever you say, Ma'am." Peter bowed at Kristen and bent down to kiss her hand. He never made it. He lost his balance and kissed her foot instead. "Are you alright, Peter...Peter?" Peter was face down with his face on the carpet. He jumped up and kissed Kristen hard, sticking his tongue in his mouth and grabbing the back of her head. After about a minute, he pulled away. "I am now." Kristen was in shock. She put her fingers to her lips. It had been a really long time since she had been kissed like that, Even when Chris was still around. She didn't know how to feel. She just knew that at that moment, there was no place she'd rather be.

Once they were convinced Rachel had gone to sleep, they quietly proceeded to Peter's bedroom. Peter told Kristen to make herself comfortable while he took a quick shower, Kristen took this opportunity to text Nikki to make sure all was alright. "Everything is fine Mom. Bobby is in his room, talking to some girl, Nonna is still cleaning the kitchen and Nonno is snoring away in his chair. I am going to brush my teeth, watch my shows and then go to bed. Same ol, same ol. You just enjoy yourself. We're fine." Kristen couldn't believe her daughter was only fourteen at times. Sometimes she felt like the kid and Nikki was the adult. "Goodnight Nik. I love you. I'll see you in the morning before you leave for school." "I love you too Mom and please don't rush home for me. I'm fine, really." "Ok, kiddo. Buona notte." "Buona notte Mom. Ti amo." Kristen hung up with her daughter and felt a pang in her heart. Her daughter was going through this whole fiasco with her parents and she was at such a vulnerable age. It wasn't fair. The last thing Kristen wanted was for Nikki to believe that's how relationships work. She needed to understand that she deserved the best, to be adored and definitely not mistreated. Kristen let out a huge sigh.

"Everything ok?" Peter came back into the bedroom, rubbing a towel on his wet hair. "Yeah fine. I was just talking to my daughter, making sure everything was ok." "And is it, I hope?" Kristen looked up at Peter. "Yeah, I just feel a bit guilty about leaving her again since I was also here last night for the whole night. I don't want her to get the impression that because her father is out of the picture, I choose to start shacking up with other men." Peter grabbed her hand. "I don't think you are just shacking up with some guy first of all and second, I will take you back home if that's what you want. After a cup of coffee though." He laughed. "No, it's fine. She's ok. It's just me being a mom." Peter smiled. "And a good one at that. Now feel free to take a shower and get comfortable. I left one of my oversized shirts in the bathroom for you to change into if you want."

Kristen kissed Peter on his forehead and went into the bathroom. *I know this is all new but he really is a charming and respectful guy. I could get used to this. Maybe even fall in love. But I'm getting ahead of myself. Chris is coming home soon. Who knows what that will entail. I may have to put seeing Peter on pause for a while while I deal with Chris.* Kristen huffed and stepped into the shower. For the next ten minutes, she just let the hot water run over and tried to forget her problems.

After she was done in the bathroom, she walked back into the bedroom, wearing Peter's shirt. Peter was lying on the bed, reading a magazine. "I could get used to having you around, wearing my clothes, being a bed buddy," he exclaimed. "Funny, I was thinking that I could get used to this too...eventually." Kristen swallowed hard. "Come here." Peter pointed his finger toward himself and motioned for Kristen to climb on top of the bed. She did so willingly. Peter leaned over to her and kissed her deeply. For the next few hours, their bodies rocked together in unison.

The Coast is Clear

Kyla and Freddie put their kids to bed after the kids brushed their teeth and changed into pajamas. It was already their bedtime when they got back after having a nice family dinner dining out. Kyla was exhausted from all of the running around they did, but happy that everything had gone smoothly and was enjoyable. She was happy that today was a much better day than yesterday and everything seemed to return to normal. "I love you." She said to Freddie once they shut the doors to their kids' bedrooms. "I love you too Ky. It was a great day, all of us together. I really enjoyed dinner." "Me too. Even when Ceski spilled her drink." They both laughed. "I gave the waitress an extra tip. I can only imagine what the floor under the table looked like. I think Francesca dropped more than she stuffed into her mouth!" Kyla smiled. "That's my Freddie. Always looking out for others. I want to take a quick bath and get into my pjs. Wanna meet on the couch in say a half hour? We can watch tv for a bit then head upstairs. She winked at her husband. Freddie grinned. "Sure. I showered when I got back from the gym, so I'm just gonna change, and then grab us a bottle of wine. I'll be in the living room when you're ready." Kyla headed for the bathroom while Freddie went into their bedroom.

At exactly thirty minutes later, Kyla walked into the living room. She was dressed in her pajamas, her long hair tied up in a bun and she wore no makeup. Freddie looked up at her and smiled. "You are just as beautiful without all of that paint on your face." Kyla rolled her eyes. "Yeah ok, Freddie, dear. Don't worry. You don't have to lie. I will still allow you to come near me in bed." Freddie laughed. "Is that what you think I'm giving you a compliment for? No offense Ky, but I don't think I should have to make sure I compliment my wife each time I want to make love or just have sex." Kyla smirked. "Of course not. Just don't go and insult me about anything either. Because that will definitely close the shop for the evening. Bad moods don't make for love time." She winked at Freddie again.

They watched a little tv, mostly flipping the channels before turning it off. Freddie turned to Kyla. "Wanna go upstairs, Babe? There's nothing but garbage on tv anyhow." "Yeah ok." They both got up and walked to their bedroom. Kyla opened the door to check on Francesca then did the same with Anthony. Freddie was already in bed, under the covers when she got to her bedroom. "Is the coast clear?" Kyla looked at Freddie like he had two heads. "Is the coast clear for what?" Freddie threw the bed comforter and sheets off of him. He was completely naked. "For this! Wanna watch porn Ky?" Kyla laughed. Freddie frowned. "Judging from the other night, you seemed bored so I thought I would change it up." Freddie was confused. Kyla felt bad for laughing at him. "Ok, ok, you're right. Change is good. I must admit, seeing you naked in bed is turning me on. So put on some porn, while I undress too, unless you wanna do it for me."

Freddie turned on the tv and flipped on the Adult channel. They started kissing and then had sex. Freddie made sure he switched up positions this time. He flipped Kyla from her stomach to her back and vice versa. He glanced at the tv and the actress could have been

Tina's twin. Freddie became even more aroused. His mind was on Tina now. Even though it was his wife he was inside, he was envisioning Tina.

Suddenly, Kyla was put on all fours and Freddie was behind her. What has gotten into him? Did it bother him that much what I said? Freddie started moaning so loud that Kyla had to tell him to be quiet or he'll wake the kids. Freddie finally finished and rolled onto his back on his side of the bed. Kyla was in shock. She loved it but she felt like she was with someone else right now. She looked over at Freddie. He turned his head and looked at her. "Thanks Babe. That was great." Kyla was perplexed. "Where did that come from?" Freddie made a face. "What, you didn't enjoy it?" "Yes...but...it was so unlike you." Freddie sat up. "Kyla, what is it exactly that you're looking for? "First you complain that we should switch up positions, then when we do, you question it. What the fuck, Ky?" Freddie got up and went into the bathroom. Truth was, he was feeling guilty for imagining he was having sex with Tina and not his wife.

Sam stopped crying and then became angry. How dare Sal curse at her and walk out. Who the fuck did he think he was? She desperately wanted to go after him and tell him off, but she didn't want to cause a scene with the kids around. Joey would have just put his headphones on and turned up the music. Natalia however, would become emotional and start screaming herself. Last time her parents had an argument, Natalia called her grandmother, crying. Sam was scolded for weeks by her mother. She swore to never make a fuss in front of her daughter again. Not that she blamed Natalia for calling her grandmother, but she didn't need the whole family knowing about their marital issues. *Not only did that man put me in a bad mood, but he ruined my bath too. Damn him!*

She went into the bathroom to brush her teeth. Sal came back into the bedroom. "Look Sam, I apologize for saying 'Fuck you' to you. I couldn't help it. You were being such a bitch." Sam picked her head up from the sink and wiped her mouth on a towel. "That's your way of apologizing? Gee Sal, that was so sincere. I can tell that you really meant it." She brushed past Sal to get out of the bathroom. Sal followed her. "Just what has gotten into you Sam? You're being so nasty and condescending, ever since we got home. What happened? Did I do something?"

Sam couldn't believe he was asking her that after she just got done telling him that she was annoyed with him for mocking Peter today. "Do you need me to repeat myself? I am upset and down right pissed off that my grown ass husband would belittle anyone, let alone a guest in my mother's house and a friend of my sister's! How fucking dare you, Salvatore! Just who do you think you are? You also made fun of him in front of our son and nephew. Don't you know that you should be setting a good example for them? My father probably thinks you're an asshole. I am so embarrassed. I'm even embarrassed for YOU!" Sal slammed the bedroom door shut to keep the kids from overhearing them argue. "I was fucking joking around Samantha...fucking joking! Like I said before, Peter had no clue, so it's fine. The boys thought it was funny. No harm done....NONE!" Sal punched the wall, putting a small dent in it. "Wow Sal really? You even argue like a child! Are you going to fix that now, you animal? And another thing, You are probably the only one that found your joking around amusing. The boys probably just laughed to please you. You know how much Joey looks up to you. I am sure if you ask anyone else, they will find your behavior, tacky, insensitive and down right rude! I am sick of it! Grow up Salvatore Dimartino! " Sam went into the bathroom again and slammed the door shut. She even locked it. "Thanks a lot Sam. Have a good night." Sal said from the other side of the door. She heard the bedroom door open and footsteps go down the stairs. She wanted to cry but she was just too angry.

She didn't want to chance seeing Sal again before they both calmed down. Otherwise, they would be at this all night, even while they were in bed together! Sam took her time, brushing her teeth and hair. Next, she did a nighttime facial routine. When she decided the coast was clear, she opened the door to the bathroom and stepped out. Her bedroom was dark. She looked over at the bed. Sal wasn't in it. She walked into the hallway and looked down the stairs. All of the lights were off, the kitchen, the living room, etc. She didn't hear the TV either. Sam crept down the stairs quietly so she wouldn't wake up Natalia. The house was so quiet, you could hear a pin drop. Sam checked throughout the entire downstairs but Sal was nowhere to be found. She looked out the window and saw that his car was gone. If only he had been blocked in, he wouldn't have been able to leave. Sam started to cry. *I can't believe this is happening. How stupid!* Her tears didn't last long though. Sam started to get angry. *He's got some set to just walk out and leave us here. It was a stupid argument. He really does need to grow up! Perhaps when he returns, I will let him know that if he ever decides to leave again, he can stay out for good!* She walked back upstairs, locked the door to her bedroom and climbed into bed. "Good night Asshole wherever you are!"

Before she even turned around, she knew what had happened. She heard the crash and then the sound of Diamond, scurrying away. Tina turned around. Yep. She knew it! The photo frame she had just put Freddie's picture in, was on the floor, broken into a hundred pieces. "Damn you Diamond! Can't you leave anything alone?" Tina huffed and puffed as she swept up the mess off the floor. Diamond walked back over to sniff. "Get out of here!" Tina yelled. Diamond ran out of the room. Tina pulled the photo out of what was left of the frame and brushed it off. "Some might think, this is a sign of things to come, Freddie baby, but I think not. Maybe I'll just put your photo on the pillow next to me so I know you're safe from that bully Diamond.

The phone rang.. Tina picked it up. It was her sister, Sonia. "Hey girl, what's up?" Tina was delighted her sister called. They hardly got to speak anymore with the two of them having busy schedules. "Not much, T. Different day, same shit." "How's my niece? Tell her I love and miss her. Aunt T is gonna visit soon." "She's good and I'll tell her," her sister replied. So what's new? Mama called me. Told me that you and she didn't exactly have the best phone call the other day." Tina sighed. "You know Mom. Same thing as always. "When are you going to get your life together? Stop being a slut. Blah, blah, blah." Sonia laughed. "You sound just like her!" "She's a pain in the ass but she means well. Anyway, enough about her, guess what?" "What?" Tina took a deep breath. "I met a guy!"

Tina bit her lip. Sonia was silent for a second, then spoke. "Tina...." "I know....don't say it, please." "There's something different about this one though. I am getting feelings that I haven't had in a long time. "He's not married, is he?" Tina looked at Freddie's picture. "He didn't say he was." "Listen, you've heard all of this before. You're a grown woman. You know what you're doing. Just be careful, Sis. I love you. I gotta go. Someone is ringing the bell." "I love you too. Kiss that baby for me!" Tina hung up and looked at Freddie's picture again. You just wait. Sonia is gonna love you! As

Tina was getting up, she heard her phone beep. She was in such a deep conversation with her sister, that she forgot, some had sent her a text while she was on the phone. Tina picked up her phone to read the message. It was from Freddie.

They had sex before, but tonight was different....special. Usually sex felt like it was, just that...sex. Tonight however, felt like love. *Yes, Peter was definitely making love to me.* Kristen was over the moon. For once, she felt like the man appreciated her for her and not her body. He was more interested in pleasing her than himself. *Why couldn't our paths meet before? Because you were with that mother fucker, that's why.* Kristen vowed to herself to do whatever it takes to not let Peter slip away. She looked over at him. He was peacefully sleeping. "Goodnight, Peter." she whispered.

Kristen got up quietly and went into the bathroom with her phone. She couldn't chance Rachel seeing her if she went out of the room. So the bathroom would have to do. She sent her sister a text. "I think he's the one. I am finally happy." Kristen put the phone down on the sink and looked at her reflection in the mirror. She was glowing. Her phone began to buzz. It was Sam. She told her she was delighted to hear it was going so well and that she was truly happy for her sister. Kristen sent another text, thanking her and to please thank Sal for making Peter feel welcome. Sam replied with, 'I would, but here's not here. We had a fight and can you believe the shithead left? God only knows where he went.' Kristen stared at her phone. *Poor Sam!* She sent a text back asking if she was ok and if she wanted, she'd ask Peter to take her over there. Sam told her no, she was fine and they would talk tomorrow. They said their 'I love yous' and 'goodnights'. Kristen crept back into Peter's bed. She looked at Peter again. "I think I'm falling for you mister."

Knock, Knock

The sun was in her eyes. Kyla rubbed them and looked over. Freddie was already out of bed and in the shower. She looked at her alarm clock. Kyla was relieved. *Twenty minutes until I have to get the kids up and ready for school. That will give me just enough time to pee, brush my teeth and get breakfast going.*

She rose out of bed and slipped on her robe. She went into the bathroom, scaring the hell out of Freddie. "You scared me! Don't you knock woman?" Kyla rolled her eyes at her sudsy husband. "Not when it comes to you Dear. I've seen it all." She leaned in for a wet kiss. Freddie kissed her then pulled the shower back over and continued washing. Kyla sat on the toilet. Freddie peeked around the curtain again. "So classy Ky. Stop. You're turning me on." Kyla frowned. "¡Cállate! I had to pee badly and wanted to brush my teeth before the kids got up. My toothbrush is in this bathroom. "Whatever. Just don't drop a deuce." He pulled the curtain back again. "Who's the classy one now, Frederico?" She finished, brushed her teeth and left the bathroom.

Kyla went downstairs and started making breakfast. Luckily, some eggs survived from the fall the other day, when Freddie slammed the door to the refrigerator. She put on a pot of coffee and glanced at the clock. "Time to wake the rugrats!" She went back upstairs and into Francesca's room. "Wake up sleepy head. Time for school." Francesca, like her mother, rubbed her eyes and sat up. "Good morning Mommy. Mr. Weatherman showed clouds on the TV yesterday. I think it might rain today so make sure you don't give me my white sneakers to wear. I don't want to get them dirty." "Yes Mija." *She is only in pre-k but one would think she is much older with her mind and attention to detail.* "Get dressed Cheski. I have to wake

Anthony now and get back downstairs before the eggs burn." "Ok, Mommy." Next, Kyla went into Anthony's room to wake him. He just grunted so Kyla shut his door and went back downstairs.

The eggs were starting to overcook. Kyla quickly shut the burner off and moved the pan to another one. She poured juice for the kids and made their plates. She poured coffee for herself and Freddie. *They all should be here in about five minutes. That's five minutes of me, peace and coffee.* Kyla plopped into a kitchen chair and took a few sips of her coffee. "What shall I do today?" She said out loud. The only one that heard her was their macaw named Monster. He got that name because Francesca was a toddler when they got him and she was scared of him. She said he looked like a monster. So hence, Monster the macaw!

The gym was a given in Kyla's daily routine. She went first thing every morning after the kids left for school. She used to go with Freddie once the gym reopened and while Freddie was still working from home during Covid. Her sister in law would watch the kids while they went. They went in the morning but now that he has returned to working onsite, they each go alone, her in the morning, him at night.

The kids ran into the kitchen, followed by Freddie. Francesca had a bright pink sweater with neon pants. Anthony told her she looked like a watermelon. "I do not!" she screamed. Freddie covered his ears while Kyla reprimanded both kids. "Now sit down, eat your breakfast and be quiet." Freddie slowly lowered his arms down. Is it safe to talk now?" he asked. Kyla laughed. "Yes, unless you don't have anything nice to say either." "Well, I was going to ask if you could go to the store today to get the rest of the groceries we need. We are low on milk and other stuff we couldn't get yesterday." Kyla thought of her plan of seeing Tina. "Let me figure out my plan for the day and I'll let you know. Now eat your breakfast before it gets cold."

Kyla went upstairs to shower and change before she had to put the kids on the bus. She liked heading to the gym as soon as the kids left. If she got there any later, it becomes crowded. Besides, that Stevens woman went there after her Zumba class. Kyla certainly did not want to bang into that one! Good thing she was friendly with the Zumba instructor, Maria. They went to school together. Kyla knew from speaking with Maria, that Jordan was a client and knew the Zumba schedule. She liked Zumba herself but made sure she didn't attend the same sessions as Jordan. *No thanks, I'd rather puke.*

Now is a good time to text Tina to see if today is good for her to meet for lunch. Her phone went off almost instantly the second she hit send. Tina responded, telling her today would work. She took the day off from work today so anytime works for her to meet. "Great." Kyla text back. Both ladies agreed on a time and location. Shit! I'm running behind! Kyla quickly jumped in the shower and dressed in her gym clothes after.

Sam woke up and looked over to Sal's side. He wasn't there. Then it all came back to her. Her locking the bedroom door, him leaving, their fight. Sam let out a huge sigh. She felt like she was in a bad dream. She got up and walked over to the window. Sal's car was in the driveway. *At least I know that he's home.* Sam sighed once more and went downstairs.

There was the pillow and the blankets from the hall closet, folded neatly in the corner of the couch. *I guess that's where he spent the night. Serves him right for the way he spoke to me.* She walked into the kitchen to find her husband drinking a cup of coffee and looking at his phone. "Good morning." She managed to squeak out. She didn't feel like talking to him but she knew the kids were still home so she didn't want to cause a scene. "It is? I don't think so." Sal looked up from his phone and at Sam. He had an angry face. "Wait...what?" Sam was confused. Sal sighed. You said 'Good morning.' I said it is, as if I'm asking what's so good about it. "Oh." Sal looked at Sam again. "Thanks for locking me out of my own bedroom last night by the way. I appreciate it." Sal hissed. Sam put her hands on her hips. You could've knocked on the door Sal. I would of let you in." Sal laughed. "And wake the kids? Why did you lock it in the first place? To show you're the boss and was pissed off at me? What did you expect? That I would have knocked and begged from the other side of the door? " Sal clutched his hands together. "Oh please, Mighty Queen Samantha, please, please let me in. I'll behave, I promise." Sam turned red. "You're ridiculous. Where did you go anyway? And what time did you get home? Furthermore, what man leaves their wife and kids home alone and just walks out because of an argument they had? Now Sal turned red. "It's none of your business where I because I was angry with you and rather than continue arguing and having our fight escalate, especially with our kids in the house, I chose to leave and go cool off. Last time I looked, Joey is old enough to look after himself, Natalia and you! Don't give me that shit, I left you guys. You make it sound like I'm a piece of shit or a dick." Sam wanted to smack him. "None of my business Sal? Really? Newsflash! You are married to ME! Everything you say and do is my business! And had you stayed and we continued fighting? What did you envision happening? You'd hit me like you hit the wall last night? Is that what you thought might happen?" Sam was seething now. So was Sal. I have never put my hands on you and I never will! Don't go there Sam! You are crossing the line! You know what I'm thinking right now? That staying away just last night wasn't enough. I think you and I need a day or two apart to get over whatever this thing is you have going on." Sam got right in Sal's face and pointed her finger at herself. "I have going on? Salvatore, honey. You're wrong. Not only about that but about needing a day or two apart. I think it should be longer than that." Sal grabbed his car keys and walked toward the front door. He opened the door to walk out but before he did, he turned around to look at Sam. "Fine Sam. If that's what you want. You got it Babe." He slammed the door behind him, got in his car and flew out of the driveway. Sam covered her face with her hands and started to sob.

When she woke up this morning, she had to pinch herself that she wasn't dreaming. Tina was really looking forward to today. Freddie sent her a text last night, asking if she could meet him any earlier at the gym. He had some exercises that he wanted to show her to step up her workout routine. It seemed pretty basic to him when she explained what exercises she currently did. He wanted to show her ones that might get her results faster. Tina decided to take the day off from work. She wanted time to take a long bath just before heading to the gym and to just fix herself up to be ready for Freddie in general. Even though this wasn't a date in his eyes, to her, it was. If she wasn't already looking forward to today already, Kyla also sent her a text, asking if they could meet for lunch today. "It's perfect." she told Diamond. "I took the day off so I definitely can meet her. Any other day, we'd have to meet on a weekend. With two kids, I don't think that would be possible for Kyla. Unless her husband is around. I gotta ask Kyla about him today. I'm curious how life turned out for her. I'm eager to tell someone about Freddie. I'll just leave the part out about him being married. If Kyla asks me, I'll just say I don't know yet." Diamond just stared at her and jumped off the bed when Tina got out of it. He followed her into the kitchen, meowing to be fed.

Tina ate breakfast, then headed for the shower. *No sense in going to the gym if I'm going later. I would normally be working anyhow. Besides, I need all my mojo for Freddie.* She was in the mood to text him just to see if he responded. "Hey! It's Tina. Looking forward to our little workout session later. I'll bring the water...and the sweat! Good morning btw. Have a beautiful day! " The text was followed by a happy face emoji. She put the phone down and headed for the shower.

Twenty minutes later, Tina stepped out of the shower and looked at her phone. To her dismay, she didn't receive a text back. "Damn!" She looked at the clock. *He has to be at work by now, so I'm sure his wife didn't see the text. Next time, maybe I should keep my name out of it, to protect him...and ME! I guess if he is working, he's just busy. I will get him all to myself later anyhow!*

She sent Kyla a text next to say she was anticipating their lunch date. Tina couldn't wait to hear what her friend has been up to all these years and tell Kyla what has been going on with her. Can we become close good friends like we once were? Tina really hoped so. She needed a confidante in her life, preferably female. She had her sister but Sonia's life was hectic. Her sister was too busy for her own life, let alone Tina's! Kyla replied to Tina's text. She was looking forward to it also and agreed, they had lots to catch up on.

Peter shook Kristen. She sat up, breathing heavily. She was sweating. "Where...where...am I?" She looked around the dimly lit room. Peter was next to her. "It's ok Kristen. You were having a nightmare. You're fine. You're in my bed." He smiled. She smiled back at him but was embarrassed that he had to wake her. They just discussed last night how quiet they had to be with Rachel in the house and then this happened. "What were you dreaming about? Were you being attacked by one of your mother's meatballs?" Peter chuckled and Kristen whacked him with a pillow. "No!" she whispered. "I spoke to my sister last night. She had an argument with Sal when they got home. He left the house. I dreamt that he left for good and she had to move in with my parent's house too. We were all fighting because the house isn't big enough for all of us." She looked at Peter. "I know, stupid right?" Peter grinned. "No, the thought of moving back in with my parents sends chills down my spine. No thanks, being on a schedule for dinner, being reprimanded if I stay out too late, my underwear being folded by my MOTHER!" Kristen laughed and then covered her mouth.

Peter climbed out of bed. "Stay here for a bit and relax. Rachel should be getting ready to leave soon. I'll come back up when she's gone so you can rise and shine." He leaned over and gave Kristen a kiss. "Bye." she said as he waltzed out of the bedroom. Kristen reached into her bag on the floor just below her and grabbed her phone. She sent Sam a text. "How's it going? You ok?" Kristen sighed and laid back down. Her phone went off a minute later. Sam told her that she and Sal were still in a fight but she'll be ok. Sam was going to call her later."

The bedroom door opened ten minutes later and Peter walked in. "Ok, Rachel just got picked up by her friend and her friend's brother. The brother is older and driving them to school. I know the parents so it's cool. Feel free to take a shower. I'll be making breakfast downstairs. We'll eat something, then I'll drive you back. Cool?" Kristen nodded. Once Peter left, she grabbed her bag and headed for the shower.

The kitchen smelled like a diner serving breakfast. Kristen came downstairs after she got dressed. "This looks a whole lot like the scene from yesterday." Peter grinned. "And what would the lady like?" Peter bowed to her. Kristen bowed back. They both stood back up, looked at each other then leaned in for a kiss.

Neither one of them heard the knock at the front door. She dug in her backpack for her key. Rachel walked into the kitchen. "Dad, I forgot my homework so I came back to.....What the....."

Sneaky Sneaky

As he was putting his shoes on, Kyla kissed Freddie goodbye and wished him a good day. A few minutes later, she made sure Anthony had his coat and shoes on as well as his lunch in his backpack. She kissed her son goodbye as he ran for the school bus. Next, she put Francesca in the car and buckled her. She was ready to drop off her daughter at her pre-k school. Once she buckled herself in and started to drive, Kyla thought of her plan for the day.

First things first after I drop off Cheski, the gym! I gotta get my workout in first thing or it won't be happening. What's the saying? Never skip a Monday! I'll stay there for an hour or two, then come home quickly and shower. I'll have enough time to do that plus change and put some makeup on before I have to meet Tina. That shouldn't take all day so I can go to the grocery store after and make it back in time to pick up Francesca and meet Anthony's bus. Kyla thought about her lunch date with Tina again. *We do have a lot of catching up to do though. I just hate sneaking behind Freddie's back to do so. I feel like I'm cheating.*

She pulled into a parking space of the Little People, Big Minds Pre-School. She unbuckled Francesca and brought her inside to her classroom. "Have a good day Baby. Make sure you eat your lunch. I'll pick you up after school, ok?" "Ok, Mommy." Francesca hugged her mother. Kyla bent down and gave Francesca a kiss on her forehead. "See ya later, Alligator." Francesca laughed. "In a while Crocodile!" Francesca ran over to a group of kids playing on the floor in a corner with some toys. "Have a nice day, Mrs. Lovazzo." Francesca's teacher said to Kyla. "You too!" Kyla left the classroom and headed for her car.

"The gym is packed today!" Kyla exclaimed to herself as she drove around for a few minutes in the gym parking lot, trying to find a space. She finally found one, in the far corner of the lot. *Guess I will be getting in my steps today as well!* Kyla was already out of breath by the time she reached the gym doors. "¡Dios mío!" She huffed, trying to catch her breath from walking so far. It didn't help that it was cold out also and that made it even harder to breathe.

Once she walked through the doors, she instantly felt the heat from the gym walls. She could also smell the stench. The staff did a pretty good job of maintaining the gym's cleanliness but there was nothing that could possibly clear up the smell. It could only be masked with a more pleasant odor such as the cleaner the staff used to mop the floor and clean the equipment with.

Kyla checked in at the front desk. Brielle was working the front. "Good morning Mrs. Lovazzo. How are you today?" "Good morning Brielle. I'm good. You?" "I'm ok, thanks. Will Mr. Lovazzo be joining you?" "No, he's at work. I'm sure he'll be by later. Have a good day." Brielle smiled at Kyla. "Thanks, you too." Kyla walked toward the locker room. *Why did Brielle ask me if Freddie was coming? That's strange. Is this now a restaurant? Do you want a table for one or a table for two? She also had a peculiar look on her face too. Wonder what that's about.* Kyla was engrossed in her own thoughts so she didn't even notice her walk in. "I forgot you came here!" She felt a light tap on her shoulder. Kyla quickly snapped out of thought. She was staring back at Jodan Stevens. *Great. ¡No te jode! Just what I need.* Kyla put on a fake smile when Jordan air kissed her cheek. "I forgot also. I haven't see you here in a while Jordan." *If I was up for best actress, I'd win the Oscar.* Jordan smiled back at Kyla, revealing her overpriced bridge and crown work done on her teeth. "That's right. I'm a member of that prestigious country club across town, but they're renovating for a few weeks so I'm stuck coming here." Jordan shrugged her shoulders. Kyla clenched her fist and bit her tongue. She couldn't wait to get out of the locker room. "Oh, well, it was good seeing you. Enjoy your workout." *I hope a dumbbell falls on your foot, you DUMBass!* Kyla started to walk away. "Kyla?" Kyla sucked her teeth and turned around. "Yes Jordan?" Again Jordan flashed her fake smile. "Have you given any thought to having a playdate?" Now it was Kyla's turn for a fake smile. "Honestly Jordan, no. I am so busy with the kids and other stuff, I haven't had a chance." "Ok, please think about it. I'm sure you'll think of something. I know you don't work and don't belong to the school PTA, so you probably have more time than I do but I'll work around your schedule to make it convenient for you." Did this Coño just insinuate something? Kyla gritted her teeth. "Yes Jordan, true, I don't work and am not involved with the PTA because I am involved in many other things as well as taking care of my own children and not paying someone else to do it for me, while I play tennis or go to Zumba class. It might be a different story if I was working but if I'm free, my kids come first. Now if you'll excuse me, I have to start my workout so I can finish on time because I have things to do!" Kyla put her headphones on in case Jordan started talking again. She rushed out of the locker room. *The nerve of that bitch! I really can't stand her. I hope someone bitch slaps her real soon. I should tell Sam. Sam will do it!* Kyla laughed to herself. Sam was always ready to throw down.

Sam got up after sulking for what felt like an eternity. She was baffled by how much the argument between her and Sal had escalated. However, she was determined to not let the situation with her husband affect her. They both needed some time apart to cool down and just think. Sam was confident that all of it would just blow over in a day or two and they would be back on easy street again. She dried her tears and decided to do something that will make her feel better and take her mind off Sal...shopping.

After she brushed her teeth, Sam turned the shower on. It felt good to let the hot water run down her back. The house was quiet since everyone had left for school and work. It was peaceful now. She washed her hair and shaved her legs. She dried her hair and put some makeup on. Her face was swollen from crying. *Nothing like a good concealer to do the trick and fix.* Next, she threw on a pair of her favorite jeans and paired them with a long sweater. Sam put her shoes on, grabbed her keys and out the door she went.

Once she was in her car, she called her team. The machine came on. She had to leave a message or it they would worry. She had told them she would finally make an appearance at the office and not work from home for a change."Hi guys, it's Samantha. I am not feeling well, so I am taking the day off. I'll see you tomorrow." She disconnected the call. Sam hated lying but was it really lying though? *I feel fine physically, but mentally emotionally. I am not well.* The arguments with Sal put her over the edge for the time being even knowing it would turn out fine. Sam tried telling herself this to justify her actions for calling out. *I just need some time to myself, to take of me alone for a change.* She took a deep breath and started the car. She headed for the plaza that had tons of shops.

As soon as she parked the car, Sam jumped right out and went inside the main building. It was six floors of stores, from clothing to makeup. One floor alone was dedicated to just shoes.. *Let's see. Where to first? I need just about everything.* With her sister and two teenagers in tow this past weekend, she didn't get much accomplished for herself when she was at the mall. *I took the day off, may as well make it useful.*

Two hours and a few hundred dollars later, Sam's arms were beginning to feel like they would fall off. She was carrying so many bags. *That's enough for me for one day, I guess. I'm exhausted anyway.* She walked to her car and put all of her purchases in the trunk.

"Samantha, is that you?" Sam turned around and saw Richie looking at her. Richie Buccatini, thee Richie Buccatini that Sam had a crush on all through junior high and dated for two years in high school. They even went to Prom together and he had taken her virginity. "Richie? Oh my God. How long has it been?" They hugged and Richie kissed Sam on the cheek. "Too long, Sam. You haven't changed a bit though. You're still as beautiful as ever." Sam blushed. "You're still the sweet guy I remember. Thank you by the way." Richie moved closer to Sam. So what have you been up to...besides shopping? I see some things never change." He began to laugh. "No..no they don't. she chuckled. "I am married with two kids. My son is eighteen and my daughter is twelve going on twenty." Richie laughed again. "Good for you!" Sam was blushing. "How about you? Wife, kids?" Richie leaned against Sam's car. "No, not for me. I never married. I came pretty close though. But she got weird and insecure about herself so I called it off." Sam frowned. "I'm sorry." Richie grinned. "Nah, don't be. My life is great. I own my own shop a few miles from here. Business is booming. I still hang out with a lot of the guys from school, so I'm not the creepy old guy that is single and still hangs out with teenagers and plays video games." He laughed and continued talking. "Marriage just wasn't in the cards for me." Sam smiled at him. "I'm happy for you Richie, I really am. You were always so good to me. I'm surprised some girl didn't snatch you up for keeps. I don't know where you and I went wrong." Richie looked away. "Me either, Sam. You'll always be the one that got away." Sam felt her face getting hot. She knew it was time to go. "Take care of yourself Richie. It was good seeing you." She kissed Richie on the cheek and opened her car door. He closed it for her once she was in. She rolled down the window and he bent down. "Goodbye Samantha, Tell that husband of yours, he's one lucky guy." He tapped the roof of her car and Sam drove away. She looked back at Richie in her side view mirror. Was that a tear he just wiped from his eye?

She drove down the block and pulled over. Sam removed her sunglasses and slumped on her seat. Her emotions got the best of her again. *Seeing Richie brought back so many memories, good memories. Maybe I should have fought harder for us. Maybe I should have just let all the bullshit go back then. We were good together. I know Sal and I are too, but with Richie, it was different. I never felt the love for Sal like I did for Richie. Did I make a mistake all those years ago? I guess I'll never know.* She put her sunglasses back on and drove to the local brunch spot for lunch.

Even though she already picked out which gym outfit she was going to wear, Tina decided to try on several outfits anyway just to make sure she had chosen the right one. It had to be perfect if she was going to get Freddie's attention. Her body had become more toned and muscular in the last few weeks. An outfit that accentuated her chest and ass to the best of its ability previously, may not be the best one now.

One hour and several outfits later, she was assured she had the right one. The one she chose, gave a little tease but not enough where she would be taken for easy or seen as trashy. She put the rest of the outfits back and got ready for her lunch date with Kyla. She chose a regular pair of leggings and a simple top. She didn't want to give Kyla the wrong impression either. It was important for Kyla to know that Tina turned out to be a decent woman, not some chick that flaunted everything she had and craved attention from everyone else's man. She needed Kyla's friendship.

Her phone rang. It was her mother. "Hey Mami. Buenos dias." "Hola Christina. How are you? I wasn't sure if I'd catch you. Don't you usually go to the gym at this time?" Tina told herself to think carefully about what she said. The last thing she wanted was another lecture from her mother about her actions. "Sí. But my friend wanted to meet for lunch today. I am going to the gym later to do my workout." Tina bit her lip. She couldn't tell her mother her whole plan for the day. If she knew she had plans to be with Freddie later, there would be hell to pay. Besides, she wasn't lying. She just held back some info. Her mother seemed to be pleased with her answer too. "Oh, ok, good. You should hang out with friends. It's healthy. Is she married?" Tina sucked her teeth. She knew why her mother was asking her this. "Yes Mami, she is married." Tina held her breath. "Oh good, she will be a good influence on you. Maybe her husband has some nice friends to introduce you to. Who knows? Maybe you will get married and have a baby like your sister. Wouldn't that be nice. You're not getting any younger, Christina."

Tina's cell phone beeped in her ear. She pulled it away from her face to look at it. She had a text from Freddie. "I hate to cut you off, Mami, but I have to get ready now or I'll be late in meeting Kyla." Her mother gasped. "Kyla Torres from our old neighborhood?" "Yes, Kyla Torres. Well, she's not Torres anymore. Honestly, I don't even know her married name yet. But yeah, we ran into each other the other day and we are getting together for lunch today to catch up. I really have to go, Ma. I love you." "Love you to Mija, talk soon." Her mother blew a kiss in the phone and hung up. Tina pressed on the app for her text messages. Freddie was looking forward to meeting later too. Tina squealed with delight.

She could feel her cheeks burning. She was so embarrassed. They had been caught by Peter's daughter. *It's all my fault. I should have never agreed to spend the night. What's wrong with you, Kristen? You have a daughter yourself. You should know better.* Peter cleared his throat. "Rachel...I apologize. You weren't supposed to know about this." Rachel laughed. "Obviously Dad. It's ok, Kristen. I get it." Kristen felt a little bit better, not much though. Rachel kept talking. "Shame on you, Dad. You kept poor Kristen hidden in your bedroom? I know there's a bathroom but what if she got thirsty or I was sick and wasn't going to school today? Would you have kept Kristen in there all day? Or would you have made her jump out of the window?" Peter started to speak. "Wait Dad. Don't say anything before this becomes awkward for any of us. I know. You're an adult and have needs as does Kristen. I just want you to be happy Dad. You went through a lot with Mom. It's nice to finally see you smile again. I can tell that Kristen is the reason. I can appreciate that. And, don't worry about setting an example for my sake. I know how old I am and I know my boundaries. Now if you'll excuse me, I have to grab my homework. Jennifer and her brother are waiting. I'm already late for school." Rachel hurried past them and ran into her room to grab her homework. Peter and Kristen didn't even have time to look at one another before Rachel popped back out of her room, scurried past them and yelled "Bye!." Kristen slumped into the chair. "Oh my God. Did that really just happen?" Peter laughed. "Yes...yes it did. Of course she would have forgotten something and had to come back.

But I think I am more in shock of what she said. She sounded like a mature adult. I was the one who felt like the kid that had snuck a girl in my room and got caught." Kristen smirked. "Your daughter is definitely wise beyond her years." Peter sighed. "I know. I guess when you have had to witness and deal with what she's had to with her mother and I, it makes you that way. She had to grow up before she was ready." Kristen got up and wrapped her arms around Peter. "That may be true and I know from my own personal experience with my children and the situation with their father, that it is such. However, it does prepare you to have thick skin and teaches you how to deal with the rough moments. You learn to not sweat the small stuff. Your daughter is going to be just fine and so are my kids. I'm not worried about them. It's us that I'm worried about!" They both laughed and shared a kiss. Peter pulled away and stared at Kristen. "Well, my lady. I guess there will be no more sneaking around. I think we will be ok with Rachel seeing us together, as long as it's not constantly thrown in her face. So! Enough with this! Where were we? Ah yes, what would you like for breakfast, my lady?"

Shh!

Kyla finished her workout and rushed to her car. She was in a hurry for two reasons. The first being if she hurried, she'd have just enough time to get home, shower and change before her lunch date with Tina. She also rushed out of the gym so she wouldn't run into Jordan again. If she did, the cops would be called and she would need someone to bail her out of jail for assault. *The nerve of her! Coming out of her face, saying what she did! Eres una zorra estúpida fea. I should have just told her to shut the fuck up!* She threw her water bottle and gym bag in the car and sped off.

Once she got in her driveway, she ran in the house, stripped her sweaty clothes off and jumped in the shower. Twenty minutes later, she was back out the door again, to meet Tina for lunch. Freddie called while he was driving. "Hi Babe. What's going on?" "Nothing, went to the gym, now running errands." "Ok, be careful. I may be a little late tonight. I have a longer workout tonight and want to do some cardio also." Kyla felt a sigh of relief. "Ok, no problem. I'll see you tonight. Love you." Freddie told her he loved her also and hung up. *Great, he's gonna be late tonight. I will have plenty of time to spend it with Tina, to stop at the store, and make dinner.* She pulled into the local brunch spot that she and Tina agreed to meet at.

Tina was already there, sitting at a table on the sidewalk. Kyla walked over. "Hi Tina. Tina jumped up. "Hey Kyla!" She gave Kyla a big hug. "I hope you don't mind. I thought it was nice out so I picked a table out here. We can go inside if you prefer." Kyla smiled. "No, this is fine. It is nice out. I could go for a cocktail out here." "You got it." Tina flagged down the waiter and ordered two martinis.

"So? How the hell have you been?" Tina smiled at Kyla. She missed the friendship she had with her all these years. Kyla smiled back. "I am good, can't complain. Great husband, two wonderful kids. My life is good. You?" Tina paused. "It's good. I work a lot. I live alone but spend a lot of time with my sister and my niece, doing the aunt thing. Kyla grinned. "Good for you Tina. Any man in your life?" Tina smirked. "No, I've dated here and there, but no more than that. I did meet someone recently and I'm hoping it turns into something, but it's too early to tell yet. Shh, let's not jinx it! *Is Tina beaming? Well, good for her!* "That's awesome Tina. Best of luck. You'll have to keep me posted." "I definitely will...you and my mother! Both women laughed.

"How is your mother?" Kyla asked. "I remember Mrs. Santiago growing up. Does she still make the best arroz con gandules?" Tina grinned. "I am going there this Friday for dinner. Wanna come?" Kyla sneered. "You know, that's not a bad idea. I am having my family and my husband's family over on Sunday. I want to make traditional Puerto Rican dishes. They usually eat Italian food. I want to impress them with my boriqua skills. Who better to teach me and have me learn from?

"Speaking of your husband, you haven't said anything about him. What's his name? How did you meet him? How long have you been married? I want details! Joked Tina. Kyla opened her mouth to speak but quickly closed it as she saw her.

"Sam?" Tina turned around and saw Sam in the distance. She rolled her eyes. *Great. She's here.* Sam walked over to the women. "Hi Ky...Tina. Tina just nodded. Sam ignored her. "Sam, what are you doing here? Why aren't you at work?" Kyla knew something was up. It was the middle of the day, on a weekday. Sam should either be working remotely or at the office. Sam wasn't dressed for the office if she was on her lunch break. "It's a long story, Ky. One I can't discuss now" She glared at Tina who was pretending to look at her nails. "Will you be home later to chat?" Kyla touched Sam's hand. "Yeah sure. Call me later." Sam smiled. "Will do. Ciao Bella...Tina." Sam turned around and walked away. "I hope she's ok," Kyla said to Tina. Tina made a face. "I'm sure she's fine. Now where were we?"

Sam returned back home and took her bags out of the car. Sal's car wasn't in the driveway but Sam didn't expect it to be there anyhow. Regardless of their fight, Sal probably went to work, unlike Sam and would be gone for another couple of hours. Sam sighed and opened the front door to the house. It was even too early for the kids to be home yet.

She sat down on the couch and thought about when she banged into Kyla. Maybe *I should have called her and told her I took the day off. Perhaps she would have met me and not that butana, Tina.* Sam hated that Kyla was hanging out with her; not because Kyla was HER best friend. Sam was long past the jealous teenager stage but because Kyla was such a good friend, she didn't want to see her get hurt. Sam was convinced that Tina had the capability to do just that. *If she hurts her in any way, I will beat that bitch to a pulp.*

Her mind was racing. Although *I didn't appreciate seeing Kyla with Tina having lunch together, running into Richie was nice. It had been a long time. He brought back a lot of memories for me, good ones, back when things were simple and not so complicated. I always felt some type of way about him, even though we went our separate ways. He was one of the good guys, treated me well, had a nice family and he had goals for his future. Look at him now, owning his own shop! I guess we just weren't meant to be together. What is meant to be, is meant to be.* She sighed once again. *Speaking of complicated, I think I will call Sal and feel him out.* She hoped he felt like her and was ready to let it go and just move on. Sam was tired of being in a funk and having to deal with this bullshit.

The phone rang a few times and then it went to his voicemail. Sam hung up. She waited awhile and then tried him again. Same thing again, voicemail. Sam hung up again but this time she decided to text him. "Hey you. I just tried your cell. I wanted to say hello and see how your day was going. I don't want to fight anymore. Friends?"

She put the phone down and sighed. Sam didn't get a response until a few hours later. It was a text from Sal. "Sam, I didn't have a chance to respond earlier. Things are crazy at work today. I don't want to fight either. But it wasn't just a fight. You said things that raised so many questions in my mind. I am not ready to talk to you yet. I need some time. Because I do, I plan on staying at my sister's tonight. Please tell the kids that I am working late so they don't get concerned. If you need me for something, you know how to reach me. Otherwise, I'll call you tomorrow. Bye."

Sam stared at her phone in disbelief. Was this really happening right now? It was a stupid argument! Was he really that immature to do this, punish her? She called Kyla. She needed advice and to talk to someone. Usually she was the one, giving advice and taking control of a situation. But right now she felt weak and vulnerable. She got Kyla's voicemail. "Fuck!" Sam threw her phone. "She is probably still out with that bitch! And why do people even have phones if they don't pick up?" Sam started to cry.

The front door opened. Natalia came in. Sam was so busy worrying about the text, she didn't even realize Natalia would be coming home any minute. She didn't even hear the school bus pull up in front of the house. Sam tried to wipe her face when she saw her daughter. "Mom...Mom are you ok?" Natalia put her backpack down, took off her shoes and walked over to her mother. "Yeah, Tali.

I'm fine. I was just watching a movie. It was a real tear jerker. The mom dies at the end." Sam lied to her daughter's face but didn't want Natalia to worry. "Oh, ok, Mom. As long as you're ok. I have sooo much homework. My teachers suck!" Sam made a face. "Natalia, watch your mouth!" "Sorry Mom. I am going to start it now. See ya later for dinner. Whatcha making anyhow?" With everything going on, Sam forgot about dinner. She didn't have a plan. She had to think quickly. "Um, Daddy is working late and I think Joey is hanging out with friends. I thought we'd just order a pizza and a salad. Cool?" Natalia grinned. "Sure! Sounds good! I'll be in my room if you need me." Natalia ran upstairs and into her room. She shut her door. Sam inhaled deeply. *Thank God, that went ok. At least something did today.* She got up and went to look for the phone number for the pizza place.

Tina was excited. Here she was, spending the afternoon with her childhood friend, having lunch together. She hadn't seen Kyla in years and it felt good to see her again and spend time with her. In fact, it had been years since she did this sort of thing with any female in general. Females hated women like Tina. Women that were beautiful, had a nice physique, great career, independent and attracted the male species, were not favored among average women. Plain Janes, in other words. Some women didn't mind being average. They had a stable marriage, great kids and a beautiful home. They were secure. The majority of women however, revered women like Tina or were jealous of them. Tina appreciated both types. It made her feel superior. She didn't like not having anyone in her corner though. She needed a friend that she could confide in, vent to and get advice from. Sure, she had her mother and sister, but that wasn't the same as having a close friend. She also wasn't sure if Kyla really meant it when they spoke about getting together. Kyla may have just been polite. Tina was pretty mean to Kyla back in the day and she didn't know if Kyla still held a grudge. Clearly Samantha did! *I never liked that bitch anyway!* But Kyla had initiated the get together so apparently she had forgiven Tina and now here they were!

The delivery worker closed the door to the box truck on the corner, making a loud noise, bringing Tina out of thought and back to the table with Kyla. She was speaking. Tina was so lost in thought, she had no idea what Kyla had just said. "So, we have been married for about nine years and have two kids. I am a stay at home mom. Not much more to say, than that, I'm afraid." Kyla laughed. Tina smiled at Kyla. "Girl, please. That's a lot to be proud of. I don't have a husband or kids. I do work, and it's ok, but nothing too exciting. They won't be featuring me in People magazine anytime soon! Both women laughed. "Who knows? Maybe they'll decide to do a feature on hot latina women and we'll both be featured! Kyla joked. "Maybe. But just in case, I won't quit my day job!"

Kyla was staring at Tina and she noticed. "Is there food on my face?" she asked. Kyla turned red with embarrassment. "No, I'm sorry for staring at you. I am just looking at you and can't imagine some guy not wanting to scoop you up and make you his wife. You are such a beautiful woman with a beautiful soul." Tina looked down at her plate of food and played with her fork. "The men that I did date over the years, I never found to be that someone special, someone I could see spending the rest of my life with. There wasn't anyone that I wanted to commit to having children with." "I understand. It's a big decision. So this guy that you're seeing right now, perhaps may be the one?" Tina looked up and smiled at Kyla. Like I said, it's too early to know yet, but what I do know is that I am definitely interested. In fact, we are seeing each other tonight. I'll have to keep you posted! Kyla raised her glass. "Well, I'll toast to that! Here's to Tina and her hopefully soon to be new found love!" "¡salud!" Both women clicked their glasses together.

Peter dropped Kristen off at her house. She kissed him goodbye before getting out of the car. "I'll call you tonight. Thank you for breakfast and this past weekend in general. I had a really good time." Peter beamed. "It was my pleasure. I enjoyed this weekend as well. I hope there will be others. Until we speak again, my lady." Kristen got out and Peter backed out of the driveway. He waved at her as he pulled away. She smiled at him but was sad inside. She dreaded this moment, when their weekend came to an end. It had been the most fun she had had in a long time. She turned around to walk up to the house. She couldn't be certain but she thought she saw her mother peeking from behind the curtain in the kitchen window. Kristen shook her head and put the key in the door. Nikki was standing there, packing her bag for school.

"Hi Mom. Did you have fun at Peter's?" Kristen kissed her daughter on top of her head. "Hey Nikki! Yes I did. He really is a nice man. His daughter was there too. She seems like a nice girl. Maybe one day, you can hang out together if I keep seeing Peter." Nikki grinned at her mother. "You really like him, huh Mom? He passed the Marino family dinner so I guess he's not too bad. Besides, Nonna was raving about him when you left. Shh!" Nikki put her finger to her lips. "That's a secret though. You know how she likes everyone to think she's this tough, strong Italian lady, but deep down, she's a mush." Kristen laughed. "I won't say a word!" Kristen pretended to zip her lips. "And to answer your question, yes, I like him...a lot. Peter is different...special." Nikki frowned. "You like him better than Dad?" Kristen put her hand on Nikki's shoulder. "Nik, I loved your father. For many years, things were great. We were so in love and absolutely adored you and your brother. We both still do. Things just fell apart. We can't go back to the way things were. We just can't. We all have to move on for all our sakes. I finally found someone I believe may be worthy of being a part of not only my life but my kids' lives too. You and your brother will always come first, no matter what. My relationship with Peter has to be accepted by you guys or I won't pursue it. That's how much you mean to me. Do you understand what I'm trying to say?" Nikki looked at Kristen. "Yes Mom, I get it. I'm glad you're happy and if Peter makes you feel that way, then he makes me happy too. I love you Mom." Kristen felt tears in her eyes. "I love you more, Nik." They hugged each other. Mrs. Marino walked into the foyer, wiping her hands on her apron. She looked at her daughter and granddaughter embracing.

"Che si dice? Tutto a posto?" "Everything is ok, Ma. Nikki and I were just having a moment." Kristen looked at her daughter. "Isn't that right, Nik?" Nikki grinned at her mother and then her grandmother. "Sì Nonna, everything is better than ok." She kissed both her mother and her grandmother on their cheeks and walked away. Mrs. Marino motioned for Kristen to follow her into the kitchen. "Voglio parlare con Lei." Kristen held her breath. This could go either way. When her mother wanted to talk it meant either being praised for something or scolded for. Kristen hoped it wasn't the later of the two.

"Sit ta down and hava da cup of coffee." Her mother pointed to the kitchen chair and Kristen took a seat. "Only for a minute though Ma. I have to get ready for work." Her mother looked baffled. "You worka today? Why you stay over Pietro house then ifa you hava work?" Kristen inhaled deeply. "Because I wanted to. I had such a nice weekend with him and I wasn't ready for it to end. He invited me back to his house after dinner and my car was still there, so I went." Kristen took a gulp of her coffee and went to get up. "Sit ta down, Kristen. I'm nota done talking to you."

Here we go. Kristen held a breath. She figured her mother was going to tell her it's not proper to spend the night, I am moving too fast or she likes him, but he's not Italian. Her mother turned sound and stared at her. "You lika this guy, Pietro. I meana more than just a fun time with him?" Kristen swallowed hard. "Yes, I do, Ma. He's warm, funny and decent. He is aware of my situation and he doesn't care. We can go at whatever speed I am comfortable with. He respects the kids feelings as well. He also has a daughter to think about." Her mother clasped her hands together. "Well, alrighta then. Good lucka to you and him." Her mother did the Sign of the Cross and left the kitchen. Kristen was dumbfounded. *Well, I certainly wasn't expecting that!* She got up from the table and headed for her bedroom to get ready for work. Upon walking out the door, her mother yelled out her name. "Yeah Ma?" "Whena you have a moment, calla you sister. She hada biga fight with Salvatore and she no sound too good. I worried." Kristen groaned. "Ok, Ma, I'll call and check on her. I love you." She kissed her mother goodbye and opened her car door. *I gotta call Sam.*

251

Monsters

Once her lunch date with Tina was over, Kyla walked into the parking lot toward her car. She thought of her date with Tina. *It sure was so nice getting together with Tina and revisiting the old times. I had forgotten how much we had been through together. She was there for me when I lost my mom. I wish we had kept in touch all these years. Maybe she would have come to my wedding, been a part of my kids lives and just be a close friend. Maybe had I stayed in her life, things would have turned out differently for her. Maybe she'd be married herself, have some kids and more. It looks like she is doing well but I get looking for more out of life. Maybe her age is starting to really creep up on her. Thank God I met Freddie and began a life with him. Who knows where I'd be now!* Kyla got to her car and got in. *I have to call Sam. She didn't look right.*

The phone rang a few times and just as Kyla was preparing to leave a voicemail, Sam picked up. "Hey you." Sam answered with a solemn tone in her voice. Kyla knew right there something was up with Sam. "Hey! I called to see if you're ok. You didn't look good when I saw you. Why were you there anyway? Aren't you supposed to be working right now?" There was a brief silence. "Sam?...Sam?...can your hear me?" Kyla heard Sam breathing. "Yea, Ky, I can hear you." Kyla knew Sam was crying. "Sam, what is it? C'mon, you're scaring me." Sam took a deep breath. "Sorry Ky, it's not that serious. I'm just upset, pissed off too. Sal and I had a fight yesterday when we got home from my parent's house. He left then came home and slept on the couch. She didn't tell Kyla the part about locking Sal out of the bedroom. "Then today, he left me a message that he needs time to think and he will be staying at his sister's tonight. We've argued before, but it never got to this point." Kyla felt so bad for her friend. "Sam, don't worry about it. I'm sure it will all blow over. Sal probably needs time to get over himself. Men can be such babies! Look at Freddie!" Sam and Kyla both laughed. Kyla continued speaking. "Seriously though, it will be fine. He will probably change his mind about tonight anyhow and come home after work. What are you fighting about anyway if you don't mind me asking."

Sam sighed and told Kyla all about how Sal made fun of Peter and how her father pulled her to the side and told her. She explained to Kyla how she called him out on it when they got home and it just escalated from there. "We said mean, nasty things to each other. Not to rehash it, but I kinda said something to him like you said to Freddie the other day." "Ouch," Kyla replied. "But Sam! Look, you see? We're fine now. Take some of the advice you gave to me. Just talk it out and confide in each other about your likes and dislikes. You both will feel better. I'm sure things will be back to normal soon and you'll be back to that Dynamic Duo, I love." Sam chuckled. "Thank you Kyla. I needed this pep talk. You're a great friend. I love you." "Even if I had lunch with Tina?" Kyla squinted and held the phone away from her ear in case Sam started yelling. Instead, she heard this. "Even if you had and continue to have lunch or anything else with Tina. I'm not a fan, but I'm not your keeper either. I know our friendship is a solid one and things that we do in life, we may not approve of, but we accept because we care about one another and will always have each other's backs. "Amen to that sister! Good luck with Sal, Sam. I won't call you tonight just in case you're in the middle of something with him. Call me tomorrow. Te amo. Adiós."

She hung up with Sam and headed for home. *Where did the day go?* She had just enough time to run home, pee and put her packages away before she had to pick up the kids from their afterschool activities. Francesca was still young but enjoyed the storytime session after school so Kyla enrolled her. Kyla went in the house and plopped her bags on the kitchen counter. She glanced quickly at her phone to see if she missed any emails, calls or texts while she was with Tina. Her phone rang. It was Freddie. Kyla picked up, "Hey Honey. How's your day?" She heard Freddie sigh. "It could be better I guess. Just many things going wrong today. Hi, by the way. How's your day?" "Ok. I ran out to do some errands and now I stopped home to use the bathroom before I pick up the kids." "Did I leave you enough money to get the rest of the groceries?" The groceries! Shit! Kyla slapped her hand against her forehead. She forgot all about stopping at the store today. Now she had to explain where she was all this time. *I can't tell him about Tina, not yet. Think Kyla think!* "Actually Freddie. I didn't have a chance to go. Sam and Sal had a big fight. Sam called me, very upset. I was on the phone with her for a long time trying to console her and just make her feel better. By the time we hung up, I looked at the clock and was afraid that if I went then, I could chance being late to get the kids." There! That should suffice him. "Would you mind grabbing something for yourself on your way home? I can just make myself a sandwich and I have stuff here that the kids will eat." "Yeah, no problem. Poor Sam. I hope they make up. Are you going to go tomorrow though? We are low on a lot of things and the little monsters need snacks." Kyla smirked. "I hope they make up too, and definitely tomorrow. I am free all day.

Tina stopped at a few stores after her lunch date with Kyla. There was a little time before she had to get ready to see Freddie. She had chosen her outfit to wear tonight when she saw Freddie at the gym, but she wanted to see if she could find an even better outfit. She even went to the perfume kiosk to try a new scent. "What's your sexiest perfume? One that men are attracted to?" she asked the sales girl. Tina was pointed to one she never tried before. She tested it on her wrist and decided she wanted it. This one was a little on the expensive side but Freddie was worth it. *Plus, if this entices him to me even more, then I'll buy 5 bottles!* "I'll take it please, Does it come in body cream as well? If so, I'll take that too." The salesgirl rang up Tina's purchases and out she went. When she left the plaza, she had the perfect outfit, perfume and a new lip gloss for tonight.

"Hello Diamond baby. Miss me?" Diamond purred and rubbed against Tina's legs. I am going out in a little bit, Di. I don't know how long I'll be. Hopefully it goes well and I am gone for a long time! Tina laughed. She knew Diamond didn't have a clue about what she was saying since he was just a cat. But nevertheless, he was still her baby. A baby that could watch himself that is.

The bathtub filled with water and bubbles. Tina was going to take a long, hot bath in preparation for seeing Freddie. She wanted to shave her legs and lather her body all over with soap. Not that Freddie would be seeing or touching it, not yet anyhow. She just wanted to be prepared...just in case. Tina poured a glass of wine, chose a playlist on her music app and grabbed Freddie's photo off the night table to stare at. She slipped into the tub and took a sip of her wine. She smiled at Freddie's photo. "Soon baby...soon." She put her head back and closed her eyes. Tina thought back to seeing Kyla earlier. *I Really enjoyed getting together with Kyla. It had been too long! It felt nice to have a conversation with another female who isn't my mother or my sister for a change! It was nice going back down memory lane. I had forgotten how many great times we had before everything got messed up. Well, now that we're older, hopefully we can form a new friendship, one that becomes even better than the first. We will become so close that Kyla will turn to me for advice and the shoulder she cries on. Not that bitch Sam! What's her deal anyway?*

The pizza delivery guy rang the doorbell and Sam got up off the couch to answer it. She hadn't done much since she got home except for sitting on the couch and sulk. The sun had gone down and Sal had not come home. Usually by this time, on any given day, he called Sam to let her know whether he's stuck at work or on his way home. Maybe he really is spending the night at his sister's. Sam prayed he was coming home, he just didn't want to give her the courtesy of a phone call. He wanted her to wonder what was going through his mind, what he was planning to do. That was the problem with Sal. He enjoyed playing games and taunting, He liked having the upperhand always. She was sick of it, his immaturity and all. Sam sighed, opened the door and paid for the pizza. "Tali, come eat!" she yelled. Natalia came bouncing down the stairs. "Mom, is it ok if I bring the pizza to my room? I'm in the middle of watching a horror movie." Sam made a face. She hated when the kids had food in their rooms and she hated horror movies as well. However, she didn't have the energy to argue right now with her daughter. The last thing she needed was another family member mad at her. "Sure, Tali. Just don't make a mess." Natalia grinned and kissed her mother on the cheek. "Thanks, Mom. You rock!" She grabbed two slices of pizza and went back upstairs. "Make sure you watch something pleasant before going to bed! Otherwise you'll be dreaming about monsters in your room all night!" She yelled up at Natalia. Sam shook her head and grabbed a plate. She took a slice herself. She reached for her cell phone and pulled up the contacts in her cell phone. Sal's sister, Anissa, was listed in her contacts. Sam searched Anissa's phone number. Sam was friendly with her sister in law and knew that Anissa would confirm whether he was there or not. She sent her a text, asking such. A few minutes went by and then she got a text back from her sister in law. She told Sam that her brother was at her house and hadn't made up his mind if he was staying there yet. All he told her was that they had a fight and he needed to cool off. Anissa asked Sam to not tell her the story. She didn't want to get in the middle of it and she wouldn't feel right if she allowed anyone to talk shit about her brother, even if it was his wife. Anissa stressed how much she cared for Sam, however. She loved them both and didn't like seeing them quarrel.. Sam sent her a text her back to say,"Thank you and to have a good night." There was no need to say anything further. She was satisfied just as long as Sal was ok and Anissa requested to not know about anything. *At least he will get to see his twin nephews, Luca and Matteo,* Sam thought, Matteo had to spend a month in the hospital after birth, so the family agreed his name should be Matteo, (gift of God.) Sam put the phone back down and let out a huge breath,

Sam sat down at the kitchen table and looked at the chef statue sitting on her counter. It was a house warming gift from her mother when they bought the house. Sam raised her glass at it. "Hi, how are you? Cheers!" "Are you that lonely, Ma?" Joey asked and laughed at his mother. She hadn't heard him come in. Thank God he was by himself. Anyone else see her talk to her statue may think she was nuts! "Joey? I didn't hear you come in. You hungry? You want some pizza?" Joey's face dropped. "Since when do you order out during the week? Why aren't you cooking? You don't feel well, Ma? And where's Dad? Natalia?" Sam took a deep breath. "Natalia is eating in her room watching a movie. Joey's mouth dropped. "You let her eat in her room? Your definitely sick! Come here, let me feel your head." Sam pushed Joey's hand away. "Knock it off Joseph! I'm fine, I am not sick. I just didn't feel like arguing with your sister tonight. And you didn't tell me your plan. As for your father...well... I'll explain that one in a sec. But to answer your question, because it was just me an Tali, I decided to give myself a break from cooking and just ordered something instead. Capisce? "Gotcha. As long as you're ok."

Joey sat down next to Sam and started to inhale a slice of pizza. "Sorry, I'm late. Practice took longer than usual. Now what this about Dad?"

"There is so much traffic today!" Kristen exclaimed as she sat in bumper to bumper traffic on the highway. She should have been back at home an hour ago from work but the traffic was horrendous. Kristen thought she'd never get off the highway. *I may be sleeping in my car tonight.* The workday had been pretty hectic as well and she didn't get much done. She had already gone in late from being at Peter's. And her mother certainly didn't help any by making her sit and talk about Peter when she ran home. Luckily it had gone smoothly though. Kristen's mother can be very opinionated and judgemental at times. At forty years old, Kristen didn't need anyone to scold her or tell her how to run her life. It was hard enough moving back in with her parents and having them witness everything occurring in her life. Sam was lucky. At least she had her own home to keep her secrets. *Sam! Oh God, I forgot about her. Mom asked me to call her. She said she is upset over a fight she had with Sal. I wonder if it's the same thing as when we spoke last night.* Keeping her eyes on the road, Kristen pressed the phone button and hovered over to favorites. She selected "Sam" and dialed. A few rings later, Sam picked up. "Hey! How are you? Mom said you're upset because you're fighting with Sal. Is this the same fight from when we spoke?

Wait. Is he there now? Can you talk?" Kristen prayed that if Sal was there, he didn't hear her. Sometimes you can hear the conversation clearly on a cellphone without even having your ear to the phone. She heard Sam take a deep breath. "Hi Kristen. I'm ok and Sal's not here. Joey is here with me." Sam got up from her table and walked into the living room so her son wouldn't hear the conversation. "We just never made up from last night. It got worse. Sal is now staying at his sister's house for the night." Sam started to cry. Kristen felt terrible. "Sam it's ok. Sam? Sam, are you listening to me? "Yeah, I'm ok. I don't want Joey to hear me. Sam sniffled. Kristen's heart ached for her sister. Many, many nights she fought with Chris about shit. There were a lot of nights that he didn't come home and it left her feeling very vulnerable. Only Chris was probably staying at some buttana's house and Sam's husband is at his sister's. "I'm sure this will all blow over Sam. Every couple goes through some shit. It will probably make you guys a stronger couple. Don't give up faith. Promise? Sam gave her a weak yes. "Ok, I'm driving home from work right now. I'll call you later...if I ever get home from all this traffic that is, Kristen smirked. "Ok, Kristen, thanks for checking on me. I love you. Kiss the kids for me." "Likewise, mia sorella. Te amo." Kristen clicked off and continued driving. Traffic lightened up a little bit, just a little.

She had only passed one more exit when her phone rang. Peter's name came across the screen on the dashboard. Kristen felt herself smiling. She pressed "accept." "Why hello there. How are you?" Hey! I'm just calling to see how your day went. I know you were in a bit of a rush this morning. I also know you could have done without the Rachel thing. Are...are we ok?" Kristen was taken back. She wasn't expecting Peter to ask her that. "I...I thought we were. Why are you asking me that? Is something wrong?" Kristen's heart started to race, "No, no not at all. I was just worried that having Rachel see you in the house, may have scared you and you may want to take it slow or even back off for now." Kristen felt a sigh of relief. "No way! Besides, you're the one that needs to explain things Sir. She's your daughter, not mine, she chuckled. Peter laughed too. "Whew! That's a relief. And I'm not worried about Rachel. I know my daughter. She enjoyed seeing us together. She and I bonded a lot after the divorce. She wants me to be happy. Rachel knows you're it for me Kristen. Kristen wanted to reach through the phone and kiss him. "I am almost home but I'd like to call you tonight when I'm settled. Would that be ok?" "You better," he replied. "I'll be waiting."

I'm Starving

She made it just in time. The school was about to close. Kyla scooped up Anthony and Francesca and then headed home. Francesca began talking immediately. "How was your day Mommy? Mine was great. First we sat in our morning circle and talked about what we did over the weekend. The whole class laughed when I told them all about Daddy breaking the eggs because you didn't want to do his laundry." Kyla tried to smile at her daughter but wanted to cry at the same time. *Great. Now her teacher must think I'm an abused housewife.* "That is funny Cheski. But remember what I told you about keeping our family moments private. It's ok to tell your friends if you went to an amusement park or to the zoo, after the fact. Ok, Honey?" Kyla looked at her daughter in the rear view mirror. Francesca nodded but was pouting. "How was your day Anthony? Do you have homework?" Anthony just grunted and Kyla sighed. It was so tough to talk to him at this hour of the day. It was his witching hour, as Freddie called it. The kid was so overtired from waking up early and being in school all day. He usually came home and did his homework and played with his toys until dinnertime, but if he was unbearable, Kyla forced him to take a nap. She regretted it sometimes though because that also could mean he wouldn't go to bed as early. "Kids, Daddy is going to the gym after work and grabbing himself dinner. What do you say to some grilled cheese sandwiches?" Francesca squealed. "French fries too, Mommy." "Yes, french fries too." Anthony just groaned. "Well then it's settled. Grilled cheese and french fries here we come!" She drove away.

Tina was early...too early. She was so excited she could barely contain herself. She parked in the back so Freddie wouldn't see she got there first. She also wanted to study him without him knowing. *If he asks why I parked so far away, I'll just tell him that there were no spots when I came.* She pulled down the sun visor in her car and checked her face in the mirror for the tenth time. *It has to be perfect!* She spent much of last night, tweaking her eyebrows and giving herself a facial. She did this all in preparation for Freedie. Tina stared at her reflection for a few seconds, then blew it a kiss. "You are one sexy bitch and Mr. Lovazzo is going to realize that tonight as well. " She winked at herself and pushed the visor back up. She looked at her phone for any missed calls or messages. *Great, nothing. He's not going to cancel.* After about ten minutes, a car pulled into the lot. It drove around slowly looking for a space, when it came close to Tina's car, she realized it was Freddie. Her heart started racing and her palms got sweaty. The car itself wasn't what she normally was used to. She preferred something more luxurious and expensive but she really liked Freddie so it would have to do. Tina watched Freddie pull into a space, get out and grab his gym bag. He pulled his phone out of his pocket and started to type. Tina's phone began to vibrate in her bag. She pulled it out and saw that she had a text from Freddie. "I'm here. I'll meet you by the locker rooms. Tina smiled. She replied with, "Where we first met, lol. Seriously tho, I'll be there in a few minutes." She put her phone back, watched Freddie go inside and then grabbed her stuff.

She took her time walking across the parking lot since she told Freddie she'd be there in a few. Several gym goers glanced her way and smiled at Tina. Normally, she would smile back if they were hot, but not today. Today was all about Freddie and only Freddie.

There was no sight of Freddie in the gym. *He must be in the locker room.* Tina went into the locker room herself. She put her bag in a locker and turned around to the mirror. She fluffed her hair and made sure her makeup was perfect. Not all women agree that makeup should be worn to the gym. Tina wasn't one of those women. She felt if you look your best, you feel your best. She secretly wished some women would wear makeup to hide their ugly faces. Some women definitely needed to shower prior to coming to the gym. They smelled offensive even before they began their workouts! She reached into her bag and pulled out her body lotion. I need to smell good! Especially if he's going to be leaning over me to spot me. Tina gave herself the once over once more, then strolled out of the locker room.

To her delight, Freddie was standing outside the men's locker room, waiting for her. She walked over to him. "Hey!" He turned around and smiled at her. "Hey! How are you? I like your outfit." He could not stop staring at Tina. *This is what I was aiming for. Score!* Tina thought to herself. Freddie was so taken back by the way she looked. He had trouble speaking. "I...I thought we'd start on the machines in the back. That's if you want to." His face was flushed. Tina smiled. "If that's what you think. You're the boss. I'll do whatever you want." Freddie swallowed hard. "Um...ok, let's go over there then." He motioned for her to walk. "Ladies first." Tina nodded and started heading for the back of the gym. *Either he's a gentleman or wants to stare at my ass. Or maybe it's both!* Tina was fine with either.

The gym was busy with many people doing their workouts after work. Freddie and Tina had to wait for the machine to become available. They waited to the side and chatted while they waited. Freddie spoke first. "So Tina, tell me about yourself. Come here often?" They both let out a laugh. "I'm sorry, that's so cliché isn't it? But seriously, I haven't seen you here before. Did you just join?" Tina looked at Freddie. There was something charming and sincere about him. She rarely saw that in a guy. "No, I've been coming here for a while now. I live close by. My work schedule varies, so it can vary when I'm here too." Freddie frowned. Tina saw that and kept talking. "But! If I have someone to workout with now, I'll make it a priority to be on their schedule." She winked at him. Freddie smiled at her. "I'd like that." The machine became available and Freddie told Tina to hop on.

For the next hour and a half, they worked out, taking turns on the machines. Of course Freddie used more weight so they were constantly adjusting the machines. He was also a few inches taller than Tina, so the seats also had to be adjusted. Usually an hour and a half in the gym felt like an eternity to Tina but today felt like it was just a few minutes. She didn't want it to end. She was enjoying Freddie's company and the face that he seemed more into her than just her body. Freddie wiped the sweat from his forehead. "I think that's enough for today. You're gonna be sore. Tina beamed."Oh ok. Thank you for showing me a new routine. I appreciate it." "I'll be in touch. Let me take a look at my calendar and see when I can get here again. Have a good night Tina. I had fun." "Me too Freddie, till next time." Tina winked at him again. Freddie started walking away. He turned around. "Hey Tina?" Tina looked at him. "Yea Freddie?" He started walking back to her. "My wife forgot to go to the grocery store today. I'm on my own for dinner and I'm starving. Wanna grab something to eat with me?"

She hung up with her sister and went back to her son who had devoured most of the pizza pie while she was on the phone with Kristen. "Um, were you hungry, Joey?" Joey smirked and wiped the sauce from his mouth. "I was starving! I didn't have a chance to grab something after school and before practice. Anyway, I asked you about Dad before Aunt K called. Is everything ok with you guys? overheard you talking to Aunt K." Sam sat back down at the table and looked at her son. "Your father and I had a fight yesterday that has spiraled into today. Apparently he is so pissed off that he is spending the night at Aunt Anissa's. "What are you fighting about?" Sam took a deep breath. "Nonno told me that when Peter went to the bathroom, Dad preceded to make fun of him." Joey's mouth opened. "That's what you're fighting about? He did Ma, but he was joking around." Sam rolled her eyes. "That's not the point, Joseph. He is always joking around. He doesn't realize that not everything is funny or at someone else's expense. I was embarrassed when Nonno told me and I'm pretty sure both Peter and your aunt would have been too if they had known. It was the first time he was meeting the family! What the hell was he thinking?" Joey put his head down. "I'm sorry Ma. I guess you're right. Dad just didn't think. It sucks that you guys are fighting now cuz of it. I'm sure Dad will realize he was wrong and he'll apologize." Sam looked at Joey. "Sometimes I think you're the parent."

She pulled into the driveway. Traffic had been horrendous but she was home now. She missed Peter but was looking forward to seeing the kids and sleeping in her own bed tonight. Kristen opened the front door and immediately smelled the delicious aroma of garlic. Her mother was in the kitchen doing what she did best. If Kristen wasn't already starving, she was now salivating. Her mother heard her come in and greeted her in the foyer. "How wasa your day? You looka tired." Kristen sighed. "I am Ma but I'm starving! What are you making? It smells sooo good in here!" Her mother grinned. "Not ta much. I justa whip up soma meatballs with spaghetti e soma bracciole. I also mada a pot of straciatella. Oh and I found some burrata e tomato in the fridge. We can eat thata too. You like?" "That's a lot of food Ma! But yes, it sounds fantastico!" Kristen kissed her mother on the cheek. "How long till dinner? I just wanna shower and say hi to the kids first." Her mother frowned. Nikki is upa stairs but ma però, Bobby no here. He goa to see a soma girl from school. Something about the movies. It'sa nice he finda someone. I hopa she is a nice a girl." Kristen huffed. "Oh ok, I guess I'll see him when he gets home then. "Dinner will be ready when?" "Taka your time. I'm still cooking." "Ok, see you in a few Ma, thanks."

Kristen went upstairs and knocked on Nikki's door. "Come in!," her daughter shouted. Kristen opened the door and saw her daughter on her bed with her history book. "Proud Mama moment. My girl is studying or doing homework." Nikki made a face. "Test tomorrow, The Rise of Imperialism and Colonialism. Shoot me now." Kristen laughed. "I'm sure you'll do fine. You always do. She kissed her daughter on top of her head. "I'm off to take a shower then Nonna is going to call us down for dinner." "Ok Mom. Did Nonna tell you that Bobby is on a date? Nonna wants to meet her and make sure she's not a dirty girl." They both laughed. "Your grandmother is some piece of work! See you in a few." Kristen shut the door and went into the bathroom.

"I can't eat another bite, Ma," Kristen pleaded to her mother when she tried to fill Kristen's plate with another serving. Her father shook his head. "Rosemarie, she said no more. Per favore, you stopa being a...how do you say...food bully?" Nikki laughed. "Good one, Nonno." Mrs. Marino was not amused however. " "Chiudi la boca, Enzo. No ona talka to you." Enzo put his head down while Kristen and Nikki laughed. Nikki looked at her grandmother. "You guys are too funny. Nonna does have a point though, Nonna. You force everyone to eat more they can handle." Mrs Marino jumped up from the table. "Fine! I'll just leave if I'ma nuisance, she yelled and walked into the kitchen. Nikki looked at her mother. "Mom, I didn't mean to..." Kristen held her hand up. It's ok Nik. Nonna gets like this when it comes to her cooking. She is proud and feels that it's the only thing she can offer so when it's frowned upon for whatever reason, she gets insulted. She'll be fine. "Ok, ok, May I be excused then? I wanna finish studying." "Yeah sure. Just bring your dishes inside please."

After she cleaned the kitchen and apologized to her mother for upsetting her, Kristen retreated to her room. She plopped on her bed and began to look over some papers she didn't have a chance to look at when she was at work. Her cell phone rang. It was Peter.

"Hello my lady. How are you?" Kristen smiled at the sound of his voice. "I'm ok, I just finished dinner at the Marino household." "I am so jealous. That meal the other night was delicious!" Peter exclaimed. "Maybe you should have come. There would have been less food available with another body. My mother tried forcing some on me. When I refused, my father called her a food bully. Peter laughed. "Well, your mother can bully me with her food anyday!"

Kristen took a deep breath. "So I was wondering...does Rachel like Italian food?" "She loves it. Why do you ask?" Peter answered. "I was thinking that if you guys are free next Sunday, perhaps you can come to dinner again and bring Rachel with you this time. She held her breath. There was a brief moment of silence and then Peter spoke. "Sure! I'd like that and I'm sure Rachel would too. Isn't that moving too fast for you though? I don't mind but they just met me. And after our conversation this weekend, I thought you wanted to go slow." Kristen mentally prepared herself for what she was about to say. "Peter, I spent a lot of time thinking since I left you this morning. I thought about this past weekend from where we went, what we did and having your daughter seeing us together, as well as my own kids. I don't know what the future will bring, all I know is that I am happy that I met you, and being with you gives me feelings I thought I had lost. So! If you'll accept, I'd like to have you guys over and our kids can meet." Again, she held her breath. "Kristen, what you just said means so much. I am ecstatic you feel that way. I feel that way about you as well. So yes, I accept the invitation on behalf of myself and my daughter."

Best for Whom

The kids needed to bathe desperately. Kyla had Anthony take a shower and when he was finished, she ran a bath for Francesca. They went for ice cream after dinner and Francesca's shirt got more of it then her mouth did. Nevermind the ends of her hair. Anthony was just messy in general as boys usually are. They also had school tomorrow and Kyla didn't want the teacher to think they were neglected children. *She probably already thinks I'm an abused housewife, thanks to Francesca!* Kyla sighed and tested the bath water. She added bubbles and toys, otherwise it would have been a fight to get her daughter in; let alone, wash her hair. Kyla thought of Freddie being at the gym. *I sure hope he appreciates the fact that I'm here, dealing with our children while he worksout. When her bath is over, he's getting a text to stop for wine!*

While supervising Francesca in the bathtub, her cellphone rang. It was Sam. Kyla instantly got nervous. "Uh-oh. This can't be good. Why is she calling me when she should be with Sal, hashing things out." Ske picked up her phone. "Hey Sam." "Hey Kyla. I just needed to talk. You busy?" Kyla sat on top of the toilet bowl next to the tub. "No, I'm just giving Cheski a bath. We just got in." Sam sniffled. "Oh, I should let you go then." "No, no, it's fine. She is playing. I'm just watching her. "Oh ok. I don't think Sal is gonna come home tonight. Anissa told me that he's at her house but hasn't decided whether he should come home or not. What makes matters worse, is Joey now knows. He asked where his father was and saw that I was upset, so I had to tell him." Kyla wished she could take the pain away from Sam. "Sam, I am sorry that Joey found out but as far as Sal goes, maybe he should spend the night at his sisters'. I'm sure you both could use a break from one another. It will also help you to realize

276

what's important. Let this be a good thing. Stop worrying. Couples argue all of the time." Sam sniffled some more. "Thanks Ky. Kristen told me the same. Where's Freddie? How come he's not barging in the bathroom asking you who you are talking to?" Kyla grunted. "Mr. Lovazzo is currently at the gym or fetching himself dinner. I forgot to stop at the grocery store after I saw Tina, so dinner was not happening." "Well, at least you got a break from cooking," Sam said. "Finish with Francesca. I'll call you tomorrow." Kyla sighed. "Ok, Sam. keep me posted but I know it will be fine. Keep your head up. Love you." Sam blew a kiss into the phone. "Love you too girl."

Kyla let out a long breath and put the phone on the sink. She truly felt bad for Sam. She looked up towards the ceiling. "Please God. Take care of my friend." Kyla glanced down at her daughter who was squeezing the water out of her rubber duckie. "Cheski, are you ready to wash? You look like a prune." Francesca looked up at her mother and smiled. "Just a second Mommy. Mommy, is Aunt Sam ok? Is she fighting with Uncle Sal?" Kyla smiled back. *I have to remember to stop talking in front of her.* "Yes, Cheski, they had an argument." Francesca made a face. "Maybe Aunt Sam was too tired to do his laundry too."

Was she dreaming? Was this really happening? Did Freddie really just ask her out to eat? She knew he didn't mean like a date or anything, but still! Tina nodded at him but inside she was squealing.

"Great, our choices are probably limited since we're all sweaty and in our gym clothes. Any ideas?" Freddie asked Tina. Tina was too busy staring into his eyes and thinking about how they are going to be spending more time together, alone! "Tina?" Freddie noticed she wasn't listening. Tina snapped out of her trance. "I'm sorry, did you say something?" Freddie laughed. "I asked if you had any ideas of where we should go since we're kinda gross and in gym clothes. Where were you just now?" Tina blushed. "Oh, I was just thinking of where we can go, actually, when you asked me. I didn't hear you, sorry." Freddie smiled. "No worries, so, did you think of anything?" Tina grinned."I know a little spot not far from here, that serves a light menu and has good drinks. The atmosphere is cozy and dark so no one will see that we're gross!" They both laughed. "Ok, then it's settled. Meet you outside the locker room in a few?" Freddie asked her. Tina nodded and they each went into their locker rooms.

She looked at herself in the mirror. *I still can't believe this is real. I wanna jump up and down. Someone might walk in though,* she laughed to herself. Tina washed her hands and used the bathroom. She fixed her hair into a neater ponytail and reapplied her lip gloss. She then sprayed herself with the perfume in her bag. She looked in the mirror once more. Girl! You are now ready for him! Out of the locker room she went.

He was already outside his locker room waiting for her. She walked over to him. He turned around and smiled. "Ready?" Freddie asked Tina. "Yes," she replied. They walked out of the gym. Freddie held the door open for Tina. "Is your car here, Tina?" "Yes, I only live a few blocks from here so normally I walk to the gym. Gotta get that cardio in. But I was running late today and didn't want to miss our...eh...session" she lied. Freddie grinned. "I hear ya. Ok, I'm parked here too. How far is that spot again?" Tina looked at him. "It's about a five minute drive. Is that ok?" Freddie smiled at Tina and said that was fine. "We can take my car if that's ok and I'll drop you back off here after so you can pick up your car, cool?" Freddie asked her. Tina wanted to scream, "Of course it's ok!" but she refrained. Instead she replied, "Sure, that'd be great." Together they walked over to Freddie's car. He opened the car door for her and closed it. Tina was beaming. *What a gentleman! This car smells like him too. Can I have a bottle of this please?* Freddie got in the driver's side. "Ok, you're in control. Let's go." *Oh I'll be in control alright. Just you wait and see!*

It was only a five minute drive but Tina wished it was longer. It thrilled her to be in the car with him, close enough that she smelled his cologne. This was his personal property, this car and she was in it. They drove along the streets barely having much conversation since Tina had to direct him where to go. They got to the restaurant and Fredie pulled into a space. As Tina grabbed her bag, Freddie hopped out of the car and walked over to her side. He opened the door for her. Tina smiled up at Freddie. "You are one hell of a gentleman. And they say chivalry is dead. Not when it comes to you sir." Freddie grinned. "Beautiful ladies should be treated as such, a lady." Tina blushed again and grabbed Freddie's hand to help her get out of the car.

The restaurant had only a few patrons since it was the middle of the week. Most of the tables were empty. Tina requested the table in the corner. It was darker over there and more private. The hostess seated them and the waiter took their drink order. Once the waiter left, Freddie began talking.

"I wanna thank you for coming with me to dinner. If you didn't, I probably would have just grabbed a slice of pizza. So not good for clean eating and my macros budget! Besides, I like the company too." Freddie winked at Tina. Her face turned red. "Thanks for inviting me. I like this place but it's hard to find someone who will go with me." Freddie looked at her. "You...you have trouble finding someone? I find that hard to believe." Tina put her head down. "It's true. Besides, I don't accept every guys invitation to accompany them." She winked at him. "Touché! Well, I for one am flattered then," he replied. Their drinks came and the waiter took their order. Freddie raised his glass. "I'd like to make a toast. Here's to meeting new people and the start of a beautiful friendship." *I prefer a relationship but I'll take it for now,* Tina thought.

They finished eating after having an appetizer, the main course, dessert and two drinks. The waiter brought the check over. Freddie quickly grabbed it. Tina noticed but asked how much anyway. Freddie shrugged her off. "Don't worry, I got it. It's on me." Tina protested but Freddie insisted. "Hey, I invited you, remember?" Tina smiled at him and thanked him. She leaned towards him and said, "Well, if we do this again, and I hope that we do, it's on me." She winked at Freddie. He looked away, blushing. They drove back to the gym parking lot and Freddie dropped her off at her car. Tina looked over at Freddie. "I had a nice time, thank you. I'll see you soon."

"Wait!" Freddie jumped out of the car and ran to her side. He opened the door. "You said I'm a gentleman right?" Tina laughed. Freddie looked at her. He got closer. *Damn! Even after a workout, she still smells good.* Tina stared straight into his eyes. With that, he pulled her towards him and kissed her with increasing intensity. She reciprocated. After a few moments, she pulled away. *Always keep them wanting more.* Freddie just looked at her with his mouth open. "I'm..I'm sorry Tina. I don't know what got over me." She put her finger over his lips. "Shhh." Tina kissed him first this time but pulled away again moments later. She opened her car and got in. Freddie watched in astonishment. "Can I call you?" "I'd like that," she relied. She pulled out of the space and drove off, leaving Freddie standing there.

Headlights shined through the curtains in the living room. Sam moved the curtain to the side and saw Sal's truck in the driveway. She felt a sigh of relief. *I guess he decided to come home. Hopefully, he's over it too and we can move on.* She looked at herself in the mirror, smooth down her hair and quickly applied some lip gloss she found in her purse. Sam greeted Sal at the door.

Sam spoke first. "Hi. I wasn't sure if you were going to come home or not. I'm glad you did. The kids missed you...I missed you. She reached up to kiss him and put her arms around him, but he pulled away. "Samantha, I'm not staying. I realized I didn't pack anything to wear to work tomorrow so I came home to grab something. I meant what I said when I texted you. I'm spending the night at my sister's. I think it's the best thing to do right now. " Sam wanted to cry. She also wanted to smack Sal. "Best for whom? You? We have one little argument and you're ready to leave? Unreal. She tried to stop the tears forming in her eyes. Sal let out a huge sigh. "Sam, sit down." He pointed to the couch. She sat and looked at him. He turned around to face the wall so he wouldn't have to look at her.

"Things between us haven't been right for awhile now. You've become bossy, critical and more. You are always mad at me for one reason or another. I can't take it anymore." Sam open her mouth to speak. Sal stopped her. "Let me finish, please. You would think you'd want me to leave based on the way you treat me. You refer to me as another one of your kids in front of other people, you keep track of my whereabouts and you criticize everything I do. Sam, I love you very much but I don't like you. Not this Sam anyway. I liked the Sam I married. I am comfortable with you, that's it, comfortable...not excited. And I think that's how you feel also. There's a big difference between the two". Sal started breathing heavy. "Sam, I think we need to spend some time apart so you can figure out if what you want is me. All I know is that we can't go on like this. It's not good for you, me or the kids."

She stood up. "Are you finished?" she asked. The tears were now streaming down her face. Sal felt bad. He didn't want this but it had to be done. Sam looked into his eyes and started speaking. "So why all of a sudden are you laying this all on me now? If something was bothering you, you should have mentioned it. Look at us now. Are you asking me for a divorce Sal? Is that what YOU want? Sal put his hands on his hips and turned around again. "To answer your first question, I never said anything because shit always blew over before. I kept telling myself we would get past the bullshit. But we never did.

Things just kept building up until I couldn't take anymore. I am not looking for a divorce Sam, not yet anyhow. I want to spend some time away from each other to refocus and see how that goes." Sam wiped her face with the sleeve of her shirt. "Just how much time are we talking about Sal? You have commitments here." she said. Sal turned back around. "I don't know. However long it takes us to figure out what we both want." I'm going to grab my stuff now. Anissa is waiting for me to get back. She wants to turn the lights out and go to bed. Sal brushed by Sam and went upstairs. Sam sat on the couch and wept.

After she hung up the phone, she was all smiles. Peter had accepted her invitation to come back for dinner the following Sunday and he was bringing his daughter. *Now I have work to do!* First Kristen had to let her mother know they were coming. That also meant another trip to the store for food. *Sam took one for the team yesterday, so I guess it's my turn now!* Kristen laughed on how they thought taking their mother to the store was more of a chore than spending time with. *She's just impossible when it comes to her cooking.* Kristen shook her head.

She also had to tell her kids that Rachel would also be coming. Kristen wasn't too concerned about Bobby. He probably wouldn't even care but Nikki on the other hand, might object or be ready for it. Kristen looked up at the ceiling. *Why must everything be so complicated?* She opened the door to herdroom and walked downstairs, fingers crossed behind her back.

Her mother was in her usual area of the house, the kitchen. Only she wasn't cooking, she was looking out the window. "Ma, what are you doing?" Kristen asked. Her mother jumped and moved away from the window. "You scara me. No do thata no more!" Kristen laughed. "Sorry Ma. What were you doing?" Bobby is outta side. He wita that girl. I look a whata they do." Kristen gasped. "Ma! Oh marone a mi! You shouldn't be spying on him!" Her mother just looked at her. "I no spy. I maka sure thata this girl is righta for him. Lota weirdos in thisa world today." Kristen shook her head. "Oh Ma. So what do you think, is this ragazza good enough for our boy? Her mother grinned. "Whata I think? I think...amore la prima vista!" He smile a lot. He really lika this girl I think." Kristen smile. "Well good for him. Now enough with the window, capisce?" Her mother frowned. "Un guastafesta!". She held her hands up. "I justa look outta for this family. Someone has to." Kristen hugged her mother and kissed her on the cheek. "And we love you for it."

Kristen sat at the kitchen table. "Ma, everything went so well yesterday. I'd like to have Peter over again this coming Sunday, only this time bring his daughter Rachel with him. Is that ok?" She put her head down, nervous of her mother's reaction. "No problem, Kristen. Youa ready for thata though? I lika Pietro però ita mighta be too soona for you." Kristen picked her head up. "I thought about it long and hard and decided it's something that I want and are ready for. If I didn't have children of my own then maybe I would take a step back or even if she was young. But she is the same age as Nikki. I've met her and I can tell, she's comfortable with her father seeing another woman besides her mother and she's comfortable with me. That's all I need." Her mother smiled. "Ok,Kristen. Ita sounds like you know whata you doing. I hope ita works out. I lika this Pietro." "Thanks Ma. Your approval & blessing is something means more than you know." She kissed her mother again and headed towards Nikki's room.

As usual, her daughter was lying on her bed, talking smack about some other girl in school to one of friends. The friend was speaking so loud that Nikki didn't even hear her mother come in. "Ahem. Nikki Rose, stop gossiping about people. It's not polite to talk about people behind their backs." Nikki rolled her eyes and told her friend she had to go and will call her back later. Nikki looked at Kristen. "This girl was talking shit about me in school so we were talking about it." Kristen shut her eyes for a second. "First of all, watch your mouth. Second, So what? Unless she says it to you directly, who cares?" Nikki rolled her eyes again. "Did you need something Mom?"

Kristen took a deep breath and sat down on Nikki's bed. "Uh-oh, what's wrong?" Nikki asked. "Nothing. I invited Peter and his daughter over next Sunday for dinner. I wanted to make sure you were comfortable with that?" "Yeah sure Mom, whatever. And besides, what would you have done if I wasn't? You said you already asked him." "True. I guess I would have had to tell him that you're not ready yet and I'm sorry but we can't do this right now." Nikki's jaw dropped. "You would do that for me?" Kristen smiled at her. "In a heartbeat. You and your brother come first. Please know that." Nikki hugged her mother. "I love you Mom." Kristen got up and started to walk out of her daughter's room. "I love you too, Nik." As Kristen was closing the door behind her, Nikki called her. "Hey Mom?" "Yeah Nik?" "I like Peter...and I'm sure I'll like his daughter too." "Thanks Baby." Kristen shut the door and grinned down the hallway.

One last stop. But I know this will be an easy one. Kristen heard Bobby come in. *The girl he is seeing must be local if he dropped her off already.* She waited until he was settled in his room before going in. She knocked on his door and he told her to come in. "Hi. How was your date? Nonna said you were out with a girl." Bobby glared at her. "Mom, no one uses the word, "date,' anymore." Kristen rolled her eyes. "Ok, fine. How was your eh...hanging out time with this girl?" Bobby laughed. "Oh Mom. It was good. She's nice. She only lives a block away from here. We met in school. If it works out, maybe I will ask her to Prom." Kristen beamed. She was happy her son found some joy. It hadn't been easy on him either, lately. "That's great Bobby. I am happy for you. When do I get to meet her?" "Easy Mom. I'm not sure if I want to go that far just yet. Like I said, 'if it works out."

Kristen made a face. "Ok, ok. Speaking of meeting people, I invited Peter over for dinner again on Sunday. I also invited his daughter to come along too. Is that ok with you?" Bobby's jaw dropped. "Mom, really? He was just here. Now you're looking for him to come here again, and with his daughter now? You do know that Dad is getting out soon, What about that? Bobby put his head down. Kristen stood there in disbelief. She did not expect this reaction from him. She put her hand on Bobby's shoulder.

"Bobby, I know your father is getting out soon. But you have to face the fact that things will never be like they used to. Your dad and I are not getting back together. There's been so much pain. More than you know. We don't feel the same as we did all those years being together. I will do what I can to help him adjust back to civilization, but that's it. I think it's best if we keep it that way." Bobby looked at her. "Best for whom? You? You don't love Dad anymore?" Kristen wanted to die. Bobby was really upset. She hated this. "I will always love your father." She grabbed Bobby's chin. "He gave you and your sister to me. But I am not in love with him anymore. There's a difference. I really like Peter and want to explore the possibilities of being with him. For so long I was so unhappy and now I'm starting to smile again. Please understand that. But like I told your sister, "You guys come first. I want you guys to be comfortable with the situation. Is that something that you think can happen? Bobby rubbed his hand over the little amount of facial hair he had. "I guess so, Mom. But it might take awhile." Kristen grinned at him. "Nothing's happening today, tomorrow or for awhile. I'm still getting use to things myself." She kissed her son on the cheek, and walked out of his room.

Impulse

He wasn't in bed next to her and the sun was shining through the window so she knew it was morning. Kyla went to read in her bed last night after she put the kids to sleep. Freddie had not gotten home by then yet. She must have fallen asleep at some point. She jumped up and looked at the clock. Luckily it was still too early to wake the kids for school yet. Kyla put on her robe and opened the door to her bedroom. She could hear whistling coming from the kitchen. She also smelled coffee. Kyla walked into the kitchen. There was Freddie, dressed already, making himself breakfast. He turned around to face her. "Hey Babe. Good morning. Sleep well? You were out cold when I got home last night." Kyla looked at him dumbfounded. "What time did you get home? It wasn't too late but you never take that long at the gym", she asked. Freddie smirked at her. "I had to stop for dinner, remember?" "Yeah but I thought you would just call something in on your way back and just pick it up." Freddie turned around when he replied. "Yeah...I did. But... I ran into my friend Tony while I was picking up my food and we had a beer together." Kyla began wiping the crumbs off the counter. "Oh ok. I just took the kids out for a quick meal then we did our usual routine when we got home. I was tired from the day so I guess I fell asleep."

Freddie smacked her on her ass as he walked past her. "I will see you later. I'm late for work." "Ok, bye. Love you." "Love you too," he replied as he walked away. *Who is this Tony? He's never mentioned him before,* Kyla thought as she began cleaning up the mess Fredie left and started making the kids their breakfast. Little did she know that her husband was outside, thinking of what he really did last night and how he just lied to her.

I never thought I'd be lying to Kyla about anything. I feel like a shithead. I just couldn't help myself last night. Being with Tina brought out things in me that I never thought I'd feel again. She makes me feel like a man. She's into ME! Besides, it's kind of exciting. I shouldn't have kissed her though. That was going too far. I could jeopardize everything. What if someone had seen us and it got back to Kyla? I don't know how Tina felt about it either. She kissed me back but then left right away. Who knows what she's thinking? Just as he was stepping into his car, his phone buzzed. Freddie had a text from Tony.

Tina got up to get ready for work. She was up earlier than usual because she couldn't sleep. She felt like a kid on Christmas morning. Last night with Freddie was on her mind and she couldn't stop thinking about it. He had kissed her. It had been a long time since someone kissed her that she had feelings for. Tina had just about given up all hope of falling for someone a long time ago. It just wasn't in the cards for her she guessed and focused all of her energy on just having fun with rich, hot men while all the baggage and stress went to the wife. But Freddie was different. Tina liked him. She liked everything about him. The way he looked, the way he smelled, his personality and more. It didn't matter what he did for a living or what connections he had. This was so unlike her to feel this way about a guy, yet here she was, falling head over heels. Big heels too, stiletto size. She had to see him again. She just had to.

She picked up her cellphone to text him. *I probably shouldn't. What if he's still home and his phone is lying around the house somewhere. His wife might see.* Normally, Tina could care less if a wife saw, but she didn't want to cause trouble for Freddie and especially cause him to stop seeing her. "I will just word the text in a way that even if his wife does see it, it's innocent," she told Diamond as if she were looking for his approval. She began typing. "Hey! Thanks again for yesterday, showing me some new exercises and everything else. I hope we can get together again soon. Have a great day!" She put down the phone and walked to her bathroom.

Midway through brushing her teeth, her phone let out an alert to tell her she had a text message. Tina fled the bathroom, toothpaste still in her mouth, to grab her phone. The text was from Freddie. It read, "Hey! You are so welcome. It was fun. I really hope I didn't overstep last night. If not and it's all good, I'd like to meet at the gym again tonight. I'm not sure I can hang afterwards tho, my kids wanna see me before they go to bed. I didn't catch them last night. I wonder why lol. Anyway, let me know if you wanna meet up."

Tina jumped up and down on her bed, swallowing the toothpaste that was in her mouth. She was so excited. *He probably can't hang afterwards, but that's ok. I'll take what I can get!* She went back to the sink to rinse out her mouth and let Freddie sit for a minute before responding. But as soon as she was finished wiping her mouth, she reached for her phone.

"You definitely didn't overstep. If you did, then I did it right back lol. I just fled in a hurry because I didn't know what to make of it all. You're married so that makes it awkward. Anyhow, I'd like to meet you at the gym again regardless, so at the same time ok?"

She flung her phone on the bed and looked for an outfit to wear to work. Her phone went off again. It was Freddie again, telling her he'd meet her. Tina was ginning so much that her cheeks started to hurt. She could hardly contain her excitement, *I gotta tell someone or I might explode!* She picked up her phone again and called Kyla.

Kyla picked up the phone, out of breath. "Hel...lo?" "Kyla, Are you ok, it's Tina." "Yes...yes, I'm fine. I was just down on my hands and knees, picking up crumbs off the floor. I'm cleaning the kitchen. The kids just ate breakfast and I'm cleaning up before we have to schlep on over to school." "Oh, ok, I thought maybe I was interrupting you know what." Tina smirked and Kyla rolled her eyes. "Oh please, like that's happening at this hour and no offense, but I wouldn't have picked up the phone if that was the case."

"True." Tina replied. "So, what brings this phone call before work?

You took the day off again and want to have lunch?" Tina sighed. "I wish. I called you because if I don't talk to someone, I will burst!" Kyla didn't know whether to laugh or be concerned. "A good or bad burst?" Tina laughed. "Definitely all good." Kyla smiled. "Well then let's hear it."

She took a deep breath. "You know that guy I mentioned that I started seeing?" "Uh-huh." Tina took another breath. "Well, he kissed me last night and asked to see me again today." "And how did you react?" Kyla wanted to know. Tina laughed. On impulse, I kissed him back!" Kyla was so happy for her. "Oh, that's awesome Tina. I am so happy for you! You really like this guy, huh? " "I sure do. Anyway, as usual, I am running late for work. But I wanted to share. Will you be around tomorrow to call you? I may not have time later if all goes well. Fingers crossed!"

"Never act on impulse, isn't that what they say?" Sam asked herself in the mirror. Her face was swollen. Mascara had run down her cheeks. She never took her makeup off from the night before. Her hair was a mess. Sam didn't sleep at all last night. She was so upset by the fight she had with Sal. The bed was cold where he normally laid. "Well fuck that shit! He wants a few days apart? I'll give him a few days apart! She started screaming like a lunatic. Luckily, Joey and Natalia had already left for school. Sam ripped their wedding photo off the wall and tossed it in the garbage can. She pulled off her wedding rings and shoved them in her jewelry box. She picked up the empty bottle of red wine on her nightstand, ready to hurl it at the wall, but then decided against it.

"Hey Sis, can you talk for a sec?" Sam called Kristen's phone hoping to catch her sister before she left for work. Kristen picked up right away. "Hey Sam...Sam? Are you ok? What happened with Sal?" Sam inhaled deeply. "Kristen, he wants us to spend some time apart to figure things out. He's not sure for how long. Can you believe him? He thinks he can just take 'time off' from his responsibilities?" Kristen's jaw dropped. "Oh my God, Sam. I'm so sorry. Do the kids know?" "Joey knows we had a fight and his father is cooling off at his aunt's house. But that's all'" she replied. "Ok, leave it at that for now until you figure out what to do. Can I help at all?" Sam took a deep breath. "Yeah, that's why I'm calling actually. Can the kids stay with you for a few days? I'll send a note to Tali's school and make up an excuse for Mom and Dad. I just gotta get out of here for a bit, clear my head." Kristen's heart went out to her sister. "Of course Sam. But where are you going to go? And by yourself? Do you need me to take a few days off from work and go with you? I'll do it." Sam smiled. *Thank God I have the sister that I do.* "No, no Kris. That's very thoughtful and generous but no. This is something I have to do on my own." "You sure, I can take off. I have the days." Sam told her sister she really appreciated it but it wasn't necessary. She hung up with her and told her she would call her at some point. Sam sighed. She pulled her suitcase down from the closet shelf and began packing. *Ugh. Now to think of what to tell my parents and where to go.*

Well I'm depressed now. Kristen drove all the way to work with Sam on her mind. She felt bad for her sister. She knew what she was going through to an extent. Like Sam, Kristen's marriage was no picnic but it was different. Chris' actions were unjustifiable. She felt like her sister and Sal still had a chance. Their issues could be worked out. She pulled into a space at her office building. She had a few minutes to spare so she called Peter.

"Why hello there! I didn't expect to hear from you until later on today. How are you?" Peter exclaimed. "Hey Peter. I was just calling to let you know that I will be out of town for a few days. As of right now, we're still on for Sunday at my mother's. There was a brief moment of silence and then Peter spoke. "Oooookay. Is everything alright?" Kristen swallowed hard. "Yes...well for me that is. Sam and Sal are going through a rough patch right now. My sister needs to get away for a few days. I don't want her to be by herself. So I am going with her. "Aww, poor Sam. That's a really nice thing to do for your sister. Is there anything I can do?" Kristen smiled. *Sweet Peter. Adorable, caring Peter.* "No, thank you. She just needs some support and maybe a shoulder to cry on." Peter felt bad for Sam. He too, knew what it felt like to have marital problems. "Where are you going and do you know when you'll be back?" "I don't know what she is planning but I'm sure she won't want to leave the kids for too long. They're staying at my parent's house. I'll call you when I have a better idea of what we are doing", Kristen told Peter. "Ok, be careful and just take care of Sam. I'm here if you guys need anything." Kristen smiled again. "Thank you Peter. It means a lot, talk soon, bye." Kristen hung up, grabbed her things and got out of the car. Now to tell my boss, I'm leaving for a few.

Get Away and Be Free

Kyla headed for the gym once she dropped the kids off. She really wasn't in the mood to workout necessarily, but the gym was the one place she could get away and just be free for a bit. Besides, she had to maintain herself to keep her husband interested. *He's not the type to care, but he's still a man!* She thought.

Truth was she was getting up there in age and her body was starting to show signs of it. Giving birth also had left its mark on Kyla.

Several men turned their heads and stared at her as she walked through the gym, headed for the locker room. *I still got it though!* She laughed to herself. *Let's just hope Freddie thinks so too. Please don't let that crazy mujer, Jordan be here. I cannot handle another scene with that one!* "Kyla?" Kyla shut her eyes. "You hate me God, don't you?" She opened them and was staring at Brielle. "I'm sorry, I meant Mrs. Lovazzo." Brielle was saying. "What...oh no...Please call me Kyla." Brielle grinned. "Oh ok...Kyla. I was just asking how you were. I thought you came here in the evening. What Kyla didn't know was that Brielle was trying to find out if there was something going on with Mr. Lovazzo and that whore, Tina, behind Kyla's back. Not that she would ever say anything. She could lose her job. But she liked Kyla and wanted to at least make her suspicious if there was anything going on. Kyla responded. "I used to, but my husband and I had a change in schedules, so we each come here at different times. I think he prefers working out with his friends, anyhow." Kyla laughed. Brielle just gawked at her. *Does she know that her husband has been working out with Tina and she doesn't care? A good looking woman like that? Whoa! Talk about being secure!* Brielle snapped out of her trance. She nodded in agreement. "Oh ok, well it's always nice to see you, Mrs. Lovazzo...eh, Kyla I mean." Kyla smiled at Brielle. "You too, Brielle. Have a great day." Kyla went back to putting things in her locker and Brielle left the locker room, dumbfounded.

After her workout, she did some errands and returned home. She started thinking about being in the locker room with Brielle earlier. *First, she was glaring at me in the gym the other day, now she is questioning why I don't go when Freddie goes anymore. Odd. Does Brielle like Freddie or something?* Kyla laughed. *Brielle can't be much older than Sam's son, Joey.*

Kyla decided to call Freddie to say hello and see how his day was going. He picked up on the first ring. "Hey Babe. What's up?" "Not much, I just called to say 'hello.' How's work?" she responded. "It's work. Same shit, different day. What did you do today or are you gonna do?" he asked. "I went to the gym this morning after I dropped off the kids and then ran some errands. I ran into Brielle from the gym. She was asking why I don't come with you there anymore. It seems like she is paying attention to your comings and goings. I think she may have a crush on you, Honey." Freddie started to sweat. Thank God his wife was on the phone and not in person to see his reaction, "Ew, gross, Kyla. What's she like, 18?" Kyla laughed. "I think she's in her twenties, but regardless, you're taken."

Freddie finished talking to Kyla and hung up. He told her he was going to the gym after work and would be there for a few hours. He had a long workout routine to do. She told him to not overdo it and be mindful of little girls lurking at him. He wasn't amused. He knew Brielle would be lurking but not for the reason that Kyla thought she would be for. Freddie took a deep breath. *Great, now I gotta worry about this girl spying on me and Tina at the gym. Just what I don't need. But maybe if she was there working already when Kyla went, she will be gone by the time I go tonight. I will have to tell Tina to act discreetly in the gym before anything gets back to Kyla.*

Freddie dialed the gym phone number. "All City Gym." a manly voice said. Good, it's a dude. "Um hello. I'm a member of the gym. I was at the gym yesterday and asked a young lady about a week pass for a guest. She said to just ask for her when I bring the guest. Brielle, I think her name is. Will she be there tonight?" The manly voice answered. "Brielle is here now. Do you want me to paige her?" "No, no. I just need to know if I should see her when I come tonight." "Oh, ok. She's here until 5." Freddie was relieved. He and Tina were coming after that. "Ok, great. Thanks so much. Bye now." Freddie hung up and went back to work.

Tonight couldn't come fast enough for her. The anticipation was killing her. Tina's mind wandered over and over about seeing Freddie again tonight. They shared a kiss last night and who knows what else would have happened if she had stayed and he didn't have to go. She knew that he was interested. He proved that once he kissed her. The kiss itself was deep, passionate. *His wife, whoever she is, is one lucky lady. But not for long if I have any input. He will be mine soon. There's just no other way, sorry.*

Her phone rang. It was her sister. "Hey Tina! How are you? I was wondering if you could possibly babysit for me tonight? "Sonia..." Tina felt bad.She didn't want to say no to her sister. She adored her niece and always agreed to help out whenever she could. But this thing with Freddie was all she could think about. "Sonia, I'm sorry. I have a date tonight. It would be rude to cancel. He has a party to go to and wants a companion. I bought a dress and everything", she lied. "Oh, ok. I know you would if you could. No big deal. Can I book ya for next week though?" her sister laughed. "Some friends want to get together." Tina smiled. She was happy her sister was venturing out these days and not staying home all of the time, caring for her daughter. "So this date? Is this the same guy you mentioned?" "Yes. I met him at the gym. He's a nice guy." "Uh-huh. Is he married Tina?" Sonia asked sarcastically. Tina felt her face get hot. "No," she lied again. She let out a fake laugh in hopes that her sister would believe her. She hated lying to Sonia, but Tina knew that she just wouldn't understand when she told her that this time was different. Tina had developed feelings this time. Sonia would'nt believe her. "At least he told me he wasn't." Her sister sighed. "Well, then just be careful. I am happy for you. I hope it works out." "Me too. I really like him." said Tina. "Gotta go, talk soon, ok? Love you always." Her sister then hung up. Tina let deep breath. *I didn't like lying to her one bit. But she can't know he's married. And with any luck, he won't be for long and he will be MINE!"*

Once she was done throwing whatever would fit in her suitcase, Sam immediately began searching the internet for quick getaways. She started researching beach vacations, weekend getaways, rest and relaxation packages and more. She didn't know what to do or for how long to go away for. Her kids weren't babies but they still needed at least one parent to be around for guidance and supervision, especially Natalia. Sam thought about taking them with her, but now was not the time to pull them out of school. Things had to be as normal as possible for them right now. She didn't want to be the reason they had stress, as well as anxiety or even be depressed over this.

After two hours of searching through beaches, hotels and locations, even airfare, she found a quiet little spot about three hours away. It was perfect. It was the bed and breakfast type, with a spa. The old Victorian house sat on a beautiful beach. It only had five bedrooms, so there wouldn't be so many guests at any given time.

The rate included breakfast and afternoon tea. The deck on the house had several Adirondack chairs that faced the ocean. Sam was thrilled. It's *the perfect spot to clear my head and think*, she thought. There was a shopping mall not too far away and a few spots to eat; the sort of things that would keep her busy and her mind off things if she wanted. There was only so much she could take sitting in a chair, staring at one thing for too long. Not to mention a flat ass! What was even better, is that she could drive there. She wouldn't have to deal with the whole airport ordeal, not to mention the expense. Sam called the place. Luckily for her, they had a room available. She made the reservation and told the front desk she'd be there in a few hours.

Next she sent Kristen a text, pleading for her sister to explain the situation to their mother. She just didn't have it in her to deal with it. Her mother would ask a million questions, then be judgemental and critical. They would argue. Her mother felt that Sam should just bow down to her husband and give in to whatever he wanted. Sam would tell her that's an old way of thinking. Back in my day, as her mother often said, "wifes were taught to obey their husbands." Sam would roll her eyes at her mother. "That is a Catholic thing" she told her mother. Her mother would respond with, "and I raised you as a Catholic." Sam told her she converted to Atheism, pissing her mother off. Truth was, Sam only believed in half of what the Catholic religion preached. She raised the kids as Catholics nevertheless, making sure they received all their sacraments. Once they became adults, they can form their own decisions about practicing or not. At least she provided the foundation to believe in something when they were young. Besides, her mother would have hung her. Forget divorce. If that happens, her mother will have a canary!

But when it came to living in today's times, Sam was an independent woman. She believed in women having a husband at their sides, not in front. She grabbed all of her toiletries and put them in her suitcase. "Toothbrush, hairbrush, make up...wait I need toothpaste." *Little tube or big tube? I don't know if I am gonna extend my stay or if Sal has a change of heart and I will shorten it.* She thought for a second. "Big tube!" she said out loud. *No matter what, I have to keep brushing my pearly whites. She chuckled. At least I can find some humor in all of this shit.* Sam closed her suitcase and carried it down the stairs. She brought it outside to throw in her trunk. A car pulled in the driveway. It was Kristen. Kristen jumped out and walked over to a surprised Sam.

"I don't think your trunk will hold two suitcases." Kristen shouted. Sam just looked at her. "I...I only have one. What are you doing here?" Kristen ignored Sam's question. "What about my suitcase? Maybe we should take my car. And judging by what you look like right now, maybe I should drive. You may decide to pull some Thelma and Louise shit." Sam just kept staring at her sister. After a few seconds, she spoke. "Kristen…I told you not to come. This isn't your problem. I just need to get away and be free for a few." "Stai zitta! Besides, what are sisters for?" Kristen replied. Sam hugged her tight. She started to winge. "I am so lucky to have you in my life, Kris. What about your job? I don't want you to get in trouble." Kristen smiled. "First, I am thankful to have you in my life as well. You were there for me and the kids when all that bullshit went down with Chris. Secondly, I have unused personal days. I took a few. I already put in for it, so I'm good. Sam clasped her hands together in excitement. Now where are we off to?" Kristen asked. Sam told her about the B and B she found. "It sounds great, Sam. I hope you packed some nice outfits and some sexy stilettos to match. I packed mine. We are going to enjoy ourselves and have you forget all about this drama in your life right now." They hopped in the car and sped away; only arguing about who was gonna call Nonna.

Restrooms

Once again, Kyla found herself fending for herself and the kids for dinner. Her mind started wandering about Freddie and how he is going to the gym more frequently and staying longer. Then there was the other night when they had sex. If Kyla hadn't been staring at him, she would have sworn it was another man besides her husband that she was in bed with. *He could also be experimenting with new things, based on what I said last week,* she thought.

She walked into the kitchen to prepare dinner. Kyla didn't want the kids to eat fast food or take out for a second night during the week. It was also costly. The pots and pans came out of the cabinets and Kyla started chopping vegetables. She couldn't stop herself from being suspicious about Freddie. So much so, that she nicked her finger cutting a carrot. "Ow!" she screamed. She ran her finger under the faucet in the kitchen sink and then put a bandage over the cut. Luckily it wasn't too deep so she didn't need a stitch. That's all I need, to go to the E.R. with two kids in tow. What time is it anyway? Freddie, where the hell are you?" She picked up her phone and called the gym.

"All City Gym, Brielle speaking." "Brielle! You're still there. Talk about a long shift! It's Kyla Lovazzo." "Oh hi Mrs...Kyla! Yes, I'm still here. My co-worker, who is usually here in the evenings, called out sick, so I stayed. Overtime! Lol." Kyla chuckled. "Well, good for you. Make that money! I have a quick question. Do you happen to know if my husband is there? He's not answering his phone," she lied. "So I assume it's probably in his locker and he decided to listen to the gym music instead." Brielle suddenly felt uncomfortable. In the distance, she could see Freddie walking in with Tina. She wasn't sure if Kyla knew anything yet. Still, she had to say something. "Brielle, are you still there?" she heard Kyla ask. She cleared her throat. "Yes, Kyla, sorry. A member was asking me something. Yes, I see Mr. Lovazzo. He's here. Do you want me to give him a message?" Kyla didn't want Freddie to know she was spying on him. "No, that won't be necessary. I just wanted to make sure he's ok. Have a good night and I hope you get off soon! She hung up. Brielle snickered. "Your husband is better than ok, Mrs Lovazzo. I think I need to throw a little wrench in his cockiness right now!"

Brielle walked over to Freddie and Tina. They were about to go into the locker rooms. "Hi guys." Freddie instantly started sweating. Tina took notice of how jumpy he looked. Brielle looked at Freddie. "Your wife called. She said she tried your cell but when you didn't answer, she became worried. I told her you were fine and are here but you may want to call her." "Um...thank you, Brielle. Will do." Brielle walked away but not before rolling her eyes at Tina.

"What was that about?" Tina asked Freddie. "Are you ok? You look perplexed." Freddie looked at Tina. "I'm ok. That was weird though. I didn't get a call from my wife. She knew I was coming here. Brielle knows my wife. She may be playing some sort of game because she's my wife's friend and looking out for her. Brielle knows I came here with you. Tina nodded and looked over to the desk where Brielle was. Freddie was contemplating his next move. He knew

Brielle would be watching them. *"Think, Freddie, think!* A few seconds went by then Freddie looked at Tina. "Tina, what do you say, we skip the workout tonight and go catch a bite to eat and a drink? I'm not really in the mood to workout." A devilish grin came over Tina's face. "Lead the way."

Freddie started walking and then turned to Tina. "Do you mind if I use the restroom first and give a quick call to my wife and see what's up?" "Not at all, she replied." He handed her his car keys. You can go ahead and get in my car if you want. I'll be out in a few." Tina started walking away and Freddie went into the locker room.

On her way out of the gym, Tina stopped at the front desk. "Um, Brielle, can I speak to you for a minute?" Brielle swallowed hard and slowly made her way over to Tina. Tina leaned in closer to speak lower. "We both know what's happening here, right? Between Freddie and I, I mean?" Brielle nodded. "Isn't it the gym's policy to not disclose any member's information to another member, especially for personal gain?" Brielle muttered a week "yes." Tina continued. "If an employee does, isn't that grounds for immediate termination and a potential lawsuit for the company?" Brielle nodded again and Tina continued again. "Well, then we wouldn't want to do anything that would jeopardize that, would we?" "Right," Brielle said. Tina stood up. "Good, we're on the same page then. I knew I liked you, Brielle. You have a nice night." Tina sashayed her way out the door and over to Freddie's car.

"Kyla, did you call me?" Freddie asked his wife. He called her as soon as he went into the locker room. "Brielle said you called." Kyla wanted to die. *Why the hell did Brielle tell Freddie I called?* She said no to leaving a message. She sighed. *Now I gotta lie.* "I did try to call you. I guess it didn't go through. I just wanted to let you know that I'm making dinner and if I should save you a plate?" Freddie felt a sigh of relief. He laughed. "And here I thought you were checking up on me at the gym because Brielle was there!" Now it was Kyla's turn to laugh. "Oh please Freddie. You're practically old enough to be her father! I am the same age as Sam. Brielle is only a few years younger than Sam's son Joey. Freddie sneered. "Well I wasn't acting old the other night, was I Ky?"

Sam and Kristen Drove along the highway, blasting music and staring at people in their cars when they passed them. After they drove for about two hours, they got off the highway and pulled into a rest stop. "I gotta pee so bad!" Kristen wailed. Sam laughed at her. "Well, who told you to drink a Venti ice coffee just before our road trip?" Before jumping on the road, the ladies went to Starbucks for Sam's beloved Salted Caramel Cold Brew and Kristen's favorite, Iced Brown Sugar Shaken Espresso. Sam only got a Tall though because she knew better. Restroom bathrooms skeeved her out, so she avoided them as much as possible. She rather pull to the side along the highway and find a bush.

"You hungry?" Sam asked Kristen. "Yeah, you want to see what they have here?" Kristen replied. "I'd rather die." Just as much as she disliked the public restrooms, Sam disliked fast food as well. "Let's find a nice restaurant for dinner. It's my treat." Sam suggested. "That's not necessary, Sam." Sam rolled her eyes at her sister. "Shut up Kris. You came here for me. You didn't have to do that. It's the least I can do. And I won't allow my sister to eat anything I wouldn't even give to my dog." "Sam, you don't have a dog." They both laughed. "True, but you know what I mean. We're coming all this way, may as well make the best of it and enjoy ourselves." Kristen smiled. "I hear that sis." Sam smirked. "Good, cuz you're need that drink that comes with dinner after you call Mom."

They got gas and started driving again. They only had an hour left so they decided to check in first and then look for a place to eat. Sam started to chill out. Being with her sister made her feel at ease. Despite what was happening in her life right now, she was calm and content for the moment.

When they were only about ten minutes from the B and B, they started driving along the coastline. The sun was going down, making the drive that much more enjoyable. "Isn't it beautiful?" remarked

Sam. Kristen nodded. Sam stared out of the window, watching the waves crash on the shore and the boats that passed by. "I don't know why we never discovered this area before." Kristen was saying. "We're really not that far." Sam turned around and faced Kristen. "Maybe because we had husbands who sucked." Kristen took a deep breath. "Sam, I had a husband. You still have one." Sam just rolled her eyes. "So do you, Kris. You're not divorced yet." "Well, it definitely is a done deal." Kristen snapped. "Anyway," Sam said, "You should come here with Peter. He'd probably like it." "Maybe," Kristen said. Kristen felt bad talking about Peter with Sam right now. She didn't want to flaunt her relationship in front of her face, knowing her sister was going through a tough time with Sal.

They pulled up to the place and parked the car. Then they went into the lobby to check in. Both of them immediately fell in love. The place was gorgeous. The windows were from ceiling to the floor, with views of the ocean. It smelled good too. Fresh flowers were on the table and the place was spotless. "I think we're gonna like it!" Sam said as she squeezed Kristen's hand in excitement. "Can I help you?" An older lady was behind the counter, talking to them. They checked in with the woman and went to their room. It was just as beautiful, if not more than the lobby, The ladies unpacked their suitcases and whipped out their phones. "Ok, let's see where we can go eat and rock our stilettos," Sam exclaimed.

Just as she was beginning her search. Her phone rang. It was Sal. Sam looked at Kristen. "It's Sal." "Well, pick it up. I'm gonna take a walk and find out what time breakfast is." Kristen left and shut the door behind her. Unbeknownst to Sam, she crossed her fingers in hope that that phone call goes well.

She picked up on the third ring. "Hi Sal." "Sam...Where are you? Joey said you went somewhere with your sister with a suitcase and he doesn't know when you'll be back." "Hi to you too, Sam, " Sam said sarcastically. "I decided to go away for a few days with Kristen. I told him I wasn't sure for how many days yet; maybe for the weekend, maybe more. But not more than a week. Why is that a problem?" She could hear Sal huffing and puffing on the phone. "Yea, Samantha, it is. You do realize our daughter is only twelve right? You can't just pick up and leave when you want." Sam grew angry. "Really Salvatore? Like you did?" "That was different Sam. I left the kids in the house with their MOTHER. I didn't drop them off at their grandparents house and left town, telling them I didn't know when I'd be back. For our son, it's probably not a big deal. He is probably enjoying having you get off his back for a few days. But Natalia on the other hand, is a different story. You can't do shit like this." Sam was pissed. How dare he criticize her for something he started. "I didn't initiate this Sal, you did! And furthermore, don't you dare tell me what I can or can't do. You are not my father. You're not even half the man he is. So before you go criticizing someone else, look at yourself first, ok Buddy? Gotta go!" Sam ended the call and threw her phone on the bed. She began sobbing.

Kristen came back to the room moments later. "Sam, I found these great brochures in the lobby...Sam? Sam what happened? Did something happen with Sal? Kristen found her sister, sitting in the corner of the room, shaking and sobbing. Sam looked at Kristen and wiped her face. "It was horrible. All we did was scream at each other. He's mad because I left. He made it sound like I abandoned the kids. I would never do that Kristen." Kristen patted Sam's head. "I know you wouldn't, Sweetie. And that's ridiculous for him to even say. They are with their grandparents who will probably take better care of them then we can. We're not talking about babies either. Also, are you not entitled to go anywhere for a few days? Who died and made him boss? C'mon Sam. Get up, wash your face. Put on a nice outfit and those ridiculously high heels, We are going out. As I was about to tell you, I found some brochures on some cool looking places in town, Andiamo!" The women left, headed out for the night, but not before Sal sent Sam a text. "We need to talk when you get back. Call me when you're back in town."

I'm Available

After she disconnected the call with Freddie, Kyla chuckled. Freddie's question amused her. *I guess he really took it to heart when I commented on our sex life. He is really trying so hard to make sure that I stay interested. Either that, or he's cheating! But Brielle did say that he was there and that*

had to be the truth because he knew I called and called me right back. I guess it's all on the up and up.

Kyla started thinking of a way to show Freddie that she was all in this too. How could she show him that she appreciated his effort and that she herself was definitely still interested in him? *I have to put some thought into this. I gotta show him that while our day to day life is pretty much routine and dull at times, we can still enjoy things and look forward to the little moments we do get, to escape with one another.* After thinking of a few ideas, one came to mind.

Kyla dialed Sam's number. After a few rings it went to voicemail. Two minutes later, she received a text from Sam. Hi, sorry, away with Kristen for a few, Can't really talk. We're in a restaurant. It's noisy here. U ok?" Kyla replied back telling her she was ok, to have a good time and they'll chat when she gets back. Next, Kyla called her sister in law, Olivia. She glanced at the clock. It was seven o'clock. . That was a perfect time to call Olivia. She knew her sister-in-law would be free to talk right now. Dinner would be over with and the kids weren't in bed yet. Olivia answered on the first ring. "Hello Sis in Law! How are you?" "Great," Kyla said. "I have a favor to ask you though." "Sure!" "Would you by chance be available to watch the kids overnight tomorrow? I want to surprise Freddie at the gym and take him out to dinner. Then come home to an empty house for once. Olivia laughed. "Of course! You guys deserve a break. Feel free to return the favor at some point though," joked Olivia. "Absolutely, just say when." The women worked out the details and chatted briefly before hanging up. They were both due to start bathtime for the kiddos.

As she watched Francesca in the tub, Kyla thought about her plan for tomorrow. She'd wait until she knew he'd be at the gym. She would show up there and surprise him, ready to workout with him, like they used to. Then she would tell him they needed to rush home and change for dinner. They could decide who was driving but she was taking him out to a nice, romantic restaurant where there was no kid's menu. They would wine and dine and then go back home to their empty house. No kids meant no distractions. She would do things to him that she hadn't done since they were dating. She would allow him to do whatever he wanted. Olivia agreed to keep the kids through lunchtime the next day, so they could sleep in. When they woke, they'd make love. It was a perfect plan and Kyla was excited.

Francesca was done with her bath and Kyla got her ready for bed. She told her daughter that she would be hanging out with her cousins tomorrow. Francesca was excited. "Yay! Should I bring a sleeping bag, Mommy?" she asked. Kyla smiled at her daughter. "Yes, and don't forget Wiggles too. Wiggles was Francesca's favorite stuffed animal. She never slept without it. "Ok, I won't Mommy. And Mommy, can I use the extra long sleeping bag?" Kyla made a face. "Why do you want that on, Cheski?" "Because Carlo always farts. If I have the big sleeping bag, I can zip up my head to and won't smell him!" Kyla laughed. Carlo was Olivia's son and Francesca's favorite cousin. Except when he farted.

She put Francesca in bed and read her a bedtime story. Later, when Francesca had fallen asleep, she tiptoed out of her room and into her own. Kyla began rummaging through her closet, looking for the sexiest outfit she could find. Most of her wardrobe consisted of leggings and oversized sweatshirts these days but she did own a few pieces that held a statement of "I'm available." A few dresses that were hot and sexy, Kyla could no longer fit into. "Wishful thinking," she sighed. *Why I hold on to these, I don't know!*

There was one plain black dress that had a slit up the leg and the back was open. She settled on that and chose a shiny black pair of stilettos to match. Next, she looked through her drawer for a sexy teddy to put aside in one of the bathroom drawers. She could change in there if Freddie was in the bedroom. *I can just imagine the look on his face when I come out of the bathroom in one of these, only hookers wear one!* She owned a few teddies, but they never had much use with two kids barging into their bedroom all the time. "This hot number will do!" Kyla chose a sheer red teddy with a lace trim. She grabbed the thong that matched with it. Once she was done, she hid it behind the toiletries, in the bathroom so Freddie wouldn't see it.

"Everything ok?" Tina asked Freddie once he got in the car. "Yeah. She just wanted to know if she should save me a plate." Tina wanted to roll her eyes but didn't want Freddie to think she was a bitch. "Awe, that's so nice. But what did you say? I mean, we are getting something to eat now, or did you change your mind?" Freddie looked at her. "No, I definitely didn't change my mind." Tina smiled at him. Freddie started the car. "So the other night, you chose the place. Tonight, it's my turn." He drove them to a little hidden spot in a few towns over from the gym. When they got there, Freddie grabbed Tina's hand and walked them into the restaurant. The guy at the counter gave Freddie a handshake and pat on the back. He winked at Tina. Freddie asked for the table in the back, behind the plant wall. "Sure thing Freddie; right this way." They sat at the table and ordered drinks. Tina ordered a martini while Freddie had a beer. "Do you like beer?" he asked her. She leaned across the table. "Put a football game on and you better have at least a six-pack ready." He smiled and grabbed his chest. "A woman who knows how to get to a man's heart!" They ordered dinner and had another drink after they ate.

Freddie drove back to the gym afterwards to drop Tina off at her car. He got out and opened the door for her. "I could get used to this!" she exclaimed. "Well, you deserve to be treated like a lady." Tina stared into his eyes. "Freddie, thank you so much for dinner. I had a really nice time. I am so happy I met you. You're a great guy. If only you weren't married." Freddie pulled her into him and kissed her. She kissed him back. He pulled away after a few moments and looked at her. "This time, I'm not sorry." "Me either." she whispered. "Do you have to leave right now?" she asked him. "Not yet, why?" She looked down. "Well...I...I don't live too far from here. I'd like to invite you to my place for one more drink." Freddie grinned. "What did you say to me earlier...lead the way."

Tina got in her car and Freddie followed her. He knew he was doing something awful. He hated betraying Kyla but the way that he felt right now was too good to pass up. What Kyla doesn't know, can't hurt her right? Fredie told himself to justify his actions.

She stopped at a condo complex and pulled into a space. She motioned for him to park in one of the visitor spots. She waited for him while he parked and they walked to her condo together. Tina opened the door and told him to take a seat on the couch. Freddie looked around. Her place was clean, very modern and smelled as good as Tina herself. Diamond walked over to his legs and sniffed him. Then he rubbed himself against his legs. Tina saw. "Oh, I hope you're not allergic. I forgot to mention that I have a cat. He's my furbaby, Diamond." Freddie smiled. "I'm not allergic and he's very cute." He started to pet a purring Diamond.

Tina fixed them both a drink, turned on a light R&B playlist. She sat on the couch next to Freddie. "Normally, I save this playlist for my bubble baths but this is a good time for it too. Freddie sneered. "What? No gangsta rap like we listen to when we're getting our workout on?" Tina laughed. Her laugh is so sexy, Freddie thought as he stared at her. He touched her cheek with his hand. She turned and faced him. He kissed her and pulled Tina onto his lap. She kissed him back moving from his lips to his neck. Then she pulled away and stood up. She removed her top, revealing only her bra. She climbed back on him and kissed him again. He wrapped his arms around her and kissed her back, moving down her neck line towards her breasts. She hopped off of him and unclipped her bra. He stood up off the couch and picked her up. "My bedroom is down the hall," she whispered. He carried her into her bedroom and laid her on the bed. He removed her pants and thong. Then he took his clothes off. He climbed on top of her and entered her. She moaned with pleasure. Together they rocked back and forth, kissing each other and switching positions.

Afterwards, they laid in her bed. Freddie was on his back with Tina lying on his chest, rubbing him. "Tina, I hate to do this. I don't wanna be that guy. I have to go. My wife is gonna wonder where I am." She picked her head up and looked at him. "I understand. I would never expect you to do anything that would jeopardize your marriage. I did enjoy you being here with me though. I like you Freddie. I hope that you won't let your conscience get to you and not see me again." Freddie got out of the bed and put on his pants. "Tina, I like you too. I really like this. I don't want to go either. But I have to. As for my conscience, let's just say, I am already thinking about the next time we can be together. They kissed one last time and out the door he went. Tina wept.

The clerk at the inn recommended a place about two miles away. The ladies drove along the coastline, headed for it. They were dressed to kill. Kristen wore her black top with the plunging neckline and satin black pants. She had a shiny black pair of stilettos to match. Sam was dressed just as hot. Her top was a one shoulder sheer lace with black leather pants and stiletto heels only a lady of the night would be seen in. "It seems like every road around here is dirt or gravel." I hope this place has a normal parking lot. I don't wanna fuck up my heels," Sam was saying. Kristen nodded in agreement. "I know. It's like we're on the Yellowstone Ranch! "Where's Rip?" Both women laughed. "He can lasso me anyday!" Sam joked. "Beth wears heels, so I guess it's possible." Kristen said.

They pulled up to the place. Luckily there was a lot to the left of it that was paved. Kristen pulled in and found a spot. Both women got out and walked over to the main entrance. When they opened the door, it was like any movie scene where the out of towner walks in and everyone in the place turns around and stares. All eyes were on them. Men and women. Even the bartender stopped making a drink and looked at them. "Can I help you?" Sam was so tall in those heels, she had to look down to face the young lady talking to her. "Yes, we'd like a table please. We don't have a reservation." "Oh we don't take them anyway Ma'am." the hostess said. Sam looked at Kristen who shrugged her shoulders. "Follow me please." the hostess said. The ladies followed her to a table, while everyone just continued to gawk at them. When they got to the table, Sam whispered to the hostess, "What's with all the stares?" The hostess chuckled. The locals don't usually see women dressed like you two or as pretty as you ladies, around here. The men are probably in awe and the women want to kill you. Your waitress will be right over." She winked at them and walked away.

They ordered their drinks and meals and looked around. "I feel like I'm on a different planet." Sam told Kristen. Kristen grinned. "Maybe that's what you need right now. A change in scenery from it all." Sam nodded. She pulled out her phone and read Sal's text. She showed Kristen. "What do you suppose this means?" Kristen read it. She looked at her sister. "Well, it could go either way. Either he realizes that you're not taking his crap and wants to work it out or he's really sore about you leaving and wants to have a chat about maybe he or you should leave for a lot longer. Sam took a deep breath. "Obviously, I don't want it to be the latter of the two but I don't necessarily want it to be the first reason either. That would mean it takes me doing all of this to make him realize how he is acting and for him to have a reaction for fear he crossed the line." Kristen reached across the table and grabbed Sam's hand. "Sammy, I can't say that I know what to say. All I can tell you is that I've been there, under different circumstances but with the same issue. Do what you want. Do you love Sal? Do you want to fight for your marriage? Or do you feel like the best moments have surpassed and now you need to move on? Either way, that is a decision you will have to eventually make, for yourself, for the kids...and him."

Sam saw she had missed a call from Kyla. She called her back while waiting for their food."Hey Girl!" Kyla exclaimed. "Hey! Sorry, I missed your call. I went away for a few days with my sister to clear my head." Kyla was concerned. "Is everything ok?" Sam paused before answering. "Yeah, Sal and I are in a pretty nasty fight. He left for his sister's, so I left too. "Where are the kids?" Sam took a deep breath. She hoped Kyla wasn't going to scold her about sending the kids to their grandparents like Sal did. "They are with my parents." "Ok good," was all Kyla said. "I called you because I was wondering if you were around tomorrow to take mine overnight, Kyla laughed. "I want to surprise Freddie with dinner and shit." Sam felt bad. "I'm sorry." "Oh, no worries! Olivia is taking them." Sam felt better. "Ok, awesome. Have fun Ky." "You too Sam...with Kristen I mean. Don't worry about this thing with Sal. It may be taking a few, but it will blow over. I'm available if you want to talk." Sam sighed. "I hope you're right, Ky. I love you, ciao." "I love you too. Adiós." Sam looked at Kristen. "Where are we going after this? I'm done being depressed."

Sweet Dreams

Kyla woke up with Freddie staring at her. He had come home, happy, saying he had a great workout. They enjoyed a glass of wine together and watched a movie. Kyla had tried to initiate sex, but he claimed he was too tired. *That's alright. I'll get you tonight, buddy!* She mischievously thought.

"Sleep well? Did you have sweet dreams?" he asked. "Uh-huh," she replied. She got out of bed and went to check on the kids. Francesca was awake in her room playing with her dolls. Anthony was still asleep. Kyla walked back into Francesca's room and shut the door. "Remember what I told you about sleeping at Aunt Liv's house tonight so I can surprise Daddy with a date?" Francesca giggled. "Yes Mommy. It's a secret." She put her fingers to her lips. Kyla kissed her daughter. "That's right. Do you think you can keep from telling Daddy that today?" Francesca put her fingers to her lips again and pretended to zip them. "Now Mommy, you be quiet before Daddy hears you." Kyla smiled. "Oh Francesca! You are something else!" She walked out of the room and back to her bedroom. Freddie was putting on some sweats. "Kids up?" he asked. "Francesca is. She's playing. "Ok, I'm going downstairs to start breakfast. I can go in a little later today. I'll bring the kids to school to give you a little break. He kissed Kyla and smacked her ass. She looked at him in shock. "You would do that?" "Sure Why not? What are husbands for?" Little did she know, he was buttering her up because he was planning on seeing Tina again later and knew she wouldn't give him a hard time if he took a little longer. "Thanks Babe, I'm gonna wake Anthony in a few." "Ok, I'll see what our little princess wants for her breakfast." He went to Francesca's room. *Please don't let my four year old spill my plans!* Francesca was four and very mature for her age but secrets were not a strong attribute of hers. Kyla crossed her fingers.

Breakfast was being made in the kitchen and Freddie was sitting at the table with the kids, talking. Kyla heard Francesca ask her father if he'll play Candyland with her if he gets home before she goes to bed. He told her he'd love to. *Good girl!* Kyla thought. She got their lunches ready and had them put on their coats and shoes. She ushered them into Frddie's car but not before reminding them to not spill the beans on the way to school. Francesca put her hand to her forehead. "Ok, Mommy. Like they say in Spongebob, "Aye aye, Captain!" Anthony rolled his eyes at his sister. "Nerd!" he yelled. "I am not!" she yelled back. Kyla shook her head. "Guys please, It is way too early for this. Be nice to each other." They both sat in the backseat with their arms folded and pouted. "Bye Babe." Freddie said as he got in the car. "I'll call you later. I'm going to the gym tonight again so we can spend the whole day together tomorrow. Sound good?" Kyla smiled. "You bet!" *Little does he know, it will be more than just tomorrow!*

Diamond jumped on the bed, causing Tina to wake up from the dream she was having with Freddie in it. She wished she didn't have to get up and go to work. She'd rather stay in bed, sleeping and have sweet dreams about Freddie. Last night definitely wasn't a dream. Freddie really was there in her bed. She could still smell him on her sheets. It had been everything she thought and more. He was a gentleman, yet playful and frisky. Last night had been so erotic, she did not want it to end. If only he didn't have to go home to his wife. Now she wanted him to be hers more than ever. Tina was determined to steal him away no matter what it cost. She liked him too much. Judging by the way he was last night, he felt the same.

She got out of bed and took a shower to get ready for work. It was going to be another long day, waiting for tonight when she saw Freddie again. Diamond was sitting on top of the toilet waiting for her when she was done. "Hopefully, Brielle won't be at the gym this time. That nosey bitch needs to mind her own fucking business", Tina told Diamond. She got dressed and out the door she went.

The train is packed today! Tina thought as she managed to find a seat in the last car. She sat down and noticed some creep staring at her. He smiled and blew her a kiss. Tina made a face, got up and walked to the next car. *I'd rather stand, then be near that loser.* Her phone went off. She pulled it out of her bag. The text was from Freddie. "Good morning Beautiful. Looking forward to tonight. See you later." Tina smiled and dropped the phone back into her bag. *Now, I'm really not going to be able to concentrate!*

They both woke up to hearing someone knocking on their door. "Housekeeping!" Through the door, Sam asked them if they could come back in half an hour. They said they would and she crawled back to the bed. She and Kristen had a late but fun night. They drank, danced and laughed until the place closed. They met a few locals and shared stories. Sam couldn't remember when she had a good time like this, just feeling free and enjoying time with her sister. She looked over at Kristen who was rubbing her eyes. "Kris, last night was so much fun. As much as I loved it, I think I need to go back. Hopefully Sal has given it some thought and we need to hash this out. I hope you understand." Kristen nodded. "Of course I do. I want what's best for you. I want to stay too, but you should go home. We can always do this again...when you're not down in the dumps. Kyla should come too!" Sam laughed. "Yes! She has a new pair of stilettos she wants to try out, too. It would be perfect. They both got up and packed. "Lets have breakfast first, then hit the road." Kristen said. Sam agreed.

Toxic

The time was approaching. Kyla dressed in a sexy gym outfit. Next, she packed a small overnight bag for the kids. She put the bag and the kids in the car and drove over to Olivia's house. She was early but she knew Olivia was home. Her sister in law greeted her once she pulled into their driveway. Kyla and the kids got out. Olivia gave Kyla a kiss and asked her if she wanted a cup of coffee. Kyla glanced at her watch and knew Freddie was probably just leaving work. She accepted Olivia's offer so she wouldn't arrive at the gym before him. She and Olivia gossiped for the next half hour about the kids, weather, their husbands and people they couldn't stand. Kyla looked at her watch again and figured Freddie was at the gym by now. She thanked Olivia for the coffee and for taking the kids. She got in her car and headed for the gym.

Once again, Tina waited for Freddie to show up at the gym. She chose a spot in the corner, way in the back. He knew what she drove now. She didn't want him to think she was too eager. Freddie pulled into the lot, parked and went inside. Tina got out, grabbed her bag and proceeded to go in as well.

Freddie was just coming out of the Men's locker room as she was going into the Women's. "Hey! What brings you here?" he joked. Tina chuckled. "Well, it's not for the nasty stench in the air, that's for sure." Freddie sneered and told her he would be in the weight room, waiting for her. She nodded and walked into the locker room.

Tina threw her stuff in a locker, put her hair in a ponytail quickly and rushed out. She wanted to get every moment she could with him. Tina found Freddie exactly where he said he would be. He smiled when he saw her and motioned for her to lie down on the leg curl machine. He pinched her ass as she was getting on it. She moaned a bit. They both were unaware of Kyla walking in the front door of the gym.

Kyla stopped at the front desk. The employee had her back turned, writing something down. "Hello," Kyla said. "I'm checking in." The employee turned around. "Oh hi Brielle! Working late gain?" Kyla asked. Brielle was in shock. "Um...hi Kyla...yes...my co-worker is still sick. I didn't know you were coming in tonight." Kyla was surprised she said that. *Does she expect me to let her know?* "Well, here I am. Have you seen my husband?" Brielle was still in shock. She knew from her conversation with Tina last night, there was something devious definitely happening between Tina and Freddie Lovazzo. They were here in the gym together. Kyla had no idea about any of it."Yes, I saw him a while ago. I...I think he's in the back. "Thanks, Love." Kyla walked away, laughing to herself. Judging by her face and the way she spoke, I'd say she is definitely crushing on Freddie! Meanwhile Brielle watched her walk to the back of the gym. *Oh shit. Something is about to go down!*

She walked into the locker room and put her stuff in a locker. She fixed herself in the mirror and walked out to surprise her husband. From a distance, she could see Freddie talking to some other woman. As Kyla got closer, she realized it was Tina. *Those two know each other?* With their backs turned, they didn't notice her. It looked like Freddie was coaching her on a leg routine. She stood there, listening. Freddie was talking. "Tina, what you're gonna do is bend your knees and squat down. Raise the bar as you come up. This will make that ass of yours, even finer." Then Tina spoke. "I'd rather squat on you, like I did last night." Kyla's jaw dropped. "What the fuck did I just hear?" Freddie picked his head up and looked in the mirror. He saw Kyla's reflection. He whipped around so fast, it almost cost Tina to lose her balance when he let go of the weight. "Kyla?..Ky...What...what are you doing here?" Tina saw Kyla and stood up. Kyla's face was bright red. "The question, my dear husband, is what the fuck are YOU doing here?" Kyla then turned and looked at Tina. "And you! You fucking whore. What the fuck are you doing with my husband? What did you say to him, squat on him like you did last night?" Kyla turned back to Freddie. "Is that why you have been coming home late? You've been cheating on me with this puta sucia?" Fredie stuttered. "Ky...This..is..Ti...Ti...Tina. She..." "Shut the fuck up, Freddie! I know damn well who she is and WHAT she is!"

Tina backed away from the weights in case Kyla threw one at her. "Kyla, I didn't know Freddie was your husband." Kyla was seething. "Like that would have mattered, you bitch. Is my husband the man you were telling me about, that you're seeing and you really like? Well guess what, as usual, you chose a married man to fuck. He's taken Slut. So I guess you gotta move on to another victim, you toxic bitch. And another thing, Sam was right. You haven't changed. You're still the pathetic hoe we all knew back in high school; only I was too blind to see it. I guess that's what I get for helping the weak." Tina ran off into the locker room, grabbed her jacket and fled the gym. Kyla turned back to Freddie. "I hope you're happy now. You fucked up our marriage, my friendship with Tina, and a lot more. And for what, a piece of dirty ass. I thought I knew you. I guess not." She started walking away. She turned around and looked at Freddie. "Do me a favor, don't come home tonight. Oh and another thing, you may want to get yourself checked. That toxic puta probably gave you an STD or worse." Kyla walked by an astonished Brielle and out of the gym.

Kristen dropped Sam off at home. Sam saw Sal's car in the driveway. *I guess we will have our talk now then. I hope the kids are not home. I don't see Joey's car but Natalia might be here.* I don't want her to hear what we talk about. She took a deep breath before unlocking the door. Sal was standing in the kitchen talking to someone on the phone. He looked at Sam and told the person on the phone, he had to call them back. He put the phone down on the counter. "Hello Sam. I guess you decided to come home." She swallowed before responding. "Yes. I just needed a day to think. Kristen came along and listened." Sal just glared at her. "Well, I hope you had that chance to think." "Are the kids here, Sal?" Sal looked at her with disgust. "No, they are still at your parent's house. I told Joey that they need to spend another night there. I didn't know if you were coming home or not but It's probably better if they're not here if you aren't." "They're not babies, Sal. I don't always have to be here. Obviously, I just didn't skip town and abandon them." "Whatever Samantha. I'm done arguing. Can we have a civil talk without fighting?" Sam rolled her eyes. "That depends on what you have to say." Sal sighed and told Sam to take a seat in the living room. He poured them both a glass of wine and sat in the chair, facing Sam on the couch. "Sam, I am not sure where to begin. Much of the way I felt and wanted to say was said the other day. There's no need to rehash it. Sam looked at him. "So what are you saying? You said what you needed to say and now you're ready to move on and let this go?" Sam felt a sigh of relief but it was only temporary. Sal stood up and turned his back toward her. "No Sam. I did some thinking over the last few days. I've been contemplating this for a while. This was the straw that broke the camel's back however. Things, as you know, haven't been great between us for some time now. We are no longer the same person we were, all those years ago. I'm not sure how I feel about you or any of this anymore. Our relationship has become toxic." Sam felt the tears coming. "Sal"...she muttered. He turned back around to face her. "I guess what I am trying to say is that I'm moving out. I don't know if divorce is the answer or not. I'm not there yet. But we can't go on like this either." Sam started crying. "You'll see that this is the best for all of us. I packed my things while you were away. My bags are in the car. "Goodbye Sam. I'll be in touch." With that, Sal walked out the front door and locked it. Sam picked up their wedding photo on the mantle and threw it across the room. Glass shattered everywhere. Sam slumped into the chair where Sal was sitting and sobbed.

Kristen returned home and found her niece and nephew still there. "I thought you two were here last night only?" Natalia looked up at her aunt. "Dad told us we had to stay. But it's ok. We get to keep hanging out with our cousins, she grinned." Nikki chimed in. "Yeah Mom. Now if you don't mind, we were in the middle of a movie." Kristen frowned. "Sorry." She went into the kitchen to find her mother baking cookies for the kids. "Hey Ma." She kissed her mother. "Do you need me? The kids look occupied and I'd like to surprise Peter since he thought I'd be away for a few." "Go, go." her mom said. Kristen repacked a bag and left for Peter's.

She pulled into his driveway quietly as she wanted to surprise him. She tiptoed to the front door and knocked. She heard Peter ask who it is and she answered "Guess?" He opened the door and she flew into his arms. "Boy, am I glad to see you!" Peter hugged her back and then pulled her back. "I'm happy to see you but I thought you were away for a few days with your sister." "She decided to come back. Hopefully, she and Sal are making up as we speak. As for me, I missed you Sir, so can I come in?" Peter slapped his forehead. "Yes, of course. Where are my manners?" He opened the door wide and allowed Kristen to pass. "Is Rachel here? ", she asked. "No, she's at a friend's house...for the night." Kristen smirked and kissed him. He picked her up and carried him to his bedroom.

A New Day

The other side of the bed was cold and untouched. Sam placed her hand on his pillow. She thought maybe she had a nightmare at first, then realized it had been reality. Sal was gone. She sat up in bed and started to cry again. When there were no more tears left, she dialed Kyla's number. It took a few rings but then she picked. "Hey Sam." Kyla sounded like her cat just died. "Kyla, he left. Sal moved out." Sam started crying again. "I'm so sorry Sam." "If you ever need advice, don't take it from me anymore. I can't even save my own marriage." Sam stammered. "I won't be needing advice, Sam. In fact, we can shop for divorce lawyers together. Freddie has been cheating on me." Sam stopped crying. "What? Are you sure? How do you know?" She heard Kyla exhale. "It gets worse, Sam. Not only was he cheating but guess who he was cheating with?" Sam thought for a second but had no ideas. "I'm not sure Ky. Who?" Kyla paused for a second. "That bitch Tina." Sam gasped. Kyla continued talking. "Please don't tell me I told you so. I wanted to give her the benefit of the doubt. I'm a fool." Sam felt bad for both of them. Just a few days ago, they were happy, married women, living their best life. "I'm not gonna say it and I wish I had been wrong Ky. I'm sorry. Me too, Sam. What are we gonna do?" Sam thought about it for a minute then told Kyla, "For starters, you and I are meeting today for lunch and having a heart to heart. Then we figure out the rest of our lives." "Sounds good, Sam. Just tell me when and where." The ladies made plans and hung up; both weeping after.

Tina woke up and instantly thought of the events that took place the day before. She lost Freddie and to who? The one person she counted on becoming friends with again after all these years. Kyla will never be her friend ever again. She knew she fucked that one up.

Diamond saw she was awake and jumped on the bed. Tina began to pet him. "I've lost Freddie...and Kyla, Diamond. They are married. I had no idea that Freddie was her husband. I would have stayed away if I knew, honestly. Now she hates me, Freddie will probably never speak to me again, whether Kya takes him back or not. I thought I was finally getting somewhere in life. He seemed unhappy in his marriage. I thought I had a chance to make him mine, settle down and just live a normal respectable life. Now, I won't. It's all my fault. Tina got out of bed, got in the shower and sat down underneath the shower head. The water poured down on her while she cried. After sitting there for almost an hour, she stood up, washed and got dressed. She put Diamond into his carrier, packed a bag and drove to her mother's.

"I could get used to this." Peter said to Kristen once he woke up and saw Kristen sleeping beside him, in his bed. She opened her eyes and smiled at Peter. "Me too." He kissed her and they started to make love.

When they were finished, they laid there for a long while. Just staring into each other's eyes. Finally, Peter spoke. "Kristen, did you mean it when you agreed to getting used to this?" She smiled at him. "Of course. Wasn't I convincing just now?" she smirked and winked at Peter. He laughed. "You definitely were. But I'm serious. I've given this a lot of thought." He got out of bed and put on his sweatpants. Kristen sat up, concerned about where this conversation was headed.

"When my wife and I got divorced, I swore I would never go through that again, for my sake and for Rachel's. I am no spring chicken so there wasn't a need to start over. I convinced myself of that. Then you came along." Kristen started to interrupt him. "Peter..." "Please let me finish," he told her. "I knew I liked you and enjoyed our time together. But these past few days have meant something more than that. I love having you near me and feel a void when you're not." He walked over to Kristen and put his hand on her shoulder. "What I am trying to do is ask you if you would consider moving in here and living with me? Now I know we will have to speak to our kids, but I am willing to give it a shot if you are." Kristen didn't know what to say. She wasn't expecting this but wanted it more than anything. "Yes, Peter. I would love to live together." Peter exhaled deeply and took Kristen into his arms. From there, they made love again.

Not for the Weak

Sam and Kyla met for lunch at a little cafe about twenty minutes away from their town. As soon as they saw each other, they hugged and cried. Kyla looked at Sam. "We will get through this." "Together," Sam said. They ordered lunch and cocktails and talked about their futures.

Sam started speaking first. "Ky, I have been married for so long, I don't know how to act, conduct my life or even run a household without him. What happens if we do end up getting divorced?" Kyla sympathized with her friend. "I don't know Sam. It's the same for me. At least your guys are older. Joey is practically a man. And you have Kristen. The kids are tight with their cousins. You have both emotional and financial support from your family. Besides, Sal isn't abandoning the kids. You will be just fine. Me, on the other hand, may not be so lucky. My kids are young. I have both brothers but they are both consumed with their own lives. And Freddie, I never thought he'd do this, so I can't assume he'll continue taking care of the kids. His mother will turn this on me and brainwash him into believing this is my fault." Sam made an angry face. "This is not your fault! It's Tina's. Freddie probably never looked at another woman before. But Tina is dangerous. She probably spewed her venom into him and sunk her claws. That bitch is nuts but she does have a way with men. I'll give her that. Freddie always lacked esteem according to you right?" Kyla nodded. "Well, then he probably got in over his head when she showed some interest in him." Kyla's jaw dropped. "Are you saying he's innocent, Sam?" Sam was shocked. "No way! He 100% is guilty. All I am saying is that he let a weak moment of his ego get to him and from there, it escalated. Kyla sighed and picked up her fork. "Well, this bitch refuses to be with a man who is weak."

Sam picked up her sandwich. "I hear that girlfriend. Mangia."

347

Epilogue

New Adventures

"We are late! Dinner will be served in one hour. We can't piss off Nonna!" Kristen ran around the house, looking for her shoe. She finally found it, lodged under the bed. Peter was amused. "That's what you get for bringing those spikes to bed. Although, dressed in a teddy with a nice pair of stilettos, while coming to bed, does something for us guys." Kristen threw a book on her night table at him. "Are the kids ready?" she huffed. Peter yelled, "You guys ready?" "Yeah" All three of them shouted." They got in the car and left for Sunday dinner at Nonna's house.

Back in her house, Sam was getting ready to leave too. The kids had gone ahead. Joey was driving him and his sister over since they needed two cars. Sam was picking up Kyla and her kids. They were coming to Nonna's for dinner too. When Sam asked her mother if it was ok, her mother beamed. People eating and enjoying Nonna's food was like winning the lotto to her. Sam looked at a photo of her and Sal on the wall on the way out."Having Kyla and the kids there instead of you will be a new adventure; out with the old, in with the new. Note to self...take that photo down. She shut the door.

www.ingramcontent.com/pod-product-compliance
Lightning Source LLC
Chambersburg PA
CBHW030130310726
48970CB00005B/1377